I0573347

Second Chance

Jude LaHaye

A Wings ePress, Inc.
Young Adult Novel

Wings ePress, Inc.

Edited by: Jeanne Smith
Copy Edited by: Christie Kraemer
Executive Editor: Jeanne Smith
Cover Artist: Trisha FitzGerald-Jung

All rights reserved

Wings ePress Books
www.wingsepress.com

Copyright © 2021 by: Jude LaHaye
ISBN-13: 978-1-61309-538-6

Published In the United States Of America

Wings ePress Inc.
3000 N. Rock Road
Newton, KS 67114

Table of Contents

Dedication

For my brother, Mike. I miss you every day...and always will.

* * *

"If the spirit of many in body but one in mind prevails among the people, they will achieve all their goals, whereas if one in body but different in mind, they can achieve nothing remarkable."

—Many in Body, One in Mind,
The Writings of Nichiren Daishonin, vol. 1, p. 618

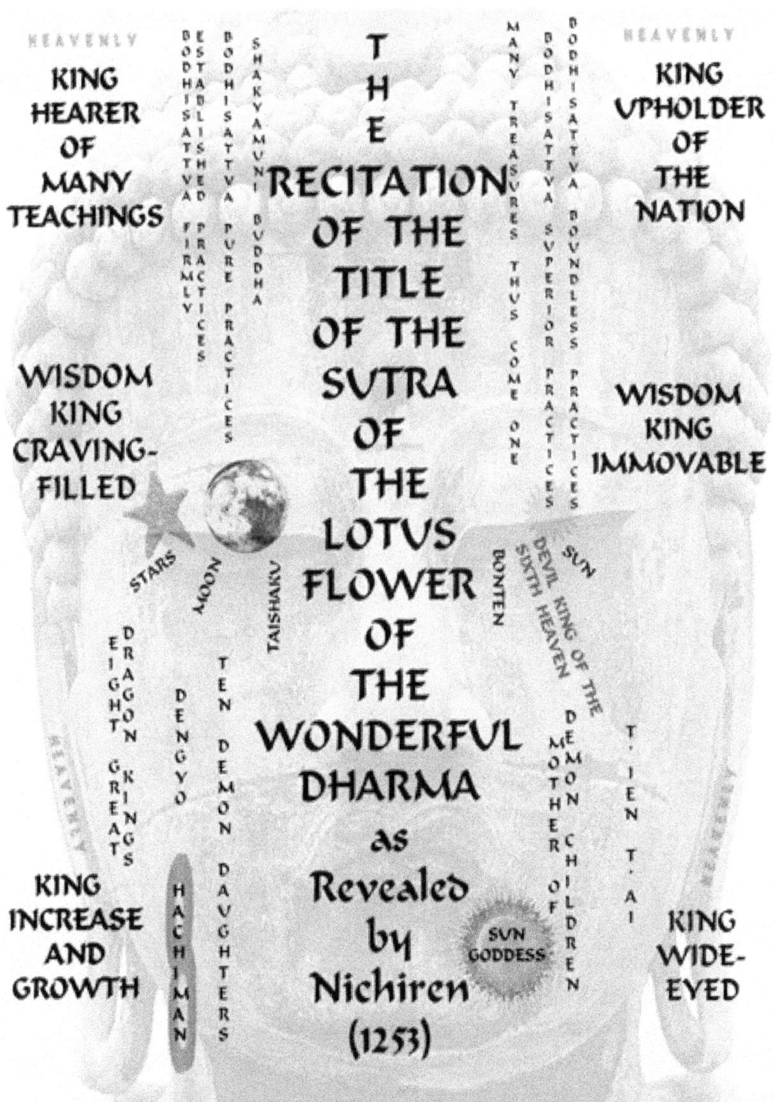

One

In Dreams...

"Durnst!" Chance cried out loud, waking himself from a troubled dream.

Now awake, well, sort of, Chance grasped at the word he had shouted. The rest of the dream dissipated entirely. He was left with just that one word.

It isn't a word, he said to himself. *It's a name. It's the name I made up for the Thorinian boy in that story I wrote last November.* In that story, Chance had created an alien world and civilization. One which used Earth to vacation, to meet partners, and to make children. Chance starred in his little narrative, as did "Durnst," an alien boy eventually revealed to be Chance's unlikely twin. This fantasy work was undertaken by a very depressed Chance Bonner, a Chance who thought he might purge his depression through expression. It hadn't worked exactly as he had hoped.

It was now February, the dreariest month of the year in Seattle, but Chance had shaken his November doldrums entirely.

He jumped out of bed and checked the weather from his bedroom window: yep, raining, a soft pattering shower. He estimated the temperature was a good ten degrees above freezing. *Sigh.* He cast out a hope into open space for some snow. It was a prayer of sorts: snow was such a rarity in the Seattle area.

His eyes widened with excitement as his nose picked up something coming from the kitchen. He inhaled a huge breath of deliciousness wafting through the air: pancakes.

Thoughts of snow completely driven out of his mind, Chance opened his bedroom door, crossed the landing, and took the stairs two at a time to arrive at the kitchen table just as his mother was putting a heaping plate of hot pancakes onto it.

"Right on time, as usual," his mother said, giving her adopted son a welcoming grin. "Dig in," she continued. "You're a growing boy, after all."

She was right about that. After worrying for a full year about his failure to mature, Chance was finally shooting up.

"You're growing like bamboo," his father said, entering the room and eagerly taking a seat. "Mmmmm, these smell just awesome, Nan!"

"You be careful. You are not a growing boy!" Nan Bonner chided her husband playfully. "You will need to run a mile for every pancake you eat."

"Oh, come on, Nan," Chaz Bonner replied. "I can eat anything I want and not gain an ounce."

Nan sighed. It was true. Chaz could do that. But she had started to realize she could no longer do the same with impunity.

Nan sat with her husband and son and watched them eat.

"Aren't you having any?" Chance asked his mother, his mouth full. He wiped some dribbling syrup from his lower lip.

"I had an egg earlier," Nan replied. "I'm fine."

"I can't hear you over the sound of your stomach growling," her witty husband said.

It was true. Her stomach was carrying on a conversation of its own.

"Well, I guess one wouldn't hurt," she replied, using her fork to help herself to the smallest pancake on the serving platter.

"I'll use this sugar-free syrup. That should be all right."

Chaz and Chance were both staring at her when she looked up from her plate.

"What? What is it?" she asked, looking from Chance to Chaz and back again.

"Are you dieting?" Chaz finally asked.

"No, of course not," Nan lied. "I am, umm, just watching my cholesterol."

Chaz hiked an eyebrow at her but dropped the subject. Silence, well at least verbal silence, reigned for the next few moments until Chaz cleared his throat to get her attention.

She had cut her tiny pancake into over a dozen really small pieces and was eating them one at a time, chewing each morsel like it was a big chunk of steak.

"You're getting too thin, Nan," Chaz said softly. "You need to eat more, not less."

"You're not the one who can't get into her jeans!" Nan snapped before she even knew she was going to speak. Chaz's comment had triggered her involuntary exclamation.

Upset, Nan rose, picked up her plate and took it to the sink where she scraped the remaining pieces of pancake into the garbage disposal.

"Honey, what's wrong?" Chaz cried, wiping his mouth with his napkin, rising, and crossing the room to put his arms around her.

She burst into tears.

Chaz tightened his grip. She turned to face him and put her arms around his neck. She buried her face in his shoulder and continued to cry.

"I'm going to get ready for school," Chance announced, rising from his seat. He flew from the room in a panic.

His mother, crying? He had never seen her cry unless there were a really good reason. A wedding. A funeral. A *Star Wars* movie. A stubbed toe.

What was she crying about? Getting fat? Chance had not noticed she was getting fat. If anything, he thought she had been looking pale and weak lately...

A moment later, Chance realized he only had twenty minutes to get dressed and get to school. In his haste to do so, he completely forgot about his mother's emotional outburst.

He arrived at school with forty-five seconds to spare.

"Where were you?" red-headed Kelly O'Hara whispered to him from her seat in the back of their science lab. The friends usually walked to school together in the morning.

"Mom made pancakes," he whispered back to his next-door neighbor and best friend. Kelly was a tomboy. She liked climbing trees and playing video games as much as she liked reading and watching old sitcoms she had on tapes and DVDs, just like Chance did. Their friendship had developed before Chance even knew Kelly was a girl.

"Oh," Kelly said.

"Yeah, 'oh.' Awesome as usual," Chance said, his eyes communicating his intent to tease her.

"I bet. Man, you're making me hungry."

"I'm stuffed."

"You're mean is what you are," she replied, but she was laughing. Chance joined her...and then remembered his mother bursting into tears over a pancake.

He had an unsettled day. It was so unsettled he forgot to think about the word...no, name...which he had shouted out just as he woke up.

But his shout had caught the attention of someone—or something—who was watching him. This someone—or something—seemed to always be watching Chance, looking for an opportunity to trip the boy up.

The watcher was The Beast, of course. And his trusty minions, Lucinder and Denny, and now also his new, recalcitrant, incompetent minion, Arthur Dillow, who pretended to be a friend and classmate to Chance Bonner.

Denny was on duty when Chance cried out. This was fortunate for Chance because Denny was on his side. Denny did not wish for any harm to come to him.

Denny kept this hidden from Lucinder and The Beast, however. If he did not, he would be removed from the team and banished.

Banished from his beloved Lucinder.

"That is not going to happen," the monkey promised himself. "I will never leave her side. Never."

The portal into Chance's world was a wet, hot cavern which opened up into his bedroom. Humans could not see the cavern, nor could they see its denizens: The Beast, Denny, Lucinder, and a number of their sub-minions.

Denny crossed the cavern and slid open a door which shielded a virtual closet abutting the actual closet in Chance's room. Instead of clothes and a variety of sporting goods and shoes, the closet in the cavern held a sewing machine on a rickety table. At the sewing machine, seated on a three-legged stool, was an old crone—or was it? She was a she and she was old...

But she wasn't human, was she? She had huge eyes and a wide mouth. Her middle was bulky, but her legs were long and lean.

Because she was shoeless, her webbed feet were exposed for all to see and admire.

Each of the toenails on those feet was painted a different shade of blue, and all of them managed to perfectly complement her greenish-blackish-brownish skin tone.

She wore a diaphanous gown, also of blue, its folds and billows disguising much of her shape.

"How are you doing, Ribetta?" Denny asked solicitously.

"Nearly done, nearly done," the old creature croaked.

"Done with what, dear?"

"Lucinder has me taking in Nan Bonner's clothes an eighth of an inch a night," Ribetta replied. "It's tiresome, I tell you. Every night I have to make the same adjustments!" She stopped pedaling the sewing machine and stared up at Denny, a look of naked panic washing over her face.

"I know this work is important," she sputtered. "I am not complaining. Please, don't tell Lucinder I said a word…"

"I understand completely," Denny replied, patting the little woman on her lumpy shoulder.

It should be said that some of the lumps were bunches of her blue gown. But some of them were her own.

Smooth she was not.

Her over-large eyes were magnified even further by the thick, round glasses which perched precariously on her wide, flat nose.

"You are a kind monkey," she told Denny.

"Don't let that get around!" he said, only half in jest.

"Don't worry," she replied with a smile and a wink. "Your secret is safe with me!"

They both jumped when, with a "poof" and a sulfurous cloud, Lucinder popped into the cavern.

"Denny!" she screamed when she saw him. "Leave my seamstress alone. She has an important mission."

"Yes, Lucinder," Denny replied, turning to face the waspish woman with a look of joy transforming his plain brown face. "I was just checking to see if she needed anything."

"Well, do you?" Lucinder demanded of the now-squirming little woman.

"Do I what?" she asked pitifully.

"DO YOU NEED ANYTHING?" Lucinder demanded, her voice ratcheting up to a near scream.

"Well. Umm, well, uhh."

"Oh, dear Devil King, what is it?! Speak up!"

"Well, umm, I am getting low on spider webs."

"Spider webs? What in the ten worlds do you do with spider webs?"

"They are my threads," Ribetta responded. "They are an essential ingredient in my art."

"Oh, you're calling it 'art' now?" Lucinder paused her nastiness to do some thinking.

"Denny," she said suddenly, turning to face him once more. "Go collect some spider webs for Ribetta."

Denny blanched. He cringed. He clasped his hands together and brought them up to his quaking chin.

"Spider webs?" he squeaked. "Lucinder, you know I am terrified of spiders!"

"I didn't ask you to play with spiders, Denny," Lucinder growled. "I told you to collect spider webs. Now get to it! Tick-tock, Denny." She waited a moment and glanced at a non-existent watch on her very real right wrist. The same right wrist which now sported a clenched fist.

"...and you're still not moving." She began to tap her left foot in a menacing manner.

"I'll go with him!" Ribetta piped up, rising to her feet and squelching across the cavern to look Lucinder in the eyes. "He won't know how to do it properly. I'll teach him. You know, for the next time I run out of thread."

Lucinder didn't blink. "Just this once, then," she acquiesced. "Be quick."

"Will do," Ribetta replied, snapping to attention and executing a smart salute. "Come on, Denny," she said, putting her hand on the monkey-man's coat sleeve. "I'll take you to my favorite spot and show you how it's done."

"OK," Denny replied weakly. His face had a definite greenish tint to it.

"Perfect camouflage for the marsh!" Ribetta cried.

Denny made little shrieks in his throat as he was propelled from the cavern into the human world.

"Be very quiet or you'll scare the spiders away," Ribetta cautioned him.

"That's good to know," Denny mumbled. "Thanks."

~ * ~

They materialized in a fen. Denny recognized immediately that they had not transitioned to a truly human world after all.

There was magic here.

And spiders the size of his hand. Everywhere. All of them in motion, spinning and weaving webs of enormous size and elaborate design.

"We want the blue webs," Ribetta whispered to him. "They have the strongest magic."

"Magic?" Denny asked, turning his head constantly to keep track of the spiders' locations. "What kind of magic?"

"The kind that binds, my dear monkey," she replied, turning her head also, but only to search for the blue spider silk she sought. "The kind that binds…"

"I see something blue over there," Denny said, his voice shaking. "And there is a huge black spider in the middle of it."

"Come with me," Ribetta instructed Denny. "I need to teach you how to collect the silk properly. I am impressed that you found the blue web so easily. You're a natural!"

"A natural? A natural what?" the frightened monkey-man asked as the couple threaded their way around marsh plants and spider webs.

"A natural spider-seeker, of course!" The little seamstress punched Denny playfully on his arm. "You've done this before, haven't you?"

"Never," he protested. "And I don't intend to do it again!"

"Do what again?" a loud voice asked. The voice came from a mossy old tree directly behind Denny's left ear.

He jumped, Denny did. Then the voice jumped. It jumped with its owner, a very large, very green, many-eyed spider.

He jumped onto Denny's shoulder.

This spider was so big that Denny felt the weight of it impact his shoulder. His terror froze him in place. His squeaking ceased as his throat clamped shut.

The only signs of his complete, abject terror were the tremors which shook his body.

"Ribetta," the spider said. "Are you here to raid our blue webs again?"

"You well know I only take what I need," the seamstress responded. They were conversing normally. They did not argue. They seemed comfortable with one another.

"So you won't take our largest, fattest, juiciest fly with you this time?" the spider asked.

Ribetta sniffed a little as if she had been unjustifiably accused of some breach of etiquette.

"I have just eaten," she insisted. "I do not require even your driest, thinnest fly at this time, thank you very much."

"Don't be offended," the spider responded. "I am sorry if I hurt your feelings."

"It's OK, Arachimedes," the little woman said. "I understand. I have on occasion dropped by for a snack or two. It is I who apologize to you, sir." She dropped her eyes and bowed her head toward the big arachnid.

Denny continued to tremble, but he realized he no longer felt he was in immediate danger.

"So who is your companion?" Arachimedes asked Ribetta.

"This is Denny," she replied. "He's a monkey, a very kind monkey from a Devil King's realm."

"Nice to meet you," Arachimedes said to Denny.

Denny turned his head slightly so he was looking into the multiple eyes of the gigantic spider.

"The pleasure is all mine," he said, his quavering voice betraying his fright. Despite his terror, he was mesmerized by the brilliant fractal gaze of the creature on his shoulder.

"D-d-do you bite?" he asked the creature.

"Well, yes, I do, actually," the spider responded. He sensed that Denny tensed up after hearing his reply. "Don't you mean '*will* I bite,' as in 'will I bite you?'"

"Y-y-es," Denny stuttered. "That's very observant of you. That is exactly what I meant to ask."

"Are you afraid of the answer?"

"Terrified."

"I will not bite you, monkey-man, for you are much more monkey than you are man. If you were one of those hairless, plump, soft humans, I'd be all over you, I'm afraid.

"But as it is, you are a friend of a friend and also very hairy and tough.

"Be forewarned, however, we spiders will all bite anything that threatens our environment or our lives."

"I don't think I know how to be threatening," Denny replied after some thought.

"I detect that this is true," Arachimedes replied. "Look, Ribetta is getting anxious. Let's go collect her silk."

Ribetta was, in fact, tapping her feet and sighing heavily. "Arachimedes, Lucinder sent me to get the silk," she said. "She said 'quickly.' You know what that means..."

"Lucinder?!" the spider asked. "Why didn't you say so! Let's get to work, people!"

"People?" Denny asked timidly.

"It's just a figure of speech," the spider replied with a little attitude. "Don't get all riled up about it."

~ * ~

It turns out that gathering spider webs is tricky. Especially if you are being supervised by a spider.

Arachimedes would not allow Ribetta to harvest a "working" web. He watched her with his keen eyes as she found abandoned webs with the right blue silk and carefully wound the strands around several wooden spools she had carried with her.

"Did you see how I did that?" she asked Denny.

"Yes, I think I've got it," he replied.

"Well, you harvest the next one," she told him. She handed him an empty spool. "Go ahead," she prompted.

Arachimedes still sat on Denny's shoulder. He was a light burden from a physical standpoint. Denny's mind, however, found the awareness of his nearness weighty and all-consuming.

"You have good hands," the spider told him as Denny deftly wound the bright blue strands upon his spool.

"Why, th-thank you," Denny responded, blushing just a bit. "That is very nice of you to say so."

"Yes, it is," Arachimedes replied. "I am not known for being very nice. I like you, monkey-man. I am going to make you my friend."

"Oh dear," Denny whispered to himself.

"What was that?" the spider asked. "I didn't hear you."

"I said I am flattered," Denny lied.

"To make you my friend, my true friend, I have to nip you."

"Nip me?"

"Just a little bite."

"Oh no, please no."

"It won't hurt at all. I inject a little anesthesia before I feed—I mean nibble."

Denny already felt the stab in the back of his neck. Resistance was futile. Within seconds of the stabbing sensation, however, a warm euphoria swept over him.

"It doesn't hurt at all," he told the spider.

"See? I told you," the spider said, a little blood trickling from his mouth.

"Arachimedes!" Ribetta had not been within hearing when the spider announced his intention to befriend Denny. She now saw that he had, in fact, bitten the little man.

She sighed. "Well, I guess it's nice to see you boys getting along," she allowed.

Denny's eyes were glassy and he had a silly smile plastered across his face.

"It's wonderful," he slurred. "Having a friend like Arac-Arac-Arachimedes. It's nice. Very, very nice."

"We have to go back now," Ribetta announced sternly. She knew what was happening. She would have to muscle Denny back to the cavern.

But Arachimedes decided to assist her. "Yes, my friend," he whispered in Denny's ear. "It's time for you to go. For now. If you ever want to see me, if you need my help with anything—anything at all—you need only speak my name. We are bonded, we two. Friends forever."

"I will see you soon," Denny replied as he and Ribetta faded from sight.

Arachimedes did not tell the monkey-man that the summoning went both ways. Whenever the spider wanted to see the monkey, all he had to do was to speak his name.

"Denny."

"Yes?" Denny popped back into view.

"Nothing, dear friend. Just testing. Good night. Sleep tight. Give my best to Lucinder."

After the seamstress and her apprentice were gone, the spider only had one thing to say before he holed himself back up into his old tree.

"He's afraid of me when he works for Lucinder?" He chuckled without amusement as he made himself comfortable for the night. "She's the scariest thing I know in the all of the worlds..."

Two

Armadillo Attitude

Arthur Dillow was mad. No, not crazy...angry. In truth, the little armadillo in human form pretty much resided in the World of Anger.

It's certainly not the best World to get stuck in. But Arthur was. Stuck.

He fumed almost constantly, as everything that confronted him in his daily life served to irritate, inconvenience, and provoke. He blamed the flowers for making him sneeze. He blamed the clouds for the darkness and the rain.

OK, the clouds deserved that. Sorry.

He blamed Chance Bonner for his friendlessness.

"Arthur," whispered a pretty little girl in pigtails. "Do you want to jump rope with me?"

"Get lost!" Arthur cried, little specks of spittle flying from his lips.

The little girl blanched and retreated.

"Why doesn't anyone like me?" Arthur murmured to himself. "Chance Bonner must be spreading lies about me. That has to be it. I can think of no other explanation, really..." And with those thoughts, Arthur plowed through a marble game in progress, kicking aggies and steelies around all willy-nilly while totally ignoring the cries of surprise and anger his thoughtlessness engendered amongst the disturbed players. *They're just middle-schoolers*, he told himself, shrugging off their very vocal objections.

Head down, seething with anger, Arthur just plodded along, making his way through Hawthorne Middle School's playground and into Hawthorne High School's side door. He continued down its gleaming hallways and into an empty classroom.

Since he had a good thirteen minutes before his next class would start, Arthur used his time to scheme.

~ * ~

"So, what's up with Arthur?" Kelly asked Chance as they ate their lunches together. Her question caused Chance to look around the crowded cafeteria for the small boy.

"I don't see him," he replied.

"That's what I'm saying," Kelly said. "He doesn't even try to hang out with us anymore. Not that he was all that fun or anything," she added. "But we are. Fun, I mean. He should really be trying to tag along at least. You know, like he used to...am I being too egotistical?"

"Well, maybe," Chance replied, clearly thinking about what Kelly had just said. "But also realistic." Chance looked Kelly in the eye. "He's new here. He doesn't have any friends. He got to know us because his parents asked my parents to look after him for a couple of days. We started to get kind of close, actually...then he seemed to have turned his back on me."

"On all of us," Kelly corrected him. "And we don't know why."

"I'll try harder to talk to him," Chance promised. "At least to find out if I did something to make him mad, or maybe hurt his feelings."

"Good idea!" Kelly exclaimed. *Good luck!* was what she was thinking, however.

"I have English class with him next period," Chance announced. "I'll try to catch him there."

This time she said it.

"Good luck," Kelly said.

"Thanks," Chance said dourly.

They both laughed at that and then returned to finishing their lunches.

~ * ~

"Hey, Arthur!" Chance said upon finding the smaller boy sitting alone in their English classroom.

Arthur grunted some kind of a greeting. At least, that's what Chance thought it was.

"Arthur, what's wrong?" Chance asked, pushing all caution aside. He was suddenly feeling bad about how Arthur looked and acted. "Did I do something to make you mad?" He decided not to mention the possibility of hurt feelings. It seemed too intimate somehow.

Arthur just shrugged.

"Well, whatever I did, I'm sorry," Chance offered, growing desperate. The first bell was ringing and he was running out of time.

"Why don't you come over to my house after school today?" Chance asked.

Arthur finally looked up, a strange expression on his sharp little features. He smiled a strange smile, too.

"Sure," he said. "That would be cool."

"Great," Chance replied, both pleased and oddly disappointed at the same time. "Meet me out front after the final bell and we'll walk there together."

"Will that dog be there?" Arthur asked, his strange expression morphing into something unpleasant.

"Dog? Oh, you mean Lucky?" Chance asked, smiling just at the thought of his canine companion.

Arthur nodded once.

"Well, I don't know," Chance admitted. "It's completely up to him. He comes when he wants to. So, yes, he might be there. Is that a problem?" Chance was puzzled. He didn't think it was possible that someone could dislike Lucky.

"Possibly," Arthur said somewhat mysteriously. "We'll see."

Their conversation was cut short by the start of their class.

They were reading *Lad: A Dog*.

"Ironic." Chance thought.

"Idiotic." Arthur thought.

~ * ~

Lucky was not waiting for Chance after school. It was not all that unusual. Lucky had things to do, places to go. Canines to meet. He had a girlfriend, after all, Chance reminded himself. Seemed like everybody wanted their time with Lucky. Everybody but Arthur Dillow, apparently.

"Why don't you like Lucky?" Chance asked Arthur as they started their stroll toward Chance's home. He couldn't help himself. The question asked itself, really.

"He doesn't like me," the smaller boy answered with a sniff. It was a scornful sniff, that sniff. It contained neither sorrow nor regret.

"Oh, that can't be true!" Chance objected.

"Oh, but it is true," Arthur responded with a little heat. "You'll see. He will growl when he sees me."

"I doubt that, but you're right, we'll see!" Chance said, trying to keep the conversation light and breezy. Why was that so hard to do?

~ * ~

"Well, hello, Arthur," said a surprised Nan Bonner as the boys entered her kitchen through the back door. "It's been a long time. How have you been?"

"I have been very well, Mrs. Bonner," Arthur responded without spirit.

"I didn't know your family was moving here after all," Nan continued, exuding warmth and care, neither of which she truly felt toward the boy.

"Yeah," he answered, again without much inflection. "We moved into that tiny house down on Twenty-fourth."

"Tiny house?" Nan asked. "Are you referring to the 'Spite House'?"

"Yes, the 'Spite House'," Arthur echoed. "That's what they call it. That's our home now."

"Well, I would love to see the inside of that house one day!" Nan crowed. "Please let your mother know, would you, Arthur? That house is famous throughout the city..."

"Sure," came the listless answer.

"Arthur, let's go up to my room," Chance said, heading for the stairwell himself.

"OK. Sure," Arthur said, turning to follow his companion. "See you later, Mrs. Bonner."

"I'll make some snacks for you boys," Nan called up after them.

"Thanks, Mom!" Chance shouted down.

~ * ~

Up in his room, Chance logged onto his Playstation and handed Arthur a wireless gaming controller. "Want to play some *Mario Party*?"

"Sure," Arthur responded. "If I get to be Donkey Kong."

"Done. I'll be Luigi."

"Fine."

The boys played for some time in complete silence. The game naturally had sound, but that day its players seemed to be in mute mode.

Nan Bonner came in carrying a tray with some chips and soda pops on it.

"I hope you can eat some of this," she said to Arthur, placing the tray down on Chance's cluttered desk. "I wasn't prepared for visitors..."

"Looks good, Mrs. Bonner," Arthur said, not even looking away from his screen.

"Your playing has really improved," Chance said.

"I've been practicing," Arthur admitted. He was really enjoying this gaming session. He had practiced long and hard just in order to completely dominate an opponent.

Which he did. Chance didn't have a chance.

Mario Party isn't normally a game of great skill, but Arthur had practiced on all of the challenge games until he had perfected them.

"Wow, Arthur," a somewhat dazed Chance said at the end of their session, "You really kicked my butt. That was really amazing!"

Chance's eyes shone with admiration for what the smaller boy had achieved.

Arthur was actually pleased by what Chance said and how he said it. He started to smile with sincerity in response to Chance's praise, then caught himself. His smile turned neutral.

He didn't look pleased.

He didn't look displeased.

"So, let's check the snacks out," Chance finally proposed. He was confused about Arthur's failure to respond to his feedback.

And Arthur?

He found himself conflicted. He wanted to talk to Chance about his winning strategy, his hard work, his determination...but his anger had become such a constant companion to him that he did not want to give it up. It seemed disloyal somehow. Like his anger had become a being worthy of respect. Someone deserving to be constantly stoked and stroked. At the very edge of his consciousness, Arthur knew he just might be wrong.

~ * ~

In the cavern, The Beast, Denny, Lucinder, and an exhausted Ribetta watched the boys at their game.

"Young Arthur is finally showing some promise," The Beast growled.

Denny smiled vacantly. He had no idea what was going on in this game, or how the boys made things happen—or not happen within it. Smiling vacantly was Denny's go-to move. In this case, however, his vacant smile was greatly enhanced by the residual after-glow of Arachimedes' venom.

Lucinder, on the other hand, was an avid gamer. She was enthusiastic about nearly every move their young protégé made.

She also was observant. She made a mental note to interrogate the little monkey-man later that day. He was very obviously hiding something...that stupid grin practically shouted at her.

"Masterful!" she cooed at the final play when Donkey Kong was crowned the winner. "That boy is blossoming!"

Ribetta was nodding off, perched on her precarious stool.

"Ribetta!" Lucinder shrieked, shocking the old seamstress into wakefulness and incipient heart attack. "Go home and get some sleep! You have a lot of work to do tomorrow!"

"Yes, Lucinder," Ribetta replied, disappearing with a soggy "poof." No sulfur smell accompanied her departure.

Mold.

Mildew.

Those were the smells of the small bit of fog which was all that remained of Ribetta in the cavern.

~ * ~

"Oh, Denny," a sly Lucinder said, sidling up to the smiling little monkey. They were alone, Arthur having gone home and Chance having gone downstairs to dinner. The Beast had disappeared in a huge sulfurous cloud as soon as the boys' game was over.

"What have you been up to today?" she whispered in Denny's ear. "Did the boy, Chance Bonner, have anything interesting to say or do during your shift this morning?"

Denny's smile grew wider, and he looked at Lucinder with admiration—and something more. "Oh, not much," he told her. "He cried out 'Durnst' during a dream. That's all."

"Durnst?" Lucinder pressed. "What is a durnst?"

"It's not a *what,*' Lucinder dear," Denny replied, his smile as wide as ever. "It's a *who*. Remember that story the boy wrote last November? Durnst was his twin in that story."

"Twin?"

"Twin."

"Chance Bonner has a twin?"

"Well, I can't be sure, dear, but yes, I think so."

"How do we find this twin?"

"Angelica would know."

"Angelica. Yes, she would know."

"She won't tell you."

"Well then, I won't ask her." And with that, a wickedly grinning Lucinder poofed out of the cavern to destinations unannounced.

Denny sighed and looked around to find himself alone.

"Good night, my love," he said to no one.

~ * ~

Later that night, two rooms down the hall from Chance's bedroom, Nan Bonner struggled to get into her pajamas. After finally getting them on and looking at the result in her full-length mirror, she collapsed onto the bed and cried.

Eventually, she fell asleep. Later that night, as the rest of the household slept, she went downstairs and slipped out of her pajama bottoms. She took her kitchen scissors to the seams of the tight nightwear and cut the pajama pants open at the seams.

All over the kitchen floor, dimly glowing blue threads pulsed.

Nan gasped. Then she went to the pantry, took out her broom and dustpan, and swept up the glowing remnants. She put them in a storage bag and placed it in the crisper drawer of her refrigerator.

She needed to think about this.

And she needed to take those scissors to her super tight jeans next. This she promised herself.

Three

Blue Magic

Nan Bonner got up the next morning and chanted a vigorous Gongyo.

Nan is a Buddhist. Nichiren Buddhists recite parts of two chapters of the Lotus Sutra twice each day, accompanied by the intoning of their sacred mantra. The recitation of the sutra is called Gongyo.

Nan's energy and focus that morning allowed her to finish her recitation in seven minutes flat.

Her service was not diminished by its velocity. Not a whit. It was powerful.

She had thrown on an old pair of sweatpants which she had not worn for years. On top, she wore one of Chance's old tee-shirts which had become too short for him.

They fit. The pants and the shirt. They fit.

Strangely vindicated by this, Nan took down every shirt, skirt, and pair of pants she had worn in the last month and spread them out on her bed.

With her tiny but sharp manicure scissors, Nan then carefully cut into the seams of each garment.

Blue thread.

Every item of clothing was held together with shiny blue threads.

Nan collected the pieces of thread and carried them down to the kitchen to add to the bag she had left in the crisper the night before.

The threads were gone. The baggie was there, but there were no blue threads in it.

Instead, there was a brilliant blue marble. Nan gasped when she saw the little orb. It was beautiful.

She took it out of the bag, with trepidation at first, but then with growing confidence. It practically throbbed with beauty, did this marble.

It should have been cold from being in the refrigerator overnight, but it was not. It was the exact temperature of the kitchen itself. Nan could barely feel it in the palm of her hand.

Except that it pulsed. She could feel it like her own heartbeat.

Nan put the marble in her sweatpants pocket and placed the newly harvested threads into the same baggie. This she plopped back into the crisper.

"Odd," she said aloud to herself.

"What's odd?" Chaz asked her, approaching her from behind. As was his habit, Chaz had arisen at dawn and gone for a vigorous walk. He was just returning, stopping in the kitchen for a cup of coffee before hitting the shower.

Nan grasped the marble in order to remove it from her pocket so she could show it to Chaz. She had already started talking before an urge caused her to change her mind and her message in mid-stream.

"I found this...umm...fuzz in my sweats," she said, showing Chaz some pocket lint which she had scraped up from the depths of her sweatpants pocket. She could feel the marble humming and throbbing in its hiding place.

"What's odd about that?" Chaz asked in return. He laughed. "And what's with those sweats? Aren't those from your 'Jogging Era'? You know those three days in May eight years ago when you thought you could become a runner?" He laughed again as he poured his coffee.

His laughter died in his throat when he turned to face his wife.

He had never seen such an expression on her face.

She looked scary. Remote. Distracted.

She looked strange, each of her features off just a smidge from normal.

And blue.

She looked blue.

"Honey, are you cold?" a now-concerned Chaz Bonner asked his wife. He put down his coffee to approach her and place his arms around her.

She seemed to snap out of her daze, and her color returned. Her features corrected themselves, smoothing out into their normal aspects.

"Oh, Chaz," she laughed, gently pushing him away. "I'm fine. Actually, I am great! And hungry. I'm going to make a ham and cheese omelet. You want one?"

"Uhh, no. No thanks, Nan. I gotta get ready for work," a slightly confused but appeased Chaz said. He was relieved, actually. Nan had announced that she was going to eat something! She needed to...

As Chaz went upstairs and the shower started, Nan took three eggs from their container in the fridge and cracked them one-by-one into a small bowl.

Each egg had double yolks except for the last one. It had three.

"Yummy!" Nan exclaimed to herself.

"What's yummy?" Chance asked, approaching her from behind like his father had done just a few minutes earlier. He had come down the stairs, however, not from outside. He was dressed and ready for school.

"A seven-yolk omelet," his mother replied cheerfully. "Want one?"

"Oh, no thanks, I had toast and cereal," Chance replied, shrugging into his parka and picking up his backpack. "Gotta meet Kelly and get to school," he added. "Bye, Mom!"

"Good-bye, sweetie," Nan practically chirped. "Have a great day!"

"Thanks. You, too!" and with that, the boy departed.

"Toast!" Nan repeated. "What a great idea!" And she made herself four pieces of toast to have with her enormous omelet.

She wolfed it all down.

Chaz came down dressed for work just as she carried her now-empty plate to the sink. She rinsed it and put it into the dishwasher.

"Well, so long, honey," Chaz said, crossing the room to give her a peck on her lips. "Oooh, is that blackberry jam I taste?" he teased her.

"Why, yes, it is!" she replied. "Or was, I should say!" She laughed at her little wordplay.

"Well, have a great day! I'm off," announced Chaz.

"Be careful out there today," Nan exhorted. "It's a jungle!"

They parted ways that fine morning in very good moods.

Moods which would soon prove very hard to maintain...

~ * ~

"Ribetta!" Lucinder screamed at full volume. "You fool! The woman has discovered our treachery!" The bony wasp-woman was enraged.

"Lucinder," her amphibious minion calmly but firmly replied. "We don't know any such thing! Just because she has removed my stitches doesn't mean she's discovered your plan. Calm down, will you? You're going to hurt yourself if you keep going on like this."

"Hurt myself?! Not discovered my plan? Wh-wh-what d-d-do you m-m-mean?" Lucinder was, in fact, swooning. Her rage appeared to have been too much for her, after all.

She sat on Ribetta's rickety stool with a plop. And then immediately hit the floor with a crack when the stool refused to remain upright.

"Lucinder!" Ribetta cried, rushing to help the smaller woman back onto her feet. "Lucinder, are you all right?"

"I'm fine, I am fine," Lucinder insisted, rising shakily. She pushed the seamstress away and brushed cavern moss and dirt from the back of her skinny black pants. "How do you sit on that thing?" she asked, pointing at the treacherous stool which remained on its side on the damp, steaming floor.

"Very carefully, Lucinder," Ribetta replied, somewhat primly. "Very carefully indeed."

"Funny," Lucinder intoned without a shred of humor in her voice. With a final scathing glance at the frog-woman, she then poofed out of the cavern.

"Probably to lick her wounds," Ribetta said to the stool. She stooped to lift it and balanced it carelessly on its three legs. It stood steadily. It seemed to preen itself, shuddering ever so slightly so that the cavern's detritus was shed from it back onto the floor.

It gleamed. Its seat curved upright in what seemed to be a smile.

It laughed.

Ribetta laughed with it. "Yes, that was funny, wasn't it?" she asked the stool. "Shame on you! You are a scamp. You know that, right?" And the pair of them proceeded to have a really great laugh together.

"What's so funny?" The Beast growled, entering the cavern with a sulfurous "poof" and a threatening scowl.

"Oh, nothing, nothing," Ribetta replied, sobering immediately. Until a little giggle erupted. She quickly covered her mouth, but her little gleeful outbursts were not completely smothered.

The Beast grinned. "OK, Ribetta," he snarled. "Don't tell me." He turned on his heel and trod off through the steaming cave. After four or five steps, he pivoted and nailed the frog-woman with his steely glare.

"Still not telling?" he asked slyly.

Ribetta burst out laughing. "No, no," she insisted between outbursts. "No, it's really not funny. Really." And she indulged in a real belly laugh.

The Beast continued his trip across the cave, pivoting again after a few more steps.

"Still?" he teased. He reversed course and swiftly approached his giggling minion. He lowered his huge horned face until he was eye-to-eye with her.

"I have to know," he pleaded, smiling very pleasantly. He almost looked nice.

"OK," choked out the bulgy little woman. "OK, but it's not that funny…"

"Tell me."

"Well, ha ha ha ha, Lucinder tried to sit on my stool, you see, and it threw itself on the floor and there she was rolling around in the mud and the moss, and oh, ha ha ha ha ha, well, I told you it wasn't very funny, ha ha ha ha…"

The Beast roared with laughter. "Lucinder? Lucinder fell? She rolled? Where, where?" he demanded.

Ribetta pointed to where Lucinder had fallen. The moss there was completely scattered and muddy water had collected in little pools where her fall had disturbed the ground.

"What did she do?" The Beast asked. "Did she jump up and start whacking the dirt and moss off of her backside?"

"Y-y-yes," Ribetta responded, breathless from laughing. "How did you know? She did just that, but, ha ha ha ha, her backside was still all muddy when she poofed out of here. There was moss clinging to her, too, oh, aha ha ha ha."

The two collapsed against each other, their knees growing weak with each successive wave of laughter.

"What's so funny?" Lucinder demanded from behind them.

She was close. Within a foot of them.

"N-n-nothing!" The Beast said, pivoting once again, this time to face the angry Lucinder. "N-n-nothing's funny."

"Could you just turn around for me for a quick moment?" he asked her. He and Ribetta exchanged a short glance and then burst out laughing again.

"Oh, I see," Lucinder said, realization washing across her sharp little features. "You are laughing about me. I get it. Well here," and she made a slow turn, "take a look. Laugh to your hearts' content."

They were. They were laughing as if they could not stop.

"Juveniles!" Lucinder sniffed. "I could have been hurt, you know!" Her protests, if anything, caused the laughing pair to laugh even harder. They hooted and slapped their knees.

"That's exactly why I came back," she continued. "I am going to fix this chair so it cannot hurt anyone else!" She brandished a roll of silver duct tape in one hand. She raised her other hand to display a broken broom handle in it.

"No, no!" Ribetta cried, her laughter drying up in the instant after her brain registered what Lucinder intended to do.

"No, please!" she repeated, stepping between Lucinder and the stool. "It won't happen again, I promise! Please don't harm my stool!"

"Harm?" Lucinder echoed. "I am not going to harm your chair-thingy. I am going to fix it!"

"No, please," begged Ribetta. "She'll behave herself from now on. Look! See, she has sprouted a fourth leg. She's stable now. Please, please put your devil tape away!"

Lucinder looked at the stool, slack jawed. "How did you do that?" she asked Ribetta. "How did you give it a fourth leg? And when?" She looked from Ribetta to The Beast and back again.

The Beast had sobered, too. He raised an eyebrow and eyeballed Ribetta.

"Magic?" he asked. "You are using magic here?"

"It's just a little harmless enchantment," Ribetta responded in a tiny voice. "Not magic, really..."

"Superb!" chortled The Beast, turning and walking away. "Just simply superb!" He paused his stride, turning to face the women once more. "Actually, Ribetta, I have an assignment for you! Please come see me later this morning..." And with that, he strode off into the dark recesses of the cavern, whistling as he went.

Lucinder made an involuntary noise. It expressed surprise, frustration, and embarrassment. Then she poofed away, leaving Ribetta in the arms—or legs—of her enchanted stool.

"Phew!" Ribetta told the stool. "That was close!"

The stool sagged in relief.

Then it retracted the new fourth leg and balanced happily on its remaining three.

All of which were blue. Bright, glowing blue.

~ * ~

The being who lived on the mountain top stirred, his meditation disturbed by an internal alarm.

The alarm had been triggered by events far, far away from his secluded hermitage. It had taken some significant time for the reverberations of those events to reach him.

But reach him they finally did.

He sighed.

He stood, stretching underused legs and arms.

He bent and touched his toes. He repeated this stretch ten times.

Satisfied his limbs were working, the being threw a rough brown robe over his clothing, stepped into a nearby pair of shiny brown cowboy boots, and with a final survey of his small but lofty domain, gradually eased out of existence.

Only the hardy little birds which lived on the excrescence of the native mountain goats noted his departure. They all stopped their pecking for the mere second it took for that disappearance to start and finish.

Then they resumed their meals.

Four

A Secret Revealed

Angelica Root raised her head and put her pen down on the desk in front of her. She rose and went to the ceiling-to-floor window which served as the exterior wall of her penthouse apartment.

The view was gorgeous, but Angelica's attention was not on the vista which could be seen, but rather on one much more distant.

"Almasty," she whispered. "Is that you?"

She seemed to hear something that made no sound. She sighed, but it was a sigh of satisfaction, not of regret or disappointment.

When she turned back to pick up her pen, Angelica wore a smile.

A big, even a beatific, smile.

She was writing to her friend, Samantha Swisher, who had become a close companion during and since their last adventure with Angelica's son, Chance Bonner.

It is a long story and is told in a book all of its own. It will not be retold here.

During the infancy of their friendship, Angelica had confided a secret to Samantha: she divulged the name of Chance's birth father. She had previously told no one, not one person, not ever, this close-held secret. But she found a connection to Samantha that gave her the confidence to confide.

She would never forget the look on Samantha's face when she revealed her mate's identity. This look completely vindicated Angelica's decision to keep their relationship a secret.

The look was awe.

It seemed appropriate, and Angelica was grateful to receive it, that look.

She had nearly finished her letter, so her return to it was just to add a postscript.

"He is coming," she wrote at the bottom of the already-signed missive. "He stirs! I need to contact the twin—can you help?"

She folded the letter into thirds, stuffed it into its envelope, addressed it, and put a festive forever stamp in its upper right corner.

"I'll drop this in the mail on my way out," she told herself.

And that is exactly what she had planned on doing. She left her apartment whistling, her mood gay and bright. But like the Bonners, her stellar mood was going to be really, really hard to maintain. She just didn't know it yet.

~ * ~

As Angelica made her way to her office, she stopped to mail her letter.

Simple, really. She held the letter in one hand and opened the mailbox chute with the other. She dropped the envelope through the chute and allowed the chute's door to swing shut.

How was she to know the mailbox was enchanted?

There were no outward signs. OK. There was one, but it's an obscure sign generally not recognized outside of magic circles, after all.

The mailbox was not standard USPS blue. It was blue, though. A bright and glowing blue.

Once Angelica turned the corner and was safely out of sight, the bright blue mailbox made its own disappearance.

As it "poofed" away, the magic mailbox ejected all of the letters and small packages it had collected while it waited for the single envelope it needed: Angelica's. It left the ejecta in a tidy bundle next to what it called a "dumb mailbox." You know, one of those completely normal mailboxes which possessed not a single scintilla of magic whatsoever.

Then, as commanded, it whisked its prize back to the being who controlled its magic.

~ * ~

Lucky was still enjoying the effects of the love potion he had been doused with at the end of the last battle of Good vs. Evil starring Chance Bonner.

Lucky existed only to protect Chance Bonner. He did his level best to do just that, but every once in a while, the urge to transform back into his true self and go cavorting with his new girlfriend was just too much to ignore.

His true self: it was magnificent. He was a tall, kilted Scotsman with a wild mane of strawberry blond hair. His bushy beard was a shade darker than the hair on his head. Let's call it light auburn. He nearly always sported a tan, belted raincoat and a snappy fedora. In this, his true guise, he visited his girlfriend.

She was also magnificent, but in a very exotic and petite way. She was almond brown and had very long black hair. She wore her hair oiled and elaborately braided. Her eyes were very large and the green of polished jade.

She was old. Older even than Lucky's true self. She was a Bodhisattva of the Earth. It was no accident that she and Lucky had been attracted to each other. Their true selves had known each other over many incarnations. And an old squirrel's potent love potion had not hurt the relationship, either. Not one bit.

In a word, she was irresistible.

So it was that Lucky was not at the Bonner house when Chance brought Arthur Dillow home after school.

But, back home and in his canine form, Lucky could not ignore the sensory evidence that Arthur had been in the Bonner house, and more specifically, that he had been in Chance's room.

Not having the power of human speech in his current form, Lucky had to be satisfied with performing a vigorous sniffing routine in front of Chance, really sniffing it up around the chair Arthur had used.

Then he nailed Chance with direct eye contact and tried to non-verbally communicate his distaste for the now-absent visitor.

"I know, I know, Lucky," Chance said. "Look, I know you don't like him, but I feel sorry for Arthur. I am going to try to make him my friend again."

Lucky sniffed a giant sniff upon receiving this news. He turned his head, pointedly not looking at Chance anymore.

"Oh, come on, Lucky," Chance begged. "Give the little guy a chance."

Lucky flopped to the floor in a pantomime of surrender.

"Good boy!" Chance said. "Thank you, Lucky."

Another sniff sufficed as acknowledgement. It was time for a good nap anyway. He was exhausted after his exertions of the day. That girl kept him going, what with her shopping and her high tea, her tennis games and her even more shopping.

Attending to her was hard work, but the rewards were outstanding. Lucky sighed heavily and happily just recollecting the sweet kiss she had deposited on his left cheek as he departed that day.

The spot still tingled.

Little did Lucky suspect what was soon going to happen to destroy his happy mood.

Five

Destiny Dyer was everything Chance Bonner was not.

She was short.

She was thin. Skinny, even. She was not athletic in the least.

She was blonde.

She had light brown eyes which were extremely nearsighted, and so it was she wore glasses. Big ones. "Cadillac rims," her mother called them.

She was shy, or appeared to be so. Although she never spoke of it, Destiny felt she had an internal core of strength coiled up within her just waiting to be summoned.

Oh, and she had the worst luck of anybody she knew or knew of. Her parents, when pressed, had to admit it, too. She was unlucky. Very.

And yet, she was Chance Bonner's twin. She did not know this. Her adoptive parents did not know this. Her father did not know this—well, he didn't even know either of his offspring existed, really.

But her birth mother knew. Her birth mother had spent the thirteen years since the twins' births hiding them. Rigorously hiding them from everyone, including themselves and each other.

They were special.

Just how special was another unknown, even to Angelica. She just knew they were. Special.

By now, Chance has been revealed as a boy whose karmic life is being lived backwards. He has discovered the Buddhist practice which gives him his strength in this, his first incarnation. He is experiencing his highest, most beneficial karmic existence in his first life, and will be reborn time after time throughout his future in increasingly worse conditions.

But he has cracked the code, has Chance Bonner. He understands he need only rediscover his Buddhist practice in those succeeding lives to immediately dispel his bad karma, turning it into good karma and benefit. This karmic transformation will be immediate and will be comprehensive.

He also understands how very difficult it is for a human being to find the right practice, the correct Buddhist practice in the world's current tarnished age. But he is determined.

And he is still so young! Statistically speaking, Chance should have many years in his current lifetime to prepare for a good death and rebirth.

Statistically speaking...

~ * ~

Destiny Dyer broke her third shoestring in a single week while trying to get ready to leave for school that morning.

"Destiny!" her mother called to her from downstairs. "Hurry, honey, the school bus is pulling up."

Destiny left the broken shoelace dangling. She grabbed her backpack and headed down the stairs, determined to catch that bus.

But of course, she tripped on the single dangling lace and fell the rest of the way down the stairs, breaking her glasses for good measure.

"Oh, sweetie, are you all right?" her mother asked, helping her up and checking her limbs and exposed skin for damage.

"I'm OK, Mom," Destiny insisted, shouldering her backpack once more. "That padding you put on the stairs worked really well," she added. "I didn't hurt myself at all this time." She stopped to pick up and examine her glasses. "The glasses didn't make it, though," she said sadly, holding them out to illustrate.

"Here, give them to me," her mother said. "I'll get them repaired today. Will you be able to get through one day without them?"

"S-s-sure," Destiny said, trying to sound positive.

She didn't feel so positive. Her eyesight was really bad. She stumbled several times on her way to the bus because she couldn't see any of the irregularities on the surface she traversed.

But she made it. She made it to the bus. She sighed in relief. Many of the children were laughing at her. They had witnessed her clumsy trip from her front porch to the bus and were convulsed in laughter.

"Sorry, Destiny," the bus driver said. "Kids are mean sometimes."

"I understand," Destiny replied. "Juveniles, am I right?" Destiny was distracted by the mean laughter, though. So distracted she didn't wonder how the bus driver—a substitute she had never seen before— knew her name.

"Oh, so right," the driver replied. "Juveniles. I mean, you could have been hurt, after all." And with that, the thin, waspish lady driver closed the school bus door and pulled away from the curb. Tiny black specks flew from her fingertips and nipped at several of the laughing children, who stopped laughing in order to desperately swat at the flying flecks. As the flecks and specks dissipated, so did the laughter.

"Mission accomplished," the driver said smugly to herself. "Juveniles."

~ * ~

Just before the school bus reached its destination, another cloud of black specks issued from the sharp-featured bus driver's skinny fingers. These specks went directly and solely to Destiny Dyer.

She fell fast asleep and did not wake up, even after all of the other students had gotten off the bus.

She slept still as the bus driver closed the door after the last departing student and drove off.

"Well, that wasn't as hard as it could have been," she commented to herself. "Angelica left a trail a mile wide pointing to this girl."

Her smile faded as she drove and she began to look worried.

"It's not like her," she continued. "Not like Angelica to leave any trace behind. What has her so distracted? It is completely out of character."

She drove on, her fear growing with every mile.

~ * ~

"She's gone!" Angelica cried, throwing her arms around her little friend.

"Who's gone, Angelica?" Samantha Swisher asked, embracing the taller woman in turn.

"Destiny!" Angelica replied, separating from her friend and pushing her long blonde hair out of her face. "Chance's twin—my daughter!"

"I just got your letter this morning," Samantha said, waving a very battered and torn envelope around. "And look at the state of it. It even stinks. It reeks of sulfur!"

"I smell something, too," Angelica said. "I smell a rat—oh, no offense intended, my good squirrel."

"None taken," the squirrel, Samantha Swisher replied. "Let's just concentrate on finding your little girl."

"Can you deploy your troops?" Angelica asked, her plaintive look speaking loudly of her desperation.

"Of course," Samantha responded. "Consider it done. I'll have every rodent in her region looking for her. But where should we start?"

"Roanoke, Virginia."

"I will get the root system working," Samantha promised.

"The root system?" Angelica Root asked, her curiosity breaking through her angst.

"We communicate through the root systems of plants," Samantha explained. "I can have the message to the tribal chiefs in Roanoke within just a few hours."

"How do we give them a description to go by? How can they begin to search for her?"

"We can't use a description, Angelica," Samantha explained. "We need a smell. We need to go to her home and get a clear sense of her signal—her scent."

"I have her address," Angelica responded, taking a scrap of paper from her jacket pocket.

Samantha took the scrap and glanced at it.

"I'll have a team of scent experts in this house by nightfall," she promised. "With any luck, we'll be on her trail within minutes of finding her scent."

Angelica noted the use of the word "luck" in her friend's reassurance. If anything, it worried her even further.

"Make sure your team understands there are two adult people living in that house," she instructed. "They must find the scent of the young girl who lives there. Tell them to be cautious and thorough— this girl is unlucky. Very unlucky. If anything could go wrong, it will..."

"Oh, really?" Samantha responded, a curious but pleased surprise beaming from her plain and honest face. "That is actually very helpful in a case like this."

"Oh? How so?"

"Bad luck has a smell of its own. A very strong smell. I have a feeling it's going to be the key to our victory!"

<h1 style="text-align:center">*Six*</h1>

Rodent Army

"The general has issued an order!" the old squirrel shouted. "Put out the call: the entire brigade is called forward!"

Rodent activity exploded after the ancient gray squirrel shouted out his command. Immediately, a large crowd of rats, squirrels, mice, beavers, porcupines, and chipmunks gathered in the large shady glade. Hamsters, gerbils, and guinea pigs watched from the windows of their human keepers' houses, looking inquisitive and wistful.

"Roll call!" the old squirrel bellowed. "Squirrels!"

"Here!" came the raucous response.

"Beavers!"

"Here!" came a less numerous but deeper collection of voices.

"Rats!"

"Here!" the loudest mid-range response so far resulted.

"Mice!"

"Here!" was the second loudest and squeakiest response...until with a deep breath, the old squirrel called for the chipmunks. Their ear-splitting response came in a full key higher than the mice's.

The mice grumbled a little at this. If you can call their high-pitched caviling grumbling, that is.

The porcupines were called. And they responded loudly and with spirit. They proudly represented the Rodent Army's field artillery. Fewer in number they may have been, but they all fully understood their importance in the army's winning strategy.

"We have a mission!" the old squirrel announced. "It came straight from General Swisher!"

An undercurrent of excited whispering greeted this announcement. General Swisher had led them on their last campaign all the way out west to Seattle to fight for the epic warrior, Chance Bonner. They all had their war stories from that adventure, and they recounted and embellished them often.

"We have a status update: Chance Bonner has a sister—a twin sister!" continued Swisher's senior non-commissioned officer. The grizzled old squirrel wore his rank on the walnut shell he used for a helmet. It sported a label which read "I Gave Blood Today." This helmet and its label were treasured memorabilia from his own combat activities in the Seattle war.

"She is missing!" he projected as loudly as he was able. Even the mice in the back of the assembly heard him clearly. "It is our mission to search for her! The general has dispatched two rats from the Roanoke Brigade to sniff out the girl's details. These details are forthcoming. The moment we have them in hand, we will scour our area for her scent, working our way south to team up with the Richmond Brigade. From Richmond, we will proceed directly to Roanoke." He paused to allow his words to soak in before continuing. "This girl may be sedated. She may be imprisoned in some way. It is very likely that she will not be able to help herself. She needs us. Chance Bonner needs us. We will not fail!"

Wild cheering greeted the old squirrel's speech. After some while, a small voice could barely be heard above the noise of the crowd.

"Sergeant Major!" it cried. "Sergeant Major!"

The old squirrel finally heard the voice and responded. "Yes," he answered. "What is it? What is your question, Private Squirrel?"

He was not surprised. The squirrels were always the most curious of all of the rodents. The younger they were, the more curious they were. This one was barely an adult.

"Does she have a name, Sergeant Major?"

"A name?" he responded. "Does who have a name?"

"The sister, Sergeant Major. The sister of Chance Bonner."

"Oh, yes," the ranking Brigade NCO responded. "Let's see, I have it here somewhere," and he appeared to be replaying a sound track in his head. "Yes, here it is. Her name is Destiny. Destiny Dyer."

"Dire?" the young squirrel echoed. "Dire, as in terrible?"

"No, it's not spelled that way," the old squirrel answered. "It's spelled with a 'Y.' D-Y-E-R."

"But it's pronounced the same, isn't it, SMAJ?"

The old squirrel bristled a little at the use of the familiar nickname for his exalted rank. But he was secretly pleased. To him, its use meant that he was beloved. His soldiers wanted to be more familiar with him. Closer.

"It is, son," he replied, "and her situation is dire, indeed. So, we all might remember her name and its alternative meaning," he continued, turning to address the entire assemblage of the Baltimore Brigade. "Return here at 0430 hours sharp. We will have the scent by then, and presumably an update on the poor girl's status. Dismissed!"

And the assembled brigade departed swiftly into trees, bushes, and thickets, intent on packing up their gear, and seeing to the maintenance of their households and offspring. They prepared for a major campaign, making last minute food forays so that their families would be provided for in their absence.

The wooded area around the glade settled down shortly before midnight as the nocturnal creatures fought their habits and tried to get some rest before their deployment.

The squirrels and the chipmunks needed no adjustment.

They were diurnal creatures who normally slept through night-time hours...but their excitement proved to be an obstacle to sleep. They were as tired as the nocturnal rodents the next morning.

Adrenalin would need to suffice.

For all of them.

Seven

Magic

Nan Bonner had tucked into a healthy lunch. Healthy meaning large.

She ate two helpings of everything at dinner, too. Chaz and Chance could not help but notice, but they were happy to see her eating again and said nothing. Even a well-intended side comment might spoil her mood.

"Dessert, anyone?" she asked, taking a carton of ice cream from the freezer and sticking her spoon into it.

"N-no. No, thanks, honey," Chaz said.

"I'm stuffed," Chance said. He was stunned. He had never seen his mother eat anything straight out of a container.

As Chaz retired to his office and Chance to his room, Nan Bonner removed a small, shiny blue ball from her sweatpants pocket and plopped it into the ice cream, scooping it up and swallowing it whole in her first spoonful.

"Ooooh, yum," she said, scooping up her second mouthful and sucking it off the spoon.

The empty ice cream container hit the garbage can just ten minutes later.

A very contented Nan Bonner went upstairs to do her evening Gongyo. After that, she was ready to brush her teeth and get ready for bed.

"I don't know why I'm so tired," she said to herself as she dragged herself up the stairs. "I am just bushed."

~ * ~

The happy day had not technically expired yet. So, it was that very same day when Nan Bonner woke up from a sound sleep to see that her bedside clock read 11:01.

She turned on her side and noted that Chaz had not yet come to bed.

"Still working, I bet," she said to herself.

As she approached the landing outside of the bedroom, Nan could hear Chaz talking to someone.

Curious, she crept down the stairs, peeking around the wall to see who he could possibly be talking to at this hour...and saw policemen. Chaz was explaining something intently to two uniformed men.

"She went to bed. I can see where her covers and pillow were disturbed. But when I tried to throw my arms around her, I realized she wasn't in bed anymore.

"She's not anywhere! I have looked everywhere in this house and out in the yard. I've walked up and down the street...my wife has disappeared!"

"Do you mind if we have a look?" one of the policemen asked.

"No, of course not! Please do," Chaz urged him. He used his arms to herd the men up the stairs—right past where Nan stood.

They did not see her. They walked right past her without noticing anything.

Nan could feel them pass. She could see them perfectly.

"Chaz!" she called out. "What are you doing? I am right here." She paused with a start when Chaz, too, walked right past her to follow the policemen up the stairs.

Nan looked at her hands, fingers splayed to make them occupy as much space as possible. She waggled her fingers.

She could see herself. No problem. Well, no problem except that her hands were glowing blue.

She looked down at her feet which protruded from her pajama bottoms.

Blue. They were as blue as her gleaming hands.

"That's our son's room," Chaz said in a whisper. "I've looked there, too. Go ahead and look around. He's a sound sleeper. I doubt that you will wake him."

Nan heard the sounds of Chance's creaky door opening. Then closing.

"We'll put out an APB," the taller of the two policemen told Chaz. "Are there any other family members she could have gone to?"

"Not here. Not anywhere near here," Chaz said. "She has a sister, but she lives in Baltimore. Wait—you know, she has a friend here. Brilliant. I mean Josephine. Josephine Schultz. Actually, she's dating one of you. A policeman, I mean. Olsen is his name."

"Do you mean Roger Olsen?" one of the men asked.

"Yes, yes. 'Roger.' That's his name," Chaz confirmed.

"Get Olsen on the comms," the taller man instructed the other. "See if he's on duty. If he is, ask him to go by this Josephine Schultz's place to see if Mrs. Bonner is there."

The second man left swiftly for the squad car, opening the passenger door, and picking up the handset for their communications system. He spoke into it, paused, then spoke again. He hung up the handset, replacing it in its cradle on the car's dash. He quickly came back to the Bonner house.

"Olsen's with Josephine Schultz," he informed his partner. "They have not seen Mrs. Bonner all night."

"Mr. Bonner," the first policeman said, turning and putting a reassuring hand on Chaz's shoulder. "Try not to worry. We'll find her. We'll put every available man and woman on the search."

"Thank you, Officers. Thank you. Please find her. Please find her and bring her home."

"If this is where she wants to be, we will make it happen," the shorter policeman said.

"What do you mean, 'if this is where she wants to be'?" Chaz asked, his confusion evident.

"She may have left of her own free will," the man explained.

"What?" Chaz was dumbfounded. "Nan? Leave? There is no way she would just up and leave me and Chance!"

"Chance?"

"Our son. Chance. And I'm Chaz. Well, that's my nickname of course, my real name is 'Charles'...look, I'm babbling. I am just so worried. Please don't waste another moment here listening to me carry on like some kind of idiot. Just find her. Please."

The policemen muttered further reassurances and left, their blue lights flashing as they pulled out of the Bonners' driveway and sped away.

Chaz slumped into a nearby armchair and dropped his head into his hands.

Nan approached him and put one blue hand on his shoulder.

She could feel him! She tried to push his arm, to see if she could move him.

She could not. Well, not much. Her push was enough to get him to rub his arm momentarily. He wasn't really doing it consciously, she noted. He was still distracted.

She crossed the room and tried to push the coffee table closer to her worried husband.

She couldn't budge it.

She swatted at a book that sat on the table. It flew across the room, hitting the wall with an impressive thud.

Chaz jumped out of his chair.

"What was that?" he said out loud. "Is anyone there?"

Nan yelled, "I'm here, Chaz. It's me, Nan. I am here!"

He sank back into his chair, moaning. "Where could she have gone?" he asked himself.

"Dad," a voice called down from the second floor. "Are you down there?"

"Yes, Chance, I am," Chaz responded. "Go back to bed, son. Everything is all right."

"OK," the boy said, sleepiness evident in his voice. "Good night!"

"Good night. Sleep tight," his distracted father said.

Nan followed her son's voice up the stairs. She was able to enter his room without opening the door.

"Weird," she said to herself.

And then things got weirder.

"Who are you?" Nan asked the old woman. "What are you doing in my son's bedroom?"

The old woman was so startled at Nan's appearance she nearly fell off her three-legged stool.

"Augh!" she cried. "Y-y-you c-can see me?" Her very large mouth gaped wide, and her glasses slid down her nose.

"What are you doing with my clothes?" Nan demanded, temporarily distracted from one curiosity by another one.

"W-w-why, I am m-m-mending them," the little old lady stuttered.

"Mending them?" a stunned Nan Bonner echoed. She stopped to consider something for a moment, then amended her question. "Oh, that's right," she said. "I took my scissors to them, didn't I?"

The little lumpy lady chuckled a bit at this. "Yes, you certainly did, didn't you?"

For some reason she didn't understand, Nan started chuckling, too.

A look of understanding washed over the old lady's face. "You ate them, didn't you?"

Nan gulped. "Ate what?" she deflected, responding defensively. She was aware she was not being completely truthful. After all, she had eaten something she probably shouldn't have.

"You ate the blue threads."

"I most certainly did not. It was a blue ball. I ate the blue ball."

"That's why you can see me," the lady said. "You are now a little magical."

"Magical? How can I be magical?"

"You might have been a little magical even before you ate the blue ball," the lady said, approaching Nan and observing her closely. "You're special, aren't you?"

Nan returned to chortling. She was just so happy all of a sudden! "No, I am just a normal human being," she replied. "But I have a very special philosophical practice—do you know about it? We chant the sacred mantra..."

"That's it!" the lady exclaimed. "The sacred mantra! That puts you in touch with the elemental forces in the universe, and in your own mind. No wonder the magic blooms!"

"Magic is an elemental force?" Nan asked, still smiling, an almost dreamy look in her eyes.

"Magic is what you call it," the old lady said. "It's really randomness, or perhaps chaos is a better word. You know the universe has positive and negative forces. Humans also have innate negativity, and they have the positive attributes to recognize it and overcome it.

"Then there are the forces which are neither positive nor are they negative. They respond to other forces with influence, for either evil or good. They are random. That is what you humans call 'magic'."

"Oh," Nan replied, faking an understanding she hadn't quite realized. "I see. Magic. Chaos. Respond. Influence. Yeah, got it..."

"You will, dear, don't worry," the old lady said reassuringly. "In the meantime, what do you want to do with your magic?"

"I feel a call!" Nan announced, her eyes dancing with glee. "I need to find out what it is...it's coming from this house!"

"Well, let's go find it, then," the old lady said.

They tiptoed from the room where Chance slept. He hadn't heard a single magic word, of course. They descended the stairs, feeling they were getting nearer to the call...

It was Chaz. He sat in the same chair he had plopped into earlier after the police departed.

But he was chanting.

Chaz didn't normally chant. Only Nan and Chance practiced Nichiren Buddhism in the Bonner household.

But he was chanting now. And he was focused on Nan.

This was what called her.

"Can you do something to give poor Chaz some rest?" Nan asked the old lady. "He is exhausted. Can you help him?"

"Of course, dear," the old lady replied, waving her hands around Chaz's head until it started nodding. She took a vial from a pocket, unscrewed its lid, and shook a drop of something very green on Chaz's head.

He was snoring immediately.

"What was that?" Nan asked. "Oh, gosh, I am so sorry. I have been so rude. What is your name? I am Nan. Nan Bonner."

The women shook hands. "I am Ribetta," the old lady said. "It is so very nice to meet you, Nan."

"Ribetta!" a loud voice screeched from the boy's bedroom above their heads. "Ribetta, where are you?"

It was Lucinder.

"Coming!" Ribetta responded, scrabbling up the stairs as fast as her rubbery legs would allow. "I'm coming, Lucinder!"

She stopped and turned back toward Nan. "You can come, too," she said, winking slyly. "I don't think Lucinder will be able to see you. But I think you will be very interested in seeing her."

Nan was feeling mischievous. Was this another random, magic thing? She thought it must be so, and she embraced it.

"I'm coming!" she responded, climbing the stairs nimbly and following Ribetta as closely as humanly possible. This thought made her chuckle again.

Lucinder was not alone. The Beast paced the breadth of the cave behind her. Denny stood some distance away in a dark corner, a dreamy look on his face.

Ribetta took this all in in one quick glance. "How is Arachimedes?" she asked Denny.

"Oh, good, he is good," the monkey-man replied vacantly. His smile widened if anything.

"Ribetta, where have you been?" Lucinder screamed.

"Oh, I was looking for some missing thread," the seamstress lied. "The Bonner woman cut all of her seams apart earlier today," she continued, telling the parts of the truth that served her.

"Well, did you find it? The thread?" Lucinder bullied.

"Yes, I did," the little woman said, returning to lying. She turned as if to extract something from a small cloth bag she carried. "Do you see them?" she hissed to Nan.

"No," Nan replied. "I only see you."

"Do you see the cave?"

"No, I don't see a cave."

"Oh, pooh," the old seamstress said, turning to face Lucinder once more. She held out a large spool of shining blue thread.

"You see, Lucinder?" she asked, all smiles now. "I have the thread."

"Well, get to work!" the wasp-woman shrieked.

"What's with him?" Ribetta asked her up-tight boss, nodding her head in the direction of the pacing Beast.

"I don't have a clue," Lucinder replied, dropping her antagonistic attitude. She leaned in closer to her seamstress so she could lower her voice. "He's been like that all day," she whispered.

"Oh dear," Ribetta responded sympathetically. "That explains your anxiety."

"Anxiety? What anxiety?" Lucinder asked, her voice nearing a shriek once again. "I am not anxious! I am, uhh, driven, that's it, yes, driven!"

"OK, OK, just calm down, Lucinder," Ribetta said, patting the tiny wasp-woman on her pointy shoulders.

"Who's your friend?" Denny asked from his corner.

"I can see him!" Nan shouted in fright and delight. "I see that little brown man with the monkey face!"

"Oh, hi!" Denny shouted, trying to match Nan's tone of voice. "I see you, too! Say, aren't you Chance Bonner's mother?"

Ribetta did her best to shush both Denny and Nan, but the task proved to be impossible. By the time she communicated her desire for them to be quiet, The Beast had stopped his pacing and stepped in close, his hot breath ruffling the blue material on her billowy gown.

"What is going on here?" he growled. "Who is the monkey talking to? Is this more of your magic?"

"N-n-not exactly," the little old lady said, shaking with something that was not exactly fear.

What was it if it wasn't fear?

She burst out laughing, guffawing right in The Beast's glowering face. He held his angry pose for another two seconds, and then his lips started to curl up and laughter bubbled up from deep within him.

Soon they were collapsing against each other again, laughing like drunken fools.

They were remembering Lucinder with clods of moss hanging from her backside.

They were remembering Lucinder swatting at her tight little backside in a vain attempt to remove the evidence of her debacle.

"W-w-why is this so funny?" Ribetta asked The Beast between bouts of laughter.

"I don't know," he replied, gasping for breath. "It. Just. Is."

"Juveniles!" Lucinder shouted. "I have somewhere else to be!" And she disappeared in a poof of sulfur.

Nan had crossed the room to be closer to Denny. She couldn't see the cavern. To her, the space Ribetta and Denny occupied was just an extension of Chance's bedroom.

It took a minute for The Beast and Ribetta to get control over themselves.

"Who is the monkey talking to?" The Beast asked Ribetta. He was huffing heavily, trying to regain his breath.

"Oh, he is talking to Nan Bonner," the little frog woman said.

"Chance Bonner's mother?"

"Yes, Chance Bonner's mother."

"How is this happening?"

"Well, I am afraid to tell you that Denny has become friends with a spider, and Nan Bonner has eaten a ball of blue spider webs."

"Are you going to explain what you just said?"

"Denny went with me to collect blue spider webs for my work, you know, the work Lucinder has me doing—you know, altering Nan Bonner's clothing? Remember, so that she would become so weak that you all could assume control of her?"

"Go on."

"He met an old friend of mine. Arachimedes, his name is. He is a spider."

"Just a spider?"

"Well, yes, just a spider."

"He speaks with monkeys?"

"All spiders can speak if they wish."

"I did not know that."

"Yes, they all have magic."

"All spiders have magic?"

"Yes."

"Go on."

"Well, Arachimedes took a liking to Denny, and just gave him a taste of venom. You know, like a friendly little nip."

"Like a binding pact, you mean?"

"Well, now that you put it like that, once a spider has made you a friend, you are kind of under its spell."

"Because they're magic?"

"Yes. Because they are magic."

"So, the monkey is drugged?"

"Yes. The monkey is drugged by spider venom."

"He looks happy."

"Oh, he is. He is very happy."

"And the woman?"

"She ate spider webs. Blue spider webs."

"Is it a human's habit to eat spider webs?"

"No, actually it was a total fluke. You see, she found my threads in her garments, gathered them together, put them in a baggie and placed them in her vegetable crisper."

"Is this going somewhere?"

"Oh, yes, it is going somewhere very odd and unusual."

"Please go on."

"It turns out that the crisper and the baggie combined to make a perfect environment for the magic threads to morph."

"Morph?"

"Yes, you know, change, mutate..."

"I know what morph means."

"Oh, so sorry, sir. I didn't mean to insult your intelligence. Yeah, so the threads morphed into a ball of pure magic."

"And?"

"Well, some urge caused the woman, you know, Nan Bonner, to eat the magic ball."

"She ate it?"

"In a half gallon of vanilla ice cream."

"That does sound good."

"I know, right? She really seemed to enjoy it."

"What then? So, after eating the magic ball she's magic, too?"

"It would appear so."

The pair continued to watch the human woman and the giddy monkey-man talk and laugh familiarly. Although The Beast could not actually see the woman, it was easy to tell from Denny's half of the conversation that it was a lively two-way talk. They seemed to be getting on very well.

"Like a house afire?" The Beast asked the frog-woman.

"Excuse me?" she asked.

"They seem to be getting along like a house afire."

"Oh, yes. They do."

"What are we going to do about this situation?"

"I don't have a clue," Ribetta confessed. "I've never really seen anything like this."

"Are you talking about the enthralled monkey or the magic human?"

"Both."

"Oh."

"Yeah, 'Oh.'"

They sighed.

"Well, come up with a plan by morning," The Beast said.

"What?"

"I said, come up with a plan by morning," The Beast repeated. "You're the magic one here. You're the only one who can figure out how we undo what has been done."

"I see. I guess you're right."

"Oh, and Ribetta?" The Beast said, moving closer once again and lowering his booming voice.

"Yes?"

"I want to meet these spiders of yours."

"Oh, no, sir, that would not be a good idea! I've already done one magic favor for you today. Let's not get greedy!"

"Oh, and can you tell me why not?" He leaned in with a particularly evil grin. He hiked his massive eyebrows twice for emphasis.

"Spiders do not like humans, sir."

"Are you calling me 'human'?"

"Yes, you are part of the human psyche. In the many faceted eyes of a spider, that makes you human."

"I see. I accept your explanation. But I do not accept your conclusion. I will meet a spider. It should be this Arachimedes you mentioned. Make it happen. Soon." The Beast poofed out of the cavern and the erstwhile conversation.

"Oh, no," Ribetta moaned. "This is going to be terrible."

"What is going to be terrible?" Nan Bonner asked, having approached her silently. The woman was even bluer than before, Ribetta noticed.

"Oh, nothing," Ribetta lied. "Everything is peachy. Where is Denny?"

"He got a call."

"A phone call?"

"No, he said he just got a call. Someone called him."

"Arachimedes," the frog-woman said, more to herself than to anyone else.

"Oh, his friend," Nan gushed. "He told me about him. I would love to meet him."

"No, no you wouldn't," Ribetta said curtly. "He does not like humans."

"But am I still human? Haven't I become a creature of magic like you and Arachimedes?"

"Hmmm. You may be right," Ribetta allowed. "You know, we might want to test that theory after all."

"I am ready when you are!" Nan announced happily.

"That's just it," Ribetta admitted with a sigh. "I am not sure I am ready."

And mere seconds later, both women poofed away, their destination unannounced but understood.

Eight

A School Bus

"I will show them how mature adults get things done," Lucinder muttered to herself.

She had just materialized back in the school bus she had been driving before something instinctive told her to take a break and check on happenings in the cavern.

Lucinder had gone rogue. After Denny let it slip that the possibility—or even likelihood—of Chance Bonner having a twin was real, she set out on her own to find and abduct her. She took her intel to the Devil King himself and received his sanction to acquire the person of one Destiny Dyer. She was going to make some major points with this coup!

So far, so good.

She had the girl sedated and lying comfortably in the very front bench seat of the bus where she could keep an eye on her.

Keep an eye on her...

Lucinder started. Where was the girl? She ran up and down the aisle of the bus, searching in vain for her human cargo.

"Where is she?" she wailed out loud. "She could not have escaped on her own. She was under my mesmer!"

A tiny little squeak caught the wasp-woman's attention. "What was that sound?" she said to herself, making a more thorough examination of the dark corners under the bench seats.

There! There was something!

She reached into the corner and snatched the small object. Putting her hand up to her face, she slowly unclenched her fist until she could just make out what she had captured.

A gerbil?

"Are you a gerbil?" she demanded, her angry face mere centimeters from the tiny trembling creature.

"I-I-I am," the creature piped.

"Speak up!" Lucinder shrieked.

"I am! I am a gerbil!" the little rodent said as loudly as was possible for its tiny vocal cords.

"And just what are you doing here?" Lucinder continued her interrogation. "Did one of those nasty juvenile delinquents smuggle you on board in one of their filthy knapsacks?"

"Backpacks," the creature corrected.

"What?"

"They're called backpacks."

"Alrighty then, smart aleck, did one of those nasty human children smuggle you on board in one of their filthy backpacks?"

"No. No, I didn't see any humans. I came with the army."

"The army?"

"The Baltimore Brigade. The Rodent Army."

"There's a rodent army?"

"Oh, yes, and it's fabulous! I wanted to join, but they said I was too young. So, I just followed them, you know, hidden in their supply wagon, until we found our target."

"Your target?"

"You know, our objective. Our mission. The girl. The sister of some legendary warrior. His twin, they said."

"Who said?"

"The sergeant major said that General Swisher provided the intel."

"Intel?"

"The girl's identification. And her scent."

"Oh bother! This is getting me nowhere," Lucinder screamed in frustration. "Why did you remain behind? Are you some kind of incompetent spy?"

"I think I have been accidentally mesmerized," the creature said. "I crawled inside the girl's sweater pocket, and there were some little black things there that climbed right up my nose. That's all I remember."

"Then why aren't you still in the girl's pocket?"

The little creature hung his head and sniffed back a woeful sob. "I don't recall, but they must have found me and...and...and...and left me behind!" he wailed. Now the tears came.

Lucinder found herself moved by the gerbil's display of grief.

But she also knew she could use his sense of betrayal to her own nefarious benefit.

"They treated you very unfairly," she said sympathetically.

The gerbil raised his big, teary eyes and looked at Lucinder with gratitude. "They did treat me unfairly. Cruelly, even. They left me here alone and vulnerable."

"Well, you're safe with me now," Lucinder said, patting the little rodent's head with an index finger. "I will take care of you. Now, where do you think they took that pesky little human?"

"Oh, I can tell you," the gerbil responded eagerly. "I happen to have a very good nose. If you can drive this contraption, I'll just stick my head out of the window and tell you which direction to take..."

"That sounds like a plan!" Lucinder responded, carrying the gerbil up to the driver's seat. She opened the big side window and carefully placed the creature on her left shoulder. The little rodent sniffed the air.

"Straight ahead!" he cried.

"Straight ahead it is," said Lucinder, starting the bus up and putting it in gear. "Straight ahead it is."

~ * ~

"Where are my minions?" The Beast called to no one in particular.

Ribetta was the only creature in the cave. She felt she had better respond to her boss.

"I really don't know," she replied. She returned to her sewing, hoping her lack of knowledge would cause The Beast to lose interest in her.

"So, I think I hit it off pretty well with that spider friend of yours," The Beast said insinuatingly. "I think he liked me."

"I think you are unable to perceive the truth of things when they don't flatter you," the little frog-woman replied.

"What?" The Beast roared.

"I said that you came away with a very different impression than I did," Ribetta replied. Her randomness was at play again. She was not going to allow The Beast's influence to keep her silent and complacent. Not any longer, at any rate.

This is the nature of randomness. It can react in completely different ways to the same stimulus—or not.

It is chaos. It cannot be predicted. It cannot be commanded.

And The Beast was trying to harness the chaos of the magic swamp, or of its spiders, at any rate.

It would never work.

But the favorable impact Nan Bonner had on Arachimedes...now that was going to create a significant influence. And Nan Bonner had only one major desire, and that was for the happiness of herself and others. Especially her son, Chance Bonner. It was going to be very interesting to watch, this influence. Chaos would react, that much was certain. In exactly what way, no one could say.

~ * ~

In his room, Chance awakened from a sound sleep to find the house eerily silent. No delicious smells emanated from the kitchen.

He got up and dressed quickly. He descended the stairs and found his father fast asleep in an armchair in the living room.

"Dad?" he said quietly, putting his hand on his father's shoulder.

Chaz Bonner's head merely slumped over onto his right shoulder. He did not awaken.

"What's going on here?" Chance said to himself.

"Mom!" Chance cried next, not caring if his shout caused his father to awaken. He rather hoped it might.

No response from his mother. His father did not budge.

Chance did a quick search of the house, calling now and then for his mother. Finally, with a glance at the kitchen clock, he grabbed an apple and a banana, slung his backpack over his shoulder, and left for school.

~ * ~

During his morning classes, Chance became increasingly more worried about his parents. At the lunch table where he sat, as was his custom, with Stefan Schultz, Kelly O'Hara, Millicent Lee, Sarah Stengler—and now Arthur Dillow—Chance expressed his concern to his friends.

Stefan was the first to respond. "The cops called the apartment last night looking for your mother."

"What?" Chance cried, grabbing the tall blond boy by his lab coat lapels. "Why didn't you say something earlier?"

"My sister made me swear!" Stefan said, smoothing down his crumpled garment. "She's been texting me every thirteen minutes with updates. She and Roger have been out looking for your mother since midnight..."

"And?" Chance prompted, really panicking now.

"And nothing so far," an abashed Stefan admitted. "I'm sorry, Chance, I just hoped we would have good news for you by now."

"How did the police get involved?" Kelly interrupted.

"Chance's Dad called them when he discovered his wife was missing."

Chance just sat in a daze, silently chanting the mantra his mother had taught him in an effort to calm himself. He focused on his mother and on her welfare.

He stood and stepped away from the lunch table.

"I have to go now," he announced, with a look that combined both worry and determination.

"I'm coming with you," Kelly said, also rising and stepping out of the table well.

"You're not going without me," Stefan announced, also rising.

"You'll need my powers of observation," Sarah said, getting to her feet.

"And my brains," added Millicent, also rising.

"Can I have your desserts?" Arthur Dillow asked, hungrily surveilling the goodies which were being abandoned.

The five departing teens did not bother to answer Arthur, but turned and departed almost as one.

Arthur scooped all of their cakes, cookies, and gelatin snacks into a pile in front of him and began to dig in.

"It's good to have friends," he said as he chewed and slurped noisily.

Somewhere, very deep inside, Arthur knew he just might be wrong.

~ * ~

"Stop here!" the gerbil cried. "This is where they took the human!"

Lucinder pulled the school bus to the curb. They were back in Roanoke, parked in front of a house in its suburbs.

"Isn't this the human girl's home?" Lucinder asked in outrage. "Have they brought her back from where we started?"

"It would appear so," the gerbil responded, looking Lucinder in her eyes from its perch on her shoulder. "You're pretty, did you know that?" it said, examining her worried face very closely. "I think I am developing feelings for you..."

"What? Oh, uhh, thank you, thank you very much," the distracted villain said. She was sweating. She could not be away from the cavern for very much longer. She might lose her position as head minion with the powerful Beast, after all.

Plus, she was sneaking around on missions of her own without asking his permission.

As if her thoughts had summoned him, with a mighty poof The Beast materialized in the bus, waving his arms to clear the air immediately around him of sulfurous clouds and stench.

"Boss!" Lucinder cried. "I can explain!"

"You'd better," The Beast said threateningly. "You have better have a really good explanation.

"Or a very bad one." And here he actually smiled at her.

"You're not mad?"

"Oh, I am quite mad, as you very well know," The Beast joked. Almost. "I am very impressed that you have been one step in front of me in this matter."

"Really?"

"Oh, yes, really, Lucinder. So tell me, how did you discover there was a twin? How did you find her? How did you capture her? And most importantly, how did you lose her?" His good humor had disappeared in its entirety. He now glowered at the twitchy little woman, tendrils of steam escaping his flared nostrils.

"Denny told me!" Lucinder blurted. "He came back from picking spider webs with Ribetta a changed monkey! I don't know what happened to him there, but he got all 'talky' after he returned. Said he overheard Chance calling for his twin. It all started with a story the boy wrote a few months ago. He called the twin 'Durnst,' apparently. Denny said Chance Bonner blurted out his fictional twin's name in his sleep. But you know that boy has a very unique, scary, and prescient mind, Boss. Denny knows that, too." She paused to gulp in some air. "So Denny said he was pretty certain Chance Bonner had a real twin."

"Sounds like some slim evidence to me," The Beast huffed. "Fluff. A lot of nothing, really. Why did you react to such a flimsy speculation on the monkey-man's part?"

"You had to see him, Boss. Denny, I mean. He was practically glowing...and sir," she paused to make sure she had his full attention.

"Denny is my best monkey. He is not given to speculation of any kind. He is solid. He is dependable. He is Denny. I stand behind his solid, dependable hunches." She continued this thought with something she muttered only to herself. "Even though this is his very first hunch..."

The Beast looked thoughtful. That's because he was thinking.

"As it turns out, he was right," The Beast admitted. "How did you find the twin?"

"I went through Angelica's garbage," Lucinder said. "She must have modernized...she had thrown away an old Rolodex. It had Chance's information in it. And it had identical information about the twin. Destiny Dyer. It wasn't at all difficult to figure out the relationship. There were notes about birthdates and times. Weights, lengths...you know, stuff parents care about...

"And if I may be so bold, sir, how did *you* find out about the twin?"

"I had Ribetta fashion me a magic mailbox," The Beast admitted without hesitation. "I intercepted Angelica's mail. Oh, and I got much more intel than that about the twin.

"The father of Chance Bonner and Destiny Dyer is afoot!" The Beast hooted in triumph. "We have hit the jackpot this time, Lucinder!" And he took the little wasp-woman by both hands and pulled her to her feet. He twirled her around and around, laughing and cheering all the while.

The gerbil held on to Lucinder's shoulder for dear life. When the twirling stopped, he slumped to his side and crawled inside her shirt collar where he fell into a swoon.

Lucinder and The Beast left the school bus where it was and returned to the cavern.

Neither of them was consciously aware they had a stowaway with them.

Nine

A Dog Day

Lucky awakened with a start. He had been having a marvelous dream involving his girlfriend and a very large, meaty bone when he sensed something was wrong.

He slowly pried open one eye and looked around Chance's room.

Chance was sleeping soundly. The boy was not the cause of the disturbance.

Something outside his range of vision was taking place in Chance's room.

Lucky smelled bad. No, he himself did not stink, he could smell bad elements. He could also smell good elements...that one over there, for example, smelled a lot like Chance's mother. He detected one other scent, one not either bad or good, but rather bad and good.

It's hard to explain smells to beings who do not have the nose of a dog.

He raised his head. He also heard something. It was outside.

Lucky quietly strode on all four paws to Chance's bedroom window which looked out onto the street. He nosed aside the blinds to gain a visual on the front yard and street.

There was a police car pulling out of the Bonners' driveway.

No sooner had it pulled off than five large Dodge Challengers, all black, silently drove up the street, pulling over near the curbs on both sides, right in front of the Bonner house. Their engines continued to run, albeit almost silently...and then the black muscle cars scattered. They pulled away quickly, tires squealing, and drove off in all directions...just as a turquoise Thunderbird drove up and made the turn up the Bonners' driveway.

Lucky knew what this meant: it meant trouble was brewing.

Checking on Chance once more, Lucky quickly descended the stairs and exited the front door of the house.

Well, he had to use the dog door to do this, but exit the house he did.

The door of the little Thunderbird flew open, and Lucky quickly entered and tucked himself into the carpeted protrusion that substituted for a back seat.

"I appreciate this, Lucky," Josephine Schultz said, throwing the car into reverse and backing down the driveway. "I think you remember Roger Olsen," she continued, nodding to the large man occupying the passenger seat.

Lucky nodded to the man, who looked back at him in surprise. "It's almost like he understands what you're saying," Roger said.

"You don't know Lucky yet," the beautiful blonde young woman responded, "so we'll let you go this once."

"Lucky," she segued. "Nan Bonner is missing. We are searching for her. Can you help us?"

The dog nodded once again, but was suddenly at a loss for what to do.

Didn't he just smell Nan Bonner up in Chance's bedroom? The scent was a little different than normal, but he was pretty sure...

They drove on, stopping at every street corner to have a reconnoiter. And a sniff. They drove on until the sun rose, and then drove on some more.

At precisely seven in the morning, Josephine, AKA "Brilliant" Schultz, dropped Roger off at the police station where he was shortly to go on shift. She and Lucky continued searching. They passed many other cars and drivers as they drove, but failed to notice the peculiar prevalence of black, orange, and red Dodge Challengers and white, gold, and silver Chevrolet Impalas on the road.

If they had noticed the two distinct groups of cars, they would have also noted that the Impalas herded the Challengers away from the little Thunderbird, just as a shepherd chases various threats away from its precious flock.

Brilliant stopped to text her brother every thirteen minutes, but had no news, good or bad, to share with him.

By late afternoon, she was exhausted. "I need to go home and get some shut-eye," she explained to Lucky. She had pulled up into the Bonners' driveway to let the dog out.

But Lucky put up a fit. He barked and grabbed at her sleeve with his teeth, urging her to enter the house with him.

He wanted to see if Nan Bonner's scent was still in Chance's room.

"OK, OK," the young woman finally surrendered. "I'll go in with you, stop pulling."

Lucky released her sleeve immediately and ran for the door. Seconds after he shot through the dog-door, a bleary-eyed Chaz Bonner opened the people-door to let Brilliant in.

"I feel like I've been drugged," a groggy Chaz said, closing the front door after the girl entered.

"Any word from the police?" Brilliant asked the woozy man.

"No, not a word," Chaz said sadly. "But I have been asleep almost all day in that chair, right there." He pointed at the armchair. "I can't believe I have been sleeping all of this time," Chaz continued. "It's not natural. It doesn't feel right…"

"Mr. Bonner," Brilliant interrupted, putting her hand on his shoulder. "Maybe you'd feel better if you showered and changed. While you do, I can scrounge you up something to eat and put on some coffee."

"That sounds good," Chaz responded. "No, actually, that sounds great. I'll be back down in a few minutes." He turned and slowly approached the stairs, which he took one by one until he finally reached the second floor. Eventually, Brilliant could hear the water running in the master bedroom's shower.

She went to the Bonner kitchen, where she found butter, eggs, cheese, and some ham. She assembled the ingredients and made a large pan of scrambled eggs.

"Toast! Mr. Bonner could use some carbs, too," she told herself.

She returned to the refrigerator to get more butter and jam when something else caught her eye.

There was something bright, bright blue in the vegetable crisper! Looking over her shoulder to make sure that she was still alone, Brilliant snaked the crisper drawer open and removed a small baggie. It was nearly full of little blue spheres which glowed from within and pulsed with—what, exactly?

"Power," she initially said to herself. "No," she amended. "Promise," she decided. On a sudden impulse, she took one of the blue balls from the baggie and palmed it in one hand. She resealed the baggie and returned it to the crisper.

She popped the blue ball that she held into her mouth and swiftly swallowed it. It was not an action she thought about. She very nearly couldn't resist the impulse; when she tried to resist the urge to eat the ball, her curiosity and sense of wonder completely overwhelmed the saner of the voices in her head.

~ * ~

When Chaz Bonner walked into the kitchen, he found a plate of scrambled eggs and buttered toast on a plate on the counter. Fresh coffee was still spewing into the coffee-maker's carafe.

There was no sign of Brilliant Schultz, though.

"Not another disappearance!" Chaz said to himself. "Something must have come up. Brilliant wouldn't just take off without a good reason...but then, Nan wouldn't either."

Brilliant tried to capture Chaz Bonner's attention, but she was a very intelligent young woman. The evidence of her senses told her very quickly that he could not, in fact, see or hear her.

She sat and watched him eat, pondering her next move.

On a whim, she ran up the stairs and entered Chance's room.

Impulses. Urges. Whims. They all added up to the same thing: karma. Her urges and whims had gotten her to where she was meant to be.

In a cavern.

With a large, horned creature, a small waspish woman and a man who largely resembled a monkey.

And a frog. Or a toad, she wasn't good at what the differences between them were. A frog—or a toad—wearing a filmy blue dress, sitting on a blue three-legged stool in front of an ancient sewing machine.

The frog's toenails were blue.

Her thread was blue.

And when Brilliant looked down at her own hands, she discovered that she, too, was blue. She was now a bright, glimmering blue.

"How odd," she said aloud, drawing the attention of the four beings in the cave to herself.

"The Schultz girl of many first names!" the horned creature cried. "Can you see us?"

"I have seen all of you before," Brilliant started to say. She was remembering a pair of battles in which these creatures all presented as enemies. As enemies to her and nine emanations of herself. The Ten Demon Daughters. These creatures were enemies to all of the forces supporting Chance Bonner...and they all resided inside the head of the self-same Chance Bonner.

"I have seen all of you before," she repeated. "Except for you," she nodded at the frog-seamstress. "You, frog. Or toad," she added.

"Frog," the seamstress said.

"Thanks," Brilliant responded.

"No problem," the frog-woman responded.

"So, are you saying you can see all of us now?" The Beast asked once again. "All four of us?"

"Yes, and the dank and dark rocky place where you stand...right in the middle of Chance Bonner's bedroom!" Brilliant responded, trying to remain calm and measured.

"The orbs! They must be mature!" the frog-woman crowed. "How marvelous! You are completely and permanently magical, my dear!"

"Magical?" Brilliant echoed. "Permanently?"

Ribetta smiled from ear to ear. "Yes, dear, you're one of us creatures of magic now! Congratulations on your transformation!"

"But shouldn't this transformation of yours have been my choice? My free choice?"

"Just how did you make this transformation anyway?" The Beast demanded, stalking closer to the now-magic creature, the former human being known to family and friends as Brilliant or Josephine, or JB Schultz. Her full given name was Josephine de Beauharnais Schultz, and nicknames had become the only way for her friends and family to deal with it.

Ribetta had lost some of her smile. "But you chose to eat the blue sphere, did you not?"

"Yes, but without knowing what would happen to me."

"And not knowing what would happen to you didn't slow you down one bit, did it?"

"Well, no, it didn't, actually..."

"See?"

"Well, I don't see," The Beast snarled, reminding the two women of his presence. He turned his full attention upon Brilliant. "How. Did. You. Accomplish. This. Transformation?" He stared at her, a look of feverish anticipation on his face. The look faltered when after several moments, Brilliant had still not answered him.

"Do you see me?" he cried. "Do you hear me?"

"Yes, yes, I see you quite clearly. I hear you very well," Brilliant answered. "I just don't know if I should tell you."

"Oh? And why not?" The Beast asked in surprise.

"I don't know!" Brilliant cried. She looked from Ribetta to The Beast, and then down at her own hands, pulsing blue in front of her own eyes. "I just don't feel like it!"

"Randomness!" cried Ribetta. "Chaos! That is what magic is, Stanley!"

"You dare to call me Stanley?" The Beast roared. He quieted instantly. "Wait. Wait a minute. How did you know my name was Stanley?"

"I'm magic, silly!" the frog-woman replied. "I see things most beings cannot.

"And like this young lady here," and she gestured to Brilliant at this point, "I, too, am a creature of the chaos. The time of your influence over me is at an end. I don't wish to work with you any longer."

"Not work with me? Why?" cried The Beast. "Why—and how— would you break our agreement?"

"There is no *why* to it. It is my nature. As for the *how*, it is so very easy: I will simply leave!" And off she poofed. Her stool poofed away seconds later.

Suddenly, Ribetta's head, and only her head, reappeared in the air above the stunned creatures still looking at the spot she had been standing on.

"Coming, dear?" she said to Brilliant.

The young woman smiled brightly—brilliantly, really—and said, "Yes! Yes, please!" When Ribetta's head poofed away, so did the now magically blue creature, Brilliant Schultz.

The Beast, Lucinder, and Denny stared at the now vacant spaces where the two women had once been, and then stared for a while at each other.

"Stanley?" Denny eventually said. He tittered.

Lucinder, too, began to smile, and then to laugh. "Stanley?" she repeated.

The wasp-woman and the monkey-man lost control of themselves almost immediately, laughing so hard they had to sit down on the cavern floor.

The Beast stared at them, his mouth agape. "It's a perfectly normal name," he said.

This just made the pair laugh harder than before.

"I begin to understand your use of the word juvenile," The Beast said to Lucinder. He poofed away immediately, leaving a gigantic cloud of sulfur behind.

Now the pair laughed and choked, the sulfur cloud interfering with their ability to breathe.

"St-st-stanley!" Denny managed to say, his face now looking blue.

Not from magic.

From lack of oxygen.

Lucinder grabbed the monkey's arm and wheezed, "better go now," and with a poof and a poof, the pair escaped.

~ * ~

Lucky sat in Chance's closet, the door just enough ajar to allow him to watch the empty room.

But he knew the room wasn't really empty. He could smell Brilliant Schultz, and he sensed the elements. You know, the elements of good and evil. And the one element which was neither good nor evil...and like a coating of oil, this same smell now covered the true smell of Brilliant Schultz.

There was something more. It was a common odor. It was rodent. Lucky could not see a rodent. But he knew one was near.

The puzzled dog watched and sniffed until everything vanished, and the room became truly empty. Then, exhausted by his day's efforts, Lucky fell fast asleep, oblivious to the world and the peoples—and rodents—in it.

Ten

Bad Luck

"Oh, darling, we are so happy to have you back!" Dorothy Dyer cried. "Where have you been? How did you get back here?"

"I'm afraid I wasn't able to make out much of it," Destiny answered. "You know, I didn't have my glasses."

Her mother nodded in empathy. "I know, honey. I got them fixed today." And she crossed the room to fetch the case which had the girl's glasses in it. She removed the glasses from the case and carefully put them on Destiny's nose, easing the earpieces into place.

"Whoa," Destiny cried, taking the glasses off and handing them back to her mother. "These aren't my glasses, Mom. They gave you the wrong ones! The prescription on these is even stronger than mine!"

"Oh dear," her mother said, staring at the glasses a moment before returning them to their case. "What bad luck!"

"Yeah, typical, right?" the girl responded, smiling blindly at where she thought her mother sat.

Her mother smiled back, and then remembered they had a problem to discuss. "Destiny, when the school called today to say you weren't there, I didn't know what to do! I called the police. I called your father. I called everyone we know. I was in a panic. Then suddenly, you're back! Where were you? How did you get back here?"

"Mom, I'm sorry, but I was asleep most of the time. I don't remember much of the day at all. And then, I woke up back in my own bed!"

"OK, OK," her mother reassured her. "Tell me what the last thing was you remember from this morning."

"Well, the kids were laughing at me on the bus," Destiny began.

"Why? Why would the children laugh at you?"

"They watched me walk from the house to the bus. I tripped like a hundred times. They thought it was funny, I guess. I'm used to it, Mom. I always get laughed at."

"I am so sorry, honey," her mother replied, putting her arms around her unlucky daughter. "Go on."

"The bus driver was nice. Said something about juveniles and whatever. She made me feel better about everything. But that's all I remember..."

"The bus company said your driver this morning was a substitute."

"Yeah, I had never seen her before," Destiny said. "It was funny. She was so small and skinny I wondered how she could even drive that big bus!"

"Would you recognize her if you saw her again?"

"Yeah. I got a good look at her. That is odd, isn't it? I can still sort of see her face, smiling at me, telling me to rest and relax..."

"Rest and relax?" Dorothy repeated. "That's an odd thing to say."

"I guess it is, now that you say it," Destiny mused. "And when I visualize her, she is looking directly at me...she's not driving the bus. She is standing right over me."

"Well, that does it," her mother decided. "I am calling the police, and I am calling the school district. That bus driver has a lot of explaining to do."

~ * ~

Lucinder dove into a camelia bush after she heard the girl's mother threaten her. Denny was already lying under a nearby laurel, fast asleep.

"Denny," Lucinder hissed at him. "Denny, wake up!"

Lucinder knew Denny's sleep was not natural. "He's been visiting that spider again!" she told herself. "Spider venom! He's addicted to the stuff."

She poofed away, leaving Denny snoring happily.

She failed to see a small spider hanging by a slim thread from the laurel. As she made her escape, the spider lowered itself until it hovered right over Denny's ear.

It began to whisper to the monkey-man. As its message was delivered, Denny's mouth stretched into a wide and joyful grin.

~ * ~

Two bushes away, two sleek rats watched the spider.

"Who is he talking to?" one asked the other.

"Beats me," replied the second rat. "Some little man. He seems to be asleep."

"Can you smell anything?" the first one asked.

"Yeah, but I don't believe the evidence of my nose," was the reply.

"I'll tell you what I smell, if you'll tell me what you smell," challenged the first rat.

"OK, on three," the second rat said. "One, two, three..."

"Monkey!" they both exclaimed at the same time.

"You see, that's just impossible," the first rat proclaimed. "There is no such thing as an invisible monkey."

"I must agree with you. Totally," his fellow rat replied. "So, anyhoo, the army has returned the girl to her home, and we've done our part in her rescue. I think we need to report back to brigade headquarters. Maybe there will be a reward! You know, some juicy garbage or something..."

"You are always such an optimist!" his comrade teased.

"Realist!" the other insisted.

"Well, I hope your optimism turns into realism," the first rat replied. "Because I am one hungry rat!"

"Let's go!"

"Let's!"

~ * ~

Back at the Roanoke Rodent Brigade headquarters, the pair of reconnoitering rats were rewarded for their success with a dented can of corned beef hash. It was almost full.

In what was probably a mistake in judgment, they both filed reports that mentioned the possibility of an invisible monkey in the greater Roanoke area.

~ * ~

Destiny brushed her teeth and got ready for bed, still without her glasses. So, after she climbed into bed and turned off the lamp on her night table, she was unable to see the tiny lights blinking around her like a small cloud of miniature lightning bugs. She fell asleep almost immediately and slept deeply throughout the night.

But not without dreams. It was funny, really. She had very sharp vision in her dreams, even without her glasses. She dreamed she danced gracefully across a stage to the awe and appreciation of a large audience.

And then, unlucky even in her dream, she tripped over an electrical cord and fell flat on her face. It was all right, though, because in her dream she was irredeemably happy all of the time. She laughed along with the crowd, dusted off her tutu, and resumed her dance. Its conclusion was rewarded with thunderous applause.

Back in her room, its jarring noise disguised as thunderous applause, a pickaxe broke through her wall, establishing access to another dimension. As the hole was widened by someone or something on the other side of it, a cavern was revealed. And inside the cavern were creatures who most certainly were not human.

"See, I told you, Brody," a trembling little woman in black and yellow stripes said. Well, she buzzed a little, really. "I told you that she was capable of manifesting us! She is different. One of a kind! And we are here to make it happen for her. No more bad luck for our human, no sir!" The little woman paused in her patter to look admiringly at the sleeping girl in the human world.

"You were right all along, Regina," her companion responded. He, too, was striped, but in black and white. He had a black mohawk and hooves instead of feet. Handsome and well-muscled, he stood a full two feet taller than the little buzzing woman. Even when she wasn't speaking, she buzzed and hummed. "I am sorry I doubted you."

Before the Bee-woman could respond, a bang and a huge cloud of glitter announced another arrival: The Beast.

No, not Chance's Beast. Destiny's Beast. It had but one spiral horn on its forehead and was built much like the Zebra-man holding the pickaxe. But there the resemblance ended, for Destiny's Beast sported long, flowing white hair. Its skin was a perfect white and it was simply plastered in sequins—and now glitter.

They all were.

"That glitter is a hazard," the Bee-woman chided The Beast. "It gets everywhere. It gets in places where it chafes..."

"Yeah, yeah," The Beast replied in an accent straight from the Bronx. "Go cry me a river, Regina. What have you and Brody done here? It looks fantastic!"

The Zebra-man, Brody, responded. "It is all thanks to Regina, mistress!" he crowed. "She has been talking about this since our human could form a complete sentence. We can manifest! Our human is special!" He kicked up his legs in enthusiasm.

"Calm yourself," The Beast cautioned. "You're going to give yourself a charley horse..." She paused to ponder, one delicate white hand on her chin, the other resting on her hip. She turned from staring at the human child and faced her minions. "Do you know what this means?" she asked them.

"Yes," Regina cried, a smile stretching from antenna to antenna. "We can stop her endless cycle of bad luck. We can help her!"

"Stop that nonsense at once!" The Beast screamed. "Of course, we will not help her...it is not our nature to help the human. We exist to stunt her potential, you bumbling idiot! We will harm her if we need to!"

The little woman's buzzing and humming ceased. She, however, continued to tremble even without sound.

"Harm her?" Regina echoed. "I don't wish to harm her..."

"Not physically," The Beast amended. "We need to dampen her spirit. We need to make her question her own worth, her own potential. That is our job...it is what we are here to do!"

"But her bad luck..." Brody began to object. "We don't need her to have rotten luck all of the time in order to destroy her spirit, do we?"

"I'll tell you, Brody," The Beast replied, laughing ironically, "It sure doesn't hurt! Shoot, half the time she sabotages herself without any help from us at all!"

"Well, that's not right," the plump black and yellow little woman said righteously, her buzzing ramping up several decibels. "If it's our job to trip her up, then we need to do the heavy lifting. As it is, we just lie around and wait for her to stumble, or worse."

"You may have a point," The Beast allowed, "but that's because you have failed to notice something important."

"I'm all ears."

"You don't even have any ears, but that's not to the point. You didn't notice how quickly those rodent brigades located her, did you?"

"Well, now that you mention it..."

"Yeah, that's right. They found her because her bad luck is like Stink City! It allowed those rodents to sniff out her scent in nothing flat...and that, my dear minions, does not work to our benefit."

"So, you're saying we can continue to work against her bad luck?" Brody's big black eyebrows were hiked like two giant boomerangs almost to his hairline.

The Beast threw her head back and roared with laughter.

"Good luck with that!" she taunted, disappearing in a second cloud of glitter.

"What does that mean?" a bemused Brody asked Regina.

Regina's answer stuck in her throat as The Beast's head popped back into view, hovering above her.

"Good work with this cave-thing, you two. Really top notch. I am going to bring some of my things back and set up shop."

And she popped away, another shower of glitter released with her departure. Her minions choked and gagged for several moments before the worst of the cascade was spent.

"Damned glitter!" Regina howled, trying to scrape the tiny gleaming scraps from her eyes, mouth and ears—yes, ears. In her human form, Regina had nice little ears, in fact.

"Keep dropping those hints about cotton candy," Brody encouraged her. "I think you've got her contemplating a change."

"I'll keep trying," Regina said, somewhat dispiritedly. She held out small hope—there was that word again—that she would succeed.

"That's my girl!" Brody cried, slapping Regina vigorously on one shoulder.

A cloud of glitter sprang from her garments, and the pair returned to gagging and choking.

~ * ~

"She's just fine, Mrs. Dyer," Doctor Hyde said. "There is nothing whatsoever wrong with her. Destiny has suffered no consequences from her abduction, if that's what it was."

"What do you mean, 'if that's what it was'?" Dorothy Dyer asked.

"You know how kids are," the amiable physician responded. "So, she played hooky from school one day—which of us hasn't?"

"Destiny does not play hooky," the injured mother said in a huff. "She was abducted!"

"She says she remembers nothing of her ordeal…"

"Nevertheless!" was the only thing the frustrated mother could think to say. "Good day, Doctor. Thank you for your help."

"You are more than welcome," the doctor replied, turning on his heel to enter the next examining room where he had another patient waiting.

"Mom, the doctor says that this whole abduction thing might be just in my head. What does that mean?" Destiny asked.

"Don't pay any attention to that kind of talk," her mother advised. "You were abducted. There is no doubt. We just have to find out who, and why. Well, at least you experienced no harm."

And the relieved, but shaken, mother and daughter left the medical facility to return home.

~ * ~

Down the hall, safely behind a closed door, Doctor Hyde returned to his natural form. The Beast removed his white lab coat and tossed it into a corner.

Lucinder sat on the examining table, waiting for him anxiously. "Well?" she demanded impatiently. "What happened?"

"Mission accomplished, Lucinder," The Beast responded. "The seed is planted and watered. I even forged an official report for the school authorities and police. Destiny Dyer manufactured the story of her abduction. That is my medical opinion."

"Good," the nervous little woman said.

"Is that all you have to say?" The Beast roared.

"Sorry!" she added.

"Sorry? Sorry? Do you think 'sorry' is adequate? You went rogue, Lucinder. We are a team. And guess what? I am in charge of our team. Sorry will not cut it."

"The King made me do it!" Lucinder cried. She immediately slapped both of her hands over her mouth, horrified at what she had just blurted.

"What did you say?" The Beast waited in vain for Lucinder to answer him. He moved closer to her and glared balefully at her from his great height. "Out with it, or I will banish you to the team in charge of Chance Bonner's navel..."

"The King made me do it," Lucinder repeated in a tiny little voice.

"The King."

"Yes."

"The Devil King."

"Yes."

"The Devil King of the Sixth Heaven."

"Yes, yes, yes! He summoned me. He told me to keep it secret... to tell no one."

"Even me?" The Beast yelled.

"Especially you," she confirmed meekly.

The Beast turned on his heel and began pacing the small office. It was too small to contain him, so after bumping into all four walls two or three times, with a roar The Beast transported them back to their cavern.

"Where is the monkey?" he was demanding even as they poofed back into existence.

"I left him under a laurel bush in Roanoke, Virginia," Lucinder admitted. "I can go get him. I can go right away. If you want him here, I can make it happen." She was practically chittering she was speaking so desperately fast.

"Yes, I want him. I want him now. Bring him back here and be quick about it!" The Beast howled. He had resumed his pacing.

Lucinder poofed away from the cave and arrived under the camelia bush she had previously used only to find the space under the laurel empty.

No Denny.

"Where in the worlds could he have gone?" Lucinder asked herself, sweat now dotting her dark forehead. "Oh, I know. I bet anything that venom addict has gone to his friend. His spider. Well, I can follow him there."

And "poof" off she went again.

~ * ~

The King was standing at the entrance to the magic fen when she arrived.

"Sire!" she cried. "What are you doing here?"

"I was bored," his royal highness responded, filing at a horny fingernail with a diamond rasp. The sound made Lucinder shudder. "I witnessed your failure in your mission."

"But, Sire," Lucinder began to protest.

"Shush, shush, shush, there's a good girl," the King said, looking straight at her. "I am not upset—well, not over that, I mean."

"Oh?" Lucinder replied shakily. "Then what are you upset about?"

"You told your Beast!" the King cried, his bearded face turning crimson in his fury. "I told you to keep it secret. And you just went off and blabbed."

"He coerced me into telling!" Lucinder protested. "He scared it out of me!"

"I thought you were made of sterner stuff than that," sniffed the miffed royal. He paused to straighten the tall crown on his head. "Maybe I should have trusted my task to the monkey."

"Oh, no, Sire," Lucinder objected. "Denny is not cut out for that kind of work. He doesn't have a dishonest bone in his entire body."

"But he has the sense to be more afraid of me than of The Beast!" the regent screamed. He was livid once again, his breath exiting his nostrils as flames. He gained control of himself with effort. "Actually, I was looking for young Dennison just now. How is it that I ended up in this place?" He looked around himself disdainfully.

"Denny is here," Lucinder said in a small voice.

"What?" roared the Devil King, losing his aplomb once again.

"Denny is in this marsh," Lucinder said flatly. "I have come to get him. To rescue him."

"Rescue him?" the King echoed. "What does he need rescuing from?"

"Himself, it seems," Lucinder responded sadly.

"Explain yourself."

"He has a problem, you see," she began. She took a big breath before proceeding with her explanation. "He has unwittingly become addicted to a substance."

"What substance?"

"Well, you see, Sire," she dithered. "Um, well, he has been introduced to...umm, well..."

"Out with it!"

Lucinder both jumped and winced as the King screamed his command.

"Spider venom!" she spat out. "Denny is addicted to spider venom!"

"Spider venom?" the King repeated, stroking his long black, well-groomed goatee. "That actually sounds quite delightful. What kind of high does that produce?" He appeared to be calculating something, which of course he was. The Devil King of the Sixth Heaven was always looking for ways to use other beings' efforts and products to support his own nefarious schemes. He had simply not considered that spiders had anything to offer, other than exceedingly long conversations, that is.

Until now.

"A dreamy one," Lucinder offered.

"A dreamy what?" the King had become distracted and didn't remember his own question.

"A dreamy high," she clarified. "Denny gets all happy and stupid when he's on the stuff."

"That could prove useful," the King commented. "Very useful indeed. All right then, take me to those spiders." He stepped aside and motioned for Lucinder to lead the way.

"Spider," she said.

"Hunh?"

"Denny has just the one spider," she explained.

"Oh. I see. Well, maybe I should acquire one of my own then," the King suggested.

"Sire, that sounds like a great idea!" Lucinder cried. "But you know, I have never actually been there. You should just go ahead and investigate for yourself. I am sure you will find the best spider ever born for your own special friend."

"I never thought I'd see the day when you would lose your nerve," the King told her. "Well, just go ahead on your own then. Go in and find Dennison and get him on your rehabilitation program. As for me, I am going in and I am going to make an ally. Today. Now, as a matter of fact. I certainly do not need your advice or protection. Good day to you, Lucinder. Enjoy!" And with this and a tip of his crown, the King strolled right into the fen, his head held high.

Lucinder snuck in behind him on tiptoe, both eyelids clamped shut. Her regent was already out of her sight when she found her nerve and opened her eyes again.

"What a wet and foggy place!" she observed to herself. "How am I going to find Denny? I can hardly see my hand in front of my face!"

"Lucinder!" a familiar voice drawled. It was close enough to make her jump and let out a little shriek.

"Denny!" she cried, pivoting in the direction of the voice.

"Where is your friend?" she asked. "Your big, important spider?" She heard it in her own voice: jealousy. She was jealous of Denny's spider? She shelved this thought for later. She just didn't have time to analyze her feelings at the moment.

Denny had begun sniveling. "He told me to leave," he sobbed. "Arachimedes. He said he found a bigger and better friend." He broke down completely, crying now in earnest. "Why?" he asked no one in particular. In fact, he addressed the entire steaming bog with his unanswered and unanswerable questions. "Who? What has happened to make him behave so cruelly?"

Lucinder fought with herself. She made a move to put her arms around the bereft little man, then drew back. She finally took a soiled and crumpled napkin out of one of her pockets and handed it to him. "Here, Denny," she said, not unkindly. "Use this. Wipe your nose. We're getting out of here."

And even as the little man began wiping his eyes and nose, unfortunately for him without examining the questionable napkin first, Lucinder put one hand on his right elbow and poofed both of them back to the relative dryness and safety of their cavern.

The sudden violence of their departure dislodged something from inside Lucinder's shirt collar. The small object hit the ground rolling. It extruded four little legs and ran under the nearest fern, shaking in fear and fairly trembling in confusion. Its tiny sharp teeth chattered, attracting the attention of a large spider sitting on the tree which provided shade to the fern.

"Why, hello," the spider said, silently closing the gap between himself and the gerbil. "And who might you be? I am Arachimedes. It is so nice to make a new friend."

Eleven

Good Luck

Chance and his friends had searched for his mother all day without finding even the slightest trace of her.

Desperate, they stopped by the police precinct and asked to speak to Officer Roger Olsen.

"Are you still looking for my mother?" Chance asked the moment the beefy officer entered the room.

"Actually, much more than that," a worried Roger Olsen responded. "Now I'm looking for Josephine as well."

"Josephine?" a stunned Stefan Schultz interrupted. "Josephine... as in my sister Josephine?"

"I'm afraid so, Stefan," the officer replied, putting one meaty hand on the young man's shoulder. "I can't find her. Her cell phone isn't working...it doesn't even go to voicemail. Have you by any chance heard from her?"

"No, not since this morning," Stefan said. "I just thought she stopped to get some rest or something."

"No, I've been by the apartment, and she is not there. I haven't told your parents yet, but I am going to have to...she's been missing for hours now."

"You know," Sarah Stengler said in a thoughtful tone. "I don't know two more capable ladies than Mrs. Bonner and Brilliant Schultz. It's hard to think they could be in any trouble that they couldn't handle...."

Kelly O'Hara jumped in with, "Yeah, that's right!" while Millicent Lee threw both thumbs up in the air in strong agreement.

Then all three of the young women turned to look at Chance.

Kelly spoke next. "Uhh, Chance, ummm, well, don't you have some kind of magic mojo thing you do, you know, something you and your mother do that could help?" All three of the girls continued to stare at Chance.

He looked puzzled at first, and then a look of understanding washed over his face. "Oh, you mean our chanting?" he asked.

The three young women voiced their agreement. Now Roger Olsen and Stefan Schultz turned to stare at Chance. Waiting. They were all waiting for his response.

"You know," he said with a wan smile, "I should have thought of that myself. Yes, I should chant. I will go home right now and chant for an hour. You know, it works even better if more people do it together."

"You mean we can chant?" Kelly asked. She looked surprised and a little frightened.

"Of course, you can!" Chance replied. "I won't ask you if it makes you uncomfortable, but any of you who are willing can come home with me now."

"Does that make us Buddhists?" Sarah asked. "Will our Christian God be insulted?" she looked around the group briefly and asked the question she really wanted to. "Is it a sin?"

"I am sure it's not a sin," Chance said. "I would never ask you to do anything that violates your own beliefs or principles."

"Well, that's good," Stefan said with a smile. "Because I don't have any of those." His words were greeted by laughter, which completely broke the ice.

"Well, I'm game," Kelly announced. "Let's go!"

"Me, too," said Sarah, and Millicent contributed nearly simultaneously.

"I am on duty, so I will say no," Roger announced. "I will let you know if anything comes up, and rest assured that half of the force is out looking for Nan and Josephine."

The young people left the precinct house quickly and arrived at the Bonners' twenty minutes later.

When they entered the house, they heard the sounds of chanting coming from the upstairs room where Nan Bonner kept her Buddhist altar and scroll, her prayer beads and her incense.

"It's my father!" Chance explained in hushed tones. "He never does this."

"I've seen him do it twice," Stefan announced.

At first Chance looked puzzled, but after a moment, he nodded in agreement. "You're right," he told the taller boy. "I keep forgetting." Those epic battles between all of the powers, good and bad, both inside of himself and throughout the Universe should have remained deeply etched in his memory, but they weren't. He kept forgetting about them.

Why did Stefan remember so clearly? The girls, all three of them, had been at those battles, too, but they were only just now looking like they remembered what Stefan was referring to.

"Come on," Millicent urged. "Let's get started."

"I need to teach you how to recite the mantra," Chance said. He pronounced it phonetically several times and had them repeat it.

"That's not so hard," Sarah said. "I think we've got it!"

They all climbed the stairs and quietly knelt or sat around Chaz Bonner, who was chanting with such focus that he didn't notice they were there until they all started chanting with him.

Chance focused on his mother and Stefan's sister. He chanted for all of the positive forces of the Universe to protect the two women. He chanted for both of them to return safely to their homes, none the worse for their disappearances.

The chanting started a little roughly but evened out in just a few moments until the tight little group was intoning the mantra in perfect unison.

~ * ~

Nan Bonner felt something tugging at her consciousness. It was near, very near.

She had been enjoying her stay in the magic fen, just talking with spiders and admiring ferns, moss-covered tree limbs, and brilliant blue webs. She had no concept of time...had no idea how long she had spent there.

In particular, she enjoyed the conversations—the dialogues—she was having with Arachimedes. They spoke frequently, and at length, about all things great and small across the Universe. They found that their thoughts and beliefs were aligned with one another.

Wait...there was that feeling again...a definite tug. Something familiar called to her.

"Well, I can follow it, can't I?" she thought. "I can and I will!" she announced to herself.

It took her a few moments to figure out how to follow the sound that beckoned to her, but she soon worked it out. Her magic could be directed to take her places. That's how she got to the fen in the first place, after all.

And so she found herself standing on the first-floor landing of her own home, heading toward the compelling sound as if it were a beacon, and she a ship at full sail.

She entered the room and noticed the sound increased in tempo as she arrived. She knew this sound! It was the Buddhist mantra. She fell into the stream of the chant, picking it up mid-syllable.

And as she chanted, Nan Bonner's color shifted, all of her blueness dissipating as she intoned the syllables of the sacred mantra. Within less than twenty minutes, she became visible, truly flesh and blood again.

Chaz rang the bell signifying a pause in the chanting.

"Chaz!" Nan wondered to herself. "Chaz doesn't chant!"

And then, Chaz turned around to face the group of young people who had been chanting with him and saw Nan.

"Nan, oh Nan!" he cried, jumping to his feet and rushing to throw his arms around her. "Where have you been? We've been worried sick about you." She saw that Chance had also thrown his arms around her, a glorious smile on his face. "Mom, you're back! You're back!" he cried.

Then Chance and Chaz both paused and waited for Nan to say something. "Where have you been?" Chaz repeated very softly.

Nan looked dazed. She shook her head as if to clear it of fog...or spider webs. "I don't know," she said. "I don't remember."

"Mrs. Bonner?" Stefan said. "My sister is missing. Have you seen her?"

"What? Josephine is missing? How? I mean when? I guess I really mean for how long?" Nan said, her concern for the young woman distracting her from her own predicament...her sudden, frustrating amnesia.

"She was out looking for you all night," the young man explained. "With Roger. Roger Olsen. She was texting me about every thirteen minutes until a few hours ago. We don't know where she is. Her phone is off. She's not home, and she didn't leave a message." Despite the calm manner in which Stefan delivered this information, Nan noticed his concern.

"You're worried, aren't you?" she asked.

"I am," he replied. "This is so not like her. She is in constant contact. Always hovering over me and Mom like we need adult supervision. Not having her around all of the sudden is scary.

"Where could she have gone?" and the young man crossed the room, collapsed in an armchair and dropped his head into his hands.

"I wish I knew," Nan whispered, more to herself than anyone else. "I don't even know where I have been." She addressed her husband next, raising her voice to do so. "How long was I missing?"

"A little over thirty hours," he replied.

"Thirty hours? Where could I have been for thirty hours?" she exclaimed.

Then she remembered. A color. Blue. A baggie in her vegetable crisper.

"Come with me!" she exhorted the group, leading them to the second story landing and then down the stairway.

Once they were all in the kitchen, she drew a deep breath and opened the refrigerator.

She could see the pulsing blue color before she even opened the crisper drawer. Sliding the drawer out, she used two fingers to tease the baggie out into the open. She held it out in front of her in clear view of everyone in the kitchen.

They all gasped in wonder. The baggie was full of beautiful blue orbs. They seemed to pulse, mesmerizing their observers with their brilliance.

"Power," Sarah said.

"Promise," Stefan corrected her. "It's promise."

"Chaz," Nan began. "When did you last see Josephine?"

"She was down here in the kitchen making me some scrambled eggs and coffee," her husband replied. "I went up to shower and get dressed. When I came down, the food was here, still hot, and the coffee was brewing...but Josephine was gone."

Nan waggled the baggie back and forth. "Does it appear to you that one of these balls might be missing?"

They all stared at the baggie, then back up at Nan. Stefan spoke first.

"It does," he said. "It looks like one of them might be missing."

All of them said it at the same time, even if they used a different name.

"JB," Stefan said.

"Brilliant," Chance, Kelly, Sarah, and Millicent said.

"Josephine," Nan and Chaz said.

Nan looked troubled. She was trying to remember. Did she eat one of those things? She remembered seeing a single blue orb...that's what caused her to check the crisper. But this baggie did not contain a single orb, but many. "Wait a minute!" she said aloud, startling the others. "The threads! It's the threads!"

"Nan," Chaz said, choosing his words carefully. "You're not making any sense."

"You see, I found blue threads in all of my clothes!" Nan exclaimed. "I gathered them up and put them in a baggie. I put the baggie in the crisper. The threads must have gone through some kind of transformation...it's the only possible explanation."

"Go on," her husband encouraged.

"This happened twice," Nan said, her relief at recapturing some part of her memory obvious to her audience. "First, I just cut up the seams of my pajamas. Blue. The threads were blue. I swept them up and put them in the baggie. The next morning, I cut up the rest of my clothes...you know, the ones that had gotten too tight for me to wear? And I discovered the same thing: they were all held together by blue threads.

"When I went to add the threads to the ones from my pajamas, the first batch of threads was gone. There was a single blue ball in that baggie the next morning. I took it. I took it out, and put the loose threads in. Put them in the crisper.

"I put that first blue ball in my sweatpants pocket."

She paused and resumed thinking. Her audience was hanging on her words and waiting for more to follow.

Finally, Chance broke the silence. "Mom," he said. "What did you do with that first ball?"

She was pale. Drawn. She turned her wide eyes to meet Chance's eyes, then Chaz's.

"I ate it," she said. "I put it in a half gallon of vanilla bean ice cream, and I ate it. The whole thing."

"Ooooooh," was the collective answer that greeted her confession.

She still held the bag out. One by one, each of the young people in the kitchen removed a ball. They held them in the open palms of their hands where the orbs pulsated with power or promise...or both.

As if their movements had been choreographed, all five of them popped the pulsing spheres into their mouths at the same moment...

...and vanished!

"There's only one left!" a panicking Nan Bonner said to her husband.

"I'm going with them!" Chaz announced, seizing the last ball and swallowing it. He was gone in less than a second.

Nan stood there, shocked motionless. Speechless. After just a moment or two, she seemed to remember something else and spoke.

"Are you all here?" she asked. Nothing. "If you are here, can you move the pages on the calendar?" She pointed to the colorful calendar on the kitchen wall.

Within seconds, the pages of the calendar were riffled by an invisible wind.

"Aha!" she cried. "So, look throughout the house for Josephine, then. If you find her, come back and turn those pages again. I will wait right here.

"Oh, and if you don't find her, just flip the first page, OK?" She did not expect an answer, but the calendar made a small wave at her and then fell still.

And stayed still. Nan waited for a full hour, but the calendar made no more motions.

What could have happened to her family and friends? She was at a complete loss as to what to do.

So, she went upstairs and began to chant. She chanted for two solid hours, but was not able to cause her husband, son, or any of her son's friends to re-materialize.

As she was considering what else she might be able to do, her gaze fell upon a lone blue thread which had draped itself across her Buddhist altar.

Nan grabbed the thread and ran downstairs to her kitchen, where she rolled the thread up and carefully placed it in a baggie. She sealed the baggie and put it in her vegetable crisper.

Then she waited.

Twelve

No Luck At All

Angelica Root had been on edge for days. She sensed that Almasty was moving in the world and hoped he would make his presence manifest.

As she took her daily constitutional in the local park, she put words to her feelings. She wanted to see him again, to be with him. But it was inevitable that she would have to tell him. The children were in their teens now. Their powers were beginning to influence people and events, and those powers would only grow.

He must be told.

"But he will also be angry. Angry that I bore his children. Angry that I did not tell him about them," she thought.

"He is not the only reason that the twins are abnormal," she reminded herself. "I, too, have gifts: I can interact with the children's manifestations, after all. I even use one of them, Stanley Greenleaf, to pretend to be my lawyer when I need one.

"I also have the ability to talk with animals like my friend, Samantha.

"And Almasty. I am the only human being who has captured his heart. I know he loves me. I can feel that he thinks of me still, even as he avoids the rest of humanity and meditates on his mountain top."

A tingling sensation, like that of being watched, ran from her back to her neck, and Angelica turned swiftly to look behind her.

Nothing.

But she felt it. "Was it him? Was it my beloved Almasty?"

~ * ~

The robed and hooded man blended into the woods which bordered the walking trail. It was one of the things that had made him a legend, this ability of his to move through wooded areas without being seen.

But it was his huge cowboy boots which disguised his biggest telling feature: his feet.

They were big.

Really, really big.

~ * ~

Samantha Swisher was waiting for Angelica at her office. She rose to her feet when the tall, blonde woman returned from her daily walk.

"Anything?" Samantha asked Angelica anxiously.

Angelica sighed. "Nothing."

The squirrel-woman also sighed. "I am just so excited about meeting him!" she said. "The very prospect of it has me on pins and needles!"

"I feel he is close," Angelica admitted. "The feeling is no better than a hunch, but my hunches are usually pretty good."

"Should I alert the Army to be on the lookout for him?" Samantha asked.

"No, don't do that," Angelica replied. "He can't be caught if he doesn't want to be caught. They would never be able to find him."

"Are you sure? We have some really crackerjack detectives, you know. Our sniffer rats are the best in the country."

"I know, I know, but he doesn't smell like anything they would know about," Angelica said.

"Oh? What does he smell like then?" the brown little woman asked, her curiosity piqued.

"Nutmeg," Angelica said, a wistful expression on her face. "And not nutmeg. Pine bark. Cinnamon. Ginger. Lemon grass. And yet none of those things. It's impossible to define, really!"

"Sounds yummy!" Samantha cried. "I just can't wait!"

"Me, neither," Angelica said. "Me, neither."

~ * ~

Arthur Dillow sat at home, alone and unhappy.

He had many things to do. He just didn't want to do any of them.

He had already put in his three hours of practice on various video games. He had become quite skilled in a good number of them.

He had plenty to eat. Plenty to drink.

He just missed something, that's all. He missed the attention. He hadn't seen Chance or any of his friends in days. He wanted them to watch him play games. He craved their acceptance, their admiration.

"How does Chance Bonner attract so many great friends?" he asked himself. "What does he have that I don't?"

Arthur started a list. He started with Chance. "I will write down all of his character traits," Arthur told himself. He began.

Friendly

Open

Honest

Smart

Humble

Good Listener

Fun

Happy

Then he listed his own traits. It didn't take long to figure out why Chance was popular and he, Arthur, was not. His list read:

Hostile

Secretive

A Liar
Smart
Prideful
Talks a lot
No Fun
Unhappy

"Well, at least we're both smart," Arthur said, trying to glean at least one good thing from his exercise. "That is what put us in proximity to one another: we are assigned to many of the same classes.

"Oh, drat and bother!" Arthur burst out, throwing his pencil across the room. "Why do I have to live here anyway! Why can't I go back to being an armadillo, minding my own business, searching for grubs and warming myself in the hot sun all day?"

Seemingly in response to his lamentations, a sulfurous "poof" announced the arrival of The Beast, his master. He stooped to retrieve the loose pencil, slapping it into Arthur's open palm, where it stayed.

"What is all of this belly-aching?" The Beast roared. "Why are you constantly complaining?"

Arthur used his pencil to write "constantly complaining" at the bottom of his list.

"I don't know what I am doing here!" he cried. "Give me something to do, please, I'm begging you!"

"All right. I will," The Beast responded, stroking his bony chin and wrinkling up his florid face with thought. Deep thought.

"Make yourself likeable," The Beast said. "Lucinder is always telling me some story about catching flies, although why anyone would want to do that is beyond me. I use them to pester people. They're not good for much else. Her story is about setting out some treacle or some such. Oh, and not putting out vinegar. Oh, well, anyway, her point is, I think, that if you want to be attractive, better to be sweet than sour." He looked back up at the boy. "There...does that help?"

The armadillo-boy was staring up at The Beast with a look of wonder. "Yes, actually, I think it does." He paused to look down at his list, moving his head back and forth from the list he had made for Chance, and the one he had made for himself.

"Well," he finally said. "It won't be easy, but at least I know where to start." He glanced back up at The Beast and smiled sweetly. "Thank you so much for your help!" he said, exuding good will and sincerity.

"Oh, brother," The Beast said, disappearing in another cloud of sulfurous gas. "How sickening."

Anything else he might have said could not be heard in Arthur's ears. Plus, the small boy was industriously scribbling away again, planning furiously on how he could pretend to be an honest, pleasant, fun, happy non-complainer who was a good listener.

"I can do this," he told himself. "It will be hard, but I will do my best.

"It's the only way to complete this mission and get back to my old life."

~ * ~

Back at school the next day, Arthur was disappointed that neither Chance nor any of his friends was there, for the second day in a row!

"Well, I'll have to practice on someone else until they return," he said to himself. He walked up to a familiar looking little girl. "Hi," he said. "Want to jump rope with me?"

The little girl looked up at Arthur in horror, turned on her heel and ran in the opposite direction as fast as her little legs would carry her.

Arthur shrugged. "Man, what's her problem?" he asked himself. "She could take some lessons from me, that's for sure! She'll never make friends like that."

~ * ~

Later that day, Arthur decided on a ploy to drop in on Chance Bonner.

Mrs. Bonner had expressed a desire to see his house. The Spite House, it was called. Well, he could make that happen. He would drop by and ask her if she wanted to visit his home. While in the Bonner house, he could accidentally run into Chance—and maybe some of his friends—and practice being nice and fun.

"This plan cannot fail," he congratulated himself. He just had to wait for the final bell, and he would be off.

Thirteen

Reunion

Chaz, Chance, and the rest of the now-blue search party had no idea where to look for Brilliant.

They could hear Nan Bonner upstairs chanting, but not a one of them felt the tug, the pull that Nan had described when they had chanted for her just a short while before.

They began to call out loud for Brilliant. And Josephine. And JB. After several attempts, they all felt something.

"What is happening?" Chance asked his father.

"Beats me," Chaz said, looking around him for the source of...the source of what, exactly?

"It's vibration," the observant Sarah Stengler announced. "And it's getting stronger."

With a mighty squelch, and a puff of fetid air, Ribetta poofed into being in the middle of their group.

She allowed them several moments to express their surprise at her, and the manner of her arrival. She said nothing, and merely waited for them to stop exclaiming. She watched patiently as, one by one, the humans realized that she was, in fact, waiting for them to settle down. Silence finally descended.

"Well, I see that our magic population is growing by leaps and bounds," she said, leaping and bounding now herself. "You all ate the blue spheres?"

"We did," Chaz Bonner said, speaking for the whole group. "We are still not sure what happened, though. Perhaps you are in a position to educate us?"

Her position at that moment was mid-air, as she continued to gambol around the room.

"Educate you?" she asked, halting her gyrations and staring at them.

"Please," Kelly said.

"Educate us," Millicent added.

"If you can..." Sarah said.

"Where's my sister?" Stefan demanded. He was bigger, louder, and much more anxious than the rest of the group, Ribetta noticed. Perhaps she should respond to his question first?

Being random, she simply changed her mind a split second later and decided to let him cool his heels for a while.

"You are now permanently magic," she announced to the group, taking pleasure from the exasperated look on the blond young man's face. He began ripping open and closing velcroed pockets on the laboratory coat he wore, creating a distraction, and a nuisance.

"Relax, young man," she said pointedly looking just at Stefan. "Stop that racket! Your sister is perfectly fine. She is speaking with Arachimedes and some of his closest allies. I will take you to her if you will calm down and get control of yourself."

Her admonition sobered all of the youth, but seemed to anger the lone adult.

"His sister is missing. He has every right to be anxious," Chaz

Bonner protested to the little—what, exactly? "Are you a frog?" he asked. "Or a toad?"

"Not another one," the woman muttered to herself. "Frog," she said loudly. "I am a frog."

"Frog, then," Chaz repeated. "Sorry. But what did you mean by 'not another one'?"

"Oh, that blonde girl who converted this morning," Ribetta clarified. "She said the same thing."

"That's her!" Stefan interrupted. "That blonde girl. She's my sister, JB!"

"She may go by 'Josephine'," Chaz said.

"Or 'Brilliant'," Chance added.

"Well, she has chosen another name now that she is magic," Ribetta told them. "She wants to be called 'Astra' now."

"Astra?" Stefan asked. "Why Astra?"

"Well, since you have said she went by the name 'Brilliant,' then 'Astra' makes perfect sense," the little woman replied.

"Why?" Stefan asked intently. "What's the connection?"

"'Astra' means 'like a star'," Ribetta explained. "Get it—'brilliant like a star'?" She wrinkled her forehead and waved her hands around, palms up, to encourage the young man to grasp her meaning.

"What did you mean when you said 'permanently magic'?" Chaz asked. "How could we be 'permanently magic'?"

"You all ingested a fully matured blue orb, did you not?" the little frog-woman asked.

They all nodded in the affirmative.

"Well, then, just as with your Astra, you have transitioned. You will remain magic beings for the rest of your lives, which now that you are magic will be very, very long ones at that."

"What does that even mean?" Millicent demanded, hands on her hips and chin held high.

"Oh, magic, you mean?" Ribetta asked. Millicent gave one nod of her head in reply. "Oh, magic isn't what you think it is," she replied readily. She was enjoying herself. "Magic—real magic, that is—is just randomness. Chaos. You have entered the void between worlds, really."

"The void between worlds?" Kelly repeated. "What is the void between worlds?"

"Well, worlds may be the wrong word," Ribetta admitted. "The word *spheres* is actually closer to the real meaning. There are forces in the Universe, you know," she continued. "There are positive forces, and there are negative forces.

"Then there are the forces that are neither positive nor negative... and that's us. Me, you, Astra, and many other creatures, both visible and invisible. We side with the positive or negative forces without rhyme or reason...we act on impulse."

Ribetta paused and took in the looks on the faces of her small audience. "You didn't know this before now?" she asked.

Chance answered. "I knew about the positive and negative forces in the Universe," he said. "But I did not know that chaos was a force..."

"Well, it is, and you are now part of it," the little woman primly announced. "Permanently," she added with emphasis.

"We chanted my wife out of your magic world," Chaz objected. "We can chant ourselves back to the human world."

Ribetta smiled sadly. "Your wife ate an immature orb," she informed them. "She was not permanently altered.

"You are."

After several moments of complete silence, Chaz spoke up once again.

"What now?" he asked.

"I'll take you to Astra," Ribetta responded.

"Is it far?" Stefan asked anxiously.

"We can be there in a heartbeat," the little woman replied.

"Let's go, then."

Ribetta enclosed them in a bubble of blue magic and "poof," they disappeared from the human world and reappeared in the magic fen.

"N-n-nice," Kelly said, turning herself around and staring at the eerie landscape. "Is magic always so ugly?"

"Ugly?" Ribetta repeated, becoming irate. "Ugly? This is one of my favorite spots! What do you mean 'ugly'?"

"Well, uhh, you know," stammered Chance, "this would not be your average human being's first choice of environments."

"Yeah," Sarah said, stepping forward to be in clear view of Ribetta. "It's damp."

"Dripping," Millicent confirmed.

"Stinky," Sarah said, sniffing the air noisily.

"Mildewy," Millicent confirmed.

"Dark," Sarah said, shuddering and putting her arms around herself.

"Dreary and depressing!" Millicent announced.

"And—eek! There are spiders everywhere!" Sarah screamed, her eyes wide, clearly terrified.

"Scary!" Millicent screamed, running to Sarah and throwing her arms around her.

"This is the magic fen," Ribetta said, her squat little nose in the air. "Of course, there are spiders here. They are the most magical of all creatures. This is their true realm. They come here to recharge their spidery batteries between visits to other worlds.

"This is also where I come to vacation, to get away from it all!" she exclaimed. "I cannot understand your negative reaction to this fabulous land...truly I cannot!"

"Where is my sister?" Stefan pressed, his interest elsewhere. "Where is JB...I mean 'Astra'?"

"Come with me," Ribetta instructed, turning on one webbed foot and leading them further into the fen. She squelched as she went.

Stefan walked carelessly directly behind her, followed closely by Chaz and Chance. Kelly came next. At a distant fifth and sixth place, Sarah and Millicent cautiously walked, cringing and making little screaming sounds as they went.

"Who are your noisy friends?" boomed a big voice from above Ribetta's head. "Are these more humans you bring to our world?"

"They are no longer truly human!" Ribetta replied. "They have partaken of the magic orbs!"

"I am not happy about this," grumbled the spider which climbed out of a hole in the moss-covered tree nearest them. "Not happy at all. That one you brought here earlier—she is redecorating! Do you hear me, Ribetta? She is changing things here."

"Oh, calm yourself, Arachimedes," the little frog-woman said. "Surely you exaggerate!"

"Oh, do I?" the spider challenged. "Just keep walking...you will soon see if I exaggerate!"

"OK, I will," she replied. "We're going now."

"Please do," Arachimedes replied in a sarcastic tone. "And please feel free to share your observations with me on your return."

"Oh dear," Ribetta soon muttered to herself. "I begin to see what the old spider meant." She continued leading the group. And as she became more and more distressed by what she saw, the others with her found themselves greatly cheered.

"Hey, this isn't so bad!" Kelly exclaimed. "It's much prettier in here than before."

Even Millicent and Sarah were walking singly now, seemingly no longer frightened.

The bog, with its reeds and weeds, moss, ferns, and fallen tree trunks had been, well, tamed. Water now stood only in clear ponds. Trees were upright. Ferns lay in tailored beds surrounded by bright flowers and little white mushrooms. There was the bright sound of birds chirping.

"Birds!" Ribetta exclaimed, scanning the trees and the skies. "Birds eat spiders! Big enough birds can eat frogs! Oh no! This cannot be!"

"What is amiss, Ribetta?" asked a cheerful voice. "Is this too chaotic for you?"

And with this jibe, JB AKA Josephine AKA Brilliant AKA Astra stepped out from behind one particularly beautiful flowering dogwood tree to confront the group and its froggy leader.

"How could you?" an affronted Ribetta demanded. "How could you make such changes to our beautiful fen?"

"I felt an urge I couldn't deny!" the young woman cried. "I am indulging myself—my new self—by just doing what I want. When I want. Where I want."

"This feels willful to me," the older woman complained. "You are doing it on purpose to spite me."

"Spite?" Stefan's big sister echoed. "Spite is not quite the word I would use…it's not angry enough. Spite is small. What I feel is huge!" Suddenly, the young woman noticed the group which Ribetta led.

"Stefan!" she cried. "Oh, no—Chance, Kelly, Sarah, Millicent, Mr. Bonner—what are you all doing here? Why are you all blue?"

"We came to find you," her brother responded, approaching her slowly, and hesitatingly holding his arms out to her. "I was so afraid for you," he said, putting those arms around her. She looked astonished, and not just because Stefan was there and, also, decidedly blue, but because Stefan never enjoyed displays of affection, let alone initiated them.

"You sure must have been worried," she said, gingerly putting her own arms lightly around her much taller and younger brother. "I am fine, well, as fine as you are, apparently," she said, moving her hands up to his shoulders and pushing him back to look him in his eyes. "What are Mom and Dad going to do with both of us missing?" Tears were forming in her big, blue eyes.

"We didn't know what we were doing," Stefan said.

"I didn't either," his sister replied.

"That is the nature of Chaos!" Ribetta cried. "Now let's see what we can do to get this fen back into fighting trim again!"

"No!" the distressed Astra shouted. "No, we are not changing this bog back into a bog. If this is my realm now, I am going to make it to my liking! There is plenty more of your 'fen' here that remains unchanged. I suggest you go find it."

"I am getting the impression that you are not happy here," the frog-woman ventured.

"Not happy? Not happy?" Astra was still shouting. "I—I mean we—don't belong here. We have people back in our human world who will be devastated by our disappearances. We have school to attend. We have jobs to do."

"We have missions," Chance broke in. "We are not creatures of chaos. We are human beings. We belong in the human world, not here with you and your randomness. We strive to develop life goals, and we strategize and work hard our entire lives to achieve those goals, to be the best we can be. To be happy." He paused to collect his thoughts. "And here?" he continued. "Here, we are not happy. Here? I don't see how we can ever be happy. We do not like chaos. We don't live randomly."

Ribetta dropped her defensive attitude and appeared to be thinking.

"I believe I need to go talk to the old spider," she announced, poofing away an instant later.

The blue humans looked at each other for a few moments.

"I really like what you've done with the place," Millicent finally said. They all laughed lightly at her witticism.

"Yeah, you got anything to eat?" Sarah added, in no joking manner. "Do we magic people eat?"

"I sure hope so, because I am really hungry!" Kelly contributed.

Astra smiled and spoke. "Well, there's not much, but I will certainly share what I have found. Follow me, right this way...." And she led the group further into her remodeled fen.

"I sure hope you like mushrooms..."

~ * ~

A tiny rodent watched the blue humans, but chose not to follow them.

He, too, preferred the fen in the state the blonde female human had created. He was content to eat tree nuts and mushrooms. The mushrooms here were so delicious...especially the blue ones. His blue whiskers twitched and his beady blue eyes shone with contentment. As he swiftly scurried under a sheltering fern, his shiny coat served as testimony to his well-being. It was sleek and glossy. And blue.

Fourteen

Conference

"What? What do you mean I am no longer welcome here?" The Beast growled. He was addressing two enormous spiders who guarded the entrance to the magic fen.

"No more humans are allowed by order of Arachimedes MDXXVI!" the larger of the two guards announced in a voice almost as big as The Beast's.

"But I am not human!" protested The Beast. "Tell Arachimedes that Stanley Greenleaf is here. We are friends. He will want to see me."

"Your name is on the list," the second guard said, perusing a handheld tablet. Its Apple logo gleamed white on white.

"Oh, good, so let me in then."

"You are on the list of banned humans, you dolt!"

The Beast sputtered in protest, but soon realized his objections were not moving the guards in the slightest.

This made him angry.

"You will rue the day you rejected me from your land!" he howled as he disappeared in a cloud of sulfur.

"Well, that was interesting," the slightly smaller guard said to the larger. "Did you see how big his left nostril got before he exploded?"

"Listen, Todd," the second guard replied, "I hate to be the bearer of bad news, but he did not explode."

"No?"

"No. He transports himself like that. He just 'poofed' somewhere. Somewhere else. He has not harmed himself or anyone else in the human domain. Plus, we were barely affected by that stinky cloud he left behind, either. He's all show, that one."

"Gosh, Brad, how is it you know these things?" Todd asked, batting his myriad eyelids, lashes and all. "You have got to be the smartest spider in the service."

"Get out of here, you big galoot," Brad replied, shuffling all eight of his feet in the loose bracken. "You could turn a spider's head with that kind of talk."

"Well, you deserve it," Todd gushed. "And I'm going to make sure that Arachimedes knows about you, too."

"That would be just great," Brad said. "I would love it if you could drop a couple of good words to your uncle like that."

"Consider it done!"

"Thanks. Thanks so much!"

"Please do not mention it, Brad. It is my sincere pleasure!"

~ * ~

Inside the magic fen, a conference was taking place. It had been going on for hours, its first decree being the one that the guards at the border had just enforced.

"We must move fast," Arachimedes was saying to an enormous congregation of spiders of every size and color. "I propose we appoint a special committee to investigate the reversal of the human transformation. I will call on our best scientists, the finest brains in all of our kingdom, to tackle this urgent mission."

Another large spider not twenty feet away interrupted the speaker.

"Should we not be putting the frog on trial?" he shouted. "She is the cause of this debacle. She took our webs and used them in the human world. She must be punished!"

His outburst was met by many other voices, most of them supporting what he had said.

"Order! Order!" Arachimedes cried. "Ribetta Anura is not on trial here, nor will she be! She collected those webs legally. I will hear no more of this vindictive, counterproductive talk from any of you.

"What happened with those webs she collected is unprecedented. The only explanation that holds water is that someone involved—someone in the human world—has luck. Good luck. No, phenomenal luck. The kind of luck that traverses the membrane which separates our worlds."

"That is our power!" the same speaker objected. "That's not luck, it is chaos!"

"Luck, whether good or bad, is a form of magic," Arachimedes responded. "You cannot see it because you are too close to magic yourself. You have to understand humans to see it."

"I don't want to see humans," some other wag in the back of the assembly yelled out. "I just want to eat them." This, naturally, was met with much laughter, hooting, and hollering.

This cooled tempers down. Arachimedes was pleased. He continued to speak in a calmer tone.

"This person, this phenomenally lucky human, must be discovered, for I believe this person to be the key to reversing the introduction of humans into our land. His luck is not chaos...it is consistently, and reliably, good luck at all times. I believe this unique attribute will be enough to reverse the effect of the blue orbs and return the humans to their former inglorious selves. Who will join me? How many of you here today will be part of the solution?"

The assembly exploded with sound, every spider without exception pledging his or her support to the effort.

"Very well, then," Arachimedes proclaimed. "I have drafted a list of assignments...it will be transmitted to all of you via text message. It will suggest—only suggest, mind you—meeting places and times. Each committee can make its own arrangements after its initial session.

Elect chairspiders. I know you prefer to have this important position determined by contests of strength and wile, but we can't afford to sideline any of you for the immediate future. Elections, my friends. Straight forward, no trickery, no bribery, no skullduggery elections.

"But, and mark you, this is a big 'but,' I want your preliminary reports by tomorrow night, let's say twenty-three hundred hours, shall we? We have to move out on this, spiders! The longer the magic humans remain in our realm, the greater the danger!"

"It shall be done!" the massive assembly said as one. They then immediately scattered to the winds, not being accustomed to staying in one exposed place for quite so long.

"That went well," said a tiny spider crouched on Arachimedes' head.

"It did, didn't it?" the giant old spider replied. "Well, did you give the monkey my message?"

"I did indeed," the tiny arachnid responded. "I did indeed. He has told me to assure you that he will play his part. He will pretend to be devastated at the loss of your friendship. He will come here in secret at o-three hundred hours as you requested."

"Perfect," Arachimedes said. "Just perfect. Well done, my son. Well done."

"Any time, Grandpa," the little guy said, catching the next wind with a net of delicate blue web and flying away.

~ * ~

A conference of a different sort was playing out in the cave.

Lucinder was still trying to comfort Denny, using her tried and true methods.

"Get over it, Denny!" she screeched. "He doesn't want to be your friend anymore. Just forget about him—he's gross, anyway. A spider, Denny! What were you thinking?

"Oh, wait, don't tell me. I know. You weren't thinking, were you? It's that venom he was feeding you, isn't it? Are you in withdrawal right now? Answer me, Denny!"

The monkey simply sat and moped morosely. Every few seconds, he would take a much-used napkin from his coat pocket and wipe either his eyes or his nose.

When The Beast poofed into the cave, both Denny and Lucinder were actually relieved—at first.

"You can never trust a spider!" The Beast howled, even as he was waving his arms through the air surrounding him to dispel the cloud of sulfur.

"Treacherous, faithless, traitors!" he continued, his face livid with anger.

"What has happened?" Lucinder asked.

"What has happened? What has happened?" The Beast repeated. "I'll tell you what has happened: that damned old spider gave me the boot!"

"The what?"

"The boot. He put guards at the entrance to the magic fen, and he banned me from entering. Me!"

"Look, sir, I am sorry to hear this, but Denny is in a very similar position. I hate to do this, but I have to report to the King, so could you and Denny just talk this out? I'll be back as soon as I possibly can." And "poof" Lucinder was gone.

The Beast was sputtering in rage. "She continues to defy me!" he roared. "Sh-sh-she conspires behind my back!" He suddenly noticed Denny hunched over in a corner, sitting on the damp cavern floor.

"What's wrong with you?" he asked bluntly.

"Nothing, nothing at all," the monkey replied, sniveling loudly.

"Out with it, monkey-man. Tell me. What is wrong with you?"

"Arachimedes," was all Denny could choke out before he broke out in serious tears.

"What? You, too?" The Beast asked. "What did that louse do to you?"

"He told me to leave the magic fen," Denny replied, his sobs breaking up his sentence so badly that The Beast had to piece it back together before a look of comprehension eventually washed across his face. Denny continued, "and he told me not to come back. Ever!"

The Beast sat down with a sigh next to the deflated little brown man. He sat close enough to him so they practically touched.

"Well, we have something in common, Denny," he said. His voice was low but full of menace. "And we're going to do something about it. We are going to come up with a plan to unseat that old magic bug—yes, Denny, he is only a bug. He played us. He hurt us, let us call it what it is...and now we're going to hurt him."

The two hugely mismatched creatures bent and raised their heads so they could lower their voices and plot and scheme in private. Denny sniffed and wiped his eyes continuously through the entire discussion.

~ * ~

Back in the magic fen, a second conference was beginning. This one was small—only three beings were involved.

"Ribetta," Arachimedes began. "Thank you for sharing the intelligence you collected from the blue humans. Their unhappiness could be their undoing. I have set things in motion. We will do everything in our power to reverse their magic status. They don't deserve it, and they don't even want it!"

"The lucky one," the third party interrupted. "I know who it is."

"Oh?" Arachimedes said. "How do you know?"

"I am an integral part of him," the man responded. "I am his negativity, the part of him who tries to keep him from being his best."

Arachimedes and Ribetta both nodded, indicating that this human-looking creature should continue, should elaborate.

"It is Chance Bonner," the creature said. "It should be obvious. He is a very lucky human being. Seriously. It has been my utter displeasure to have been assigned to him. I strive mightily to trip him up and bring him down—he has defeated me twice already, and I brought my entire army to bear against him each time."

"So how did he win, then?" a sly Arachimedes asked.

"Because he's lucky, I told you!" The creature had flecks of spittle flying from his mouth he was so worked up. "L-U-C-K-Y!"

The creature walked a few steps away and then pivoted to face the pair once more. "I have given you the information you need to bring you victory and to return the boy to me unchanged. It's up to you now. Don't squander this gift. Do something with it. Now!"

The creature "poofed" away, a veritable shower of odds and ends accompanying his departure.

"What is all that stuff?" the old spider asked the frog-lady. Ribetta had picked up and discarded several of the items left behind.

"Junk," she replied. "A pen with someone's name on it. A wallet with another human's identification in it. A broken model plane. A half-finished painting. Oh look! He's left half of a tuna sandwich!" She looked at Arachimedes in wonder. "I think he's a thief!" she cried. "He has stolen all of these objects, I'm sure of it!"

"Well, why hasn't he stolen any decent clothes?" the old spider asked her. "Did you catch that get-up he had on? And that hat...what was that, a crown?"

The pair laughed uproariously for a short while before returning to planning their next steps.

"I have to go now," the spider told the frog after many moments. "My monkey is due any minute."

"Yes, by all means," Ribetta replied. "Don't keep your monkey waiting!" And "pop," off she went, showering the spider in her signature scent of mold and mildew.

"What a delight!" the spider observed to himself, sniffing the cloud of stench Ribetta left behind. "She really ought to bottle that up and sell it. It would be a huge commercial success."

~ * ~

Lucinder paced, waiting for the Devil King of the Sixth Heaven to arrive, albeit late, for their appointed "conference."

When he finally appeared, "poofing" into his throne room, he seemed jubilant. He strode across the richly appointed room and threw himself into its throne.

"Good news!" he cried, addressing Lucinder. "The boy will soon be returned to us!"

"Because you have given the spider the information on his true identity?" Lucinder asked.

A cloud moved over the King's face. His smile transformed into a sneer. "No, Lucinder. Not because I have identified Chance Bonner as the lucky person. Not that." His smile morphed into a glower. "But, rather, because you are not going to disappoint me a second time. You are going to get that unlucky girl, that twin sister of Chance Bonner, and you are going to bring her to me. You will get one more chance, Lucinder, and only one. Do not fail me, is that understood?"

"Y-y-yes, Sire," Lucinder stuttered, backing out of the room and poofing back to the cavern.

It was empty.

"Now where have they gotten off to?" she asked herself. "Wait—that doesn't really matter. I have to concentrate on capturing that girl, that unlucky girl Destiny Dyer. I will use this privacy to plan."

~ * ~

One last conference was conducted that night: Arachimedes summoned Denny at 0300 sharp in a quiet secluded part of the fen.

"I am feeling a mite peckish," he announced to the monkey. "Do you mind?"

"Mind? Mind...oh, yes, I see," replied a delighted monkey. "Yes, please, help yourself. Please!"

Arachimedes restrained himself, taking only a little nibble from the back of Denny's willing neck. He naturally exchanged a good amount of his own venom for the blood he consumed.

"Thank you, my dear friend," he said, wiping his mouth clean with one bristly arm.

Denny was in an ecstasy. "Any time," he slurred. "Any time at all."

"I have something I need you to do for me," the spider said next.

"Anything," the monkey answered with a sloppy smile. "Anything at all. At any time..."

"I need you to spy on your human. This Chance Bonner character. You can do that, right?"

"I am a manifestation of part of him," the monkey said. "Of course, I can observe him any time I wish to."

"Well, I need to know what he's up to," Arachimedes explained. "He is key to our success in the campaign."

"Campaign? Will there be snacks?"

"Campaign, Denny. Not champagne."

"Oh," and the monkey giggled. "Sorry."

"Just watch him for me, will you? I will summon you when we can talk without being observed. Will that suit you?"

"To a tee," Denny replied. "Or tea. Whichever works. Yes. Yes, I will do it."

"You are a good friend, Denny," Arachimedes said, patting the monkey on his back with one hairy appendage.

"So are you, Ara-ara-arachimedes," Denny slurred. "I just need a little rest before I start." And the little brown man who was not a man fell over, face down in the fen, and began immediately to snore.

"Guards!" Arachimedes called quietly. "Watch him! Don't let him drown before he can get to work."

"Yes, Sire!" Todd and Brad said, executing smart three-handed salutes.

"I need that monkey," Arachimedes said to himself as he travelled back to his tree. "I cannot deal with these humans myself. I will need the monkey to deliver the death blow when the time comes."

Exhausted, he slept. He dreamt of a world without humans in it that night. It was a delightful dream where he had no end of tender monkeys to dine on. He slept through the day, arising only as the sun started its descent into night.

Night.

It's spider time.

Fifteen

Spite

"So, this is my home, Mrs. Bonner," Arthur Dillow said, opening the tiny house's front door and gesturing for her to enter first.

"My parents aren't home from work yet," he explained. "But they said that you could come over any time, so…"

"Oh, Arthur, it's so…so…so…oh, I don't think there's a word that's right!" Nan Bonner gushed. "It's cute but classy! You practically have to walk sideways to get from room to room, don't you?"

"Yes, it's skinny all right!" the small boy responded. "You know why it's called 'The Spite House', right?"

"I heard that the family who owned the land built two big Victorian houses on four-fifths of the family plot to try to block one sister from building on the property, so she built this skinny house in between the two big ones just to spite them," Nan said. "Is that right?"

"Close enough," the boy said. "So, is it as cool as you thought it would be?"

"Oh, yes," Nan replied. "Thank you so much for showing me around. I am sorry to look and run, but I really need to get home."

"Uhh, I was hoping to run into Chance at your place, Mrs. Bonner," Arthur admitted. "I didn't see him a school yesterday." He gulped. "Or today."

"Oh, that's right, Arthur," Nan dissembled. "He and his father had to make an emergency trip to Baltimore for a funeral."

"I am sorry to hear that," Arthur said politely. "Someone close?"

"Chaz's Uncle Henry," Nan lied. "So yes, pretty close."

"Again, my sympathies," Arthur said. He was pretty pleased with how sensitive and polite he was being.

Nan Bonner just wanted to get home. Arthur was reminding her of Eddie Haskell from *Leave it to Beaver*. OK, she told herself. Now you're really dating yourself, she thought. *Well, at least you saw that show as a re-run on Nickelodeon, not the original airing.* She remembered when Chance had found the show, again as a re-run on one of the kids' channels. Or maybe YouTube. Anyway, he had asked her what the "grey TV" was all about...

"Mrs. Bonner," Arthur said for the third time. "Mrs. Bonner, are you OK?"

"Just daydreaming, I'm afraid, Arthur dear," she replied. "And now I'm afraid I have to run. Chaz will be calling from, uhh, Baltimore any minute now, and I don't want to miss his call."

"Well, I hope you liked your tour," the boy said. "Would you tell Chance I was asking after him?"

"Sure, Arthur. I will," Nan promised.

Arthur was muttering to himself as he closed the door. "Baltimore. Sure, Mrs. Bonner. If Chance went to Baltimore for a funeral, did he take all of his friends with him?" He fumed for a moment, then deflated.

"All of his friends...except me," he said in a very little voice.

~ * ~

Denny was exceedingly glad to be reunited with the young man, Chance Bonner. Plus, since he was on a secret mission for the spider, he didn't need to hide his admiration for the youth from Lucinder or The Beast.

This was a perfect assignment.

Denny observed Chance, his father, and his friends without any fear of being observed himself. He was a monkey, after all, so up a tree he went and found a perfect perch. He could see the blue humans, but there was no way their inferior eyes and noses could detect him.

"Look!" Kelly O'Hara cried, pointing right at Denny. "Look up there in that tree! What is that? Is it a monkey? If it is, it's as big as a man!"

Denny panicked and prepared to jump from his branch to a new one when another brown man, bigger and hairier than he by far, jumped down to the ground from the branch just above his own.

"I am no monkey!" he announced in a booming voice which seemed to fill the fen. "I am Almasty!"

He was a tall creature, Denny saw. But he was not truly hairy. It was the robe he wore. It was hairy—goat hair, to be precise. And those big brown boots—cowboy boots. Odd, that, Denny thought to himself. His attention was distracted by further conversation.

"You may know me as Yeti, Sasquatch, or Bigfoot!" the creature cried, kicking off his boots to reveal two really big feet. Huge, really.

"I detect the presence of magic here," he said. "I, too, am a creature of magic, but not the blue variety you have evidently adopted."

"See here, Mr. Almasty," Chaz Bonner said, stepping forward to shield the young people from the stranger. "Would you mind telling us what you're doing here, and what you want from us? And while you're at it, you might tell us where you came from. And why we should talk to you, or trust you."

"Are you through?" the robed man asked, smiling in a kindly manner.

Chaz Bonner's chest was heaving. "Not by a long shot, but I'll pause to let you answer the first few questions."

"I have one of my own first," the man calling himself Almasty said. "Which one of you is living backwards?"

A stunned silence greeted his question.

"Oh," he said, almost to himself. "Maybe you don't know about that."

"If you're talking about karma, then you're talking about me," Chance piped up. "I am not living backwards as a human being. I am living backwards in that I have peaked, karmically, in my first incarnation. This. This life. It's my first incarnation, and I've already discovered the mystic law and recite its mantra."

"I see," responded the man. "And just who might you be?"

Chaz signaled Chance not to speak. He resumed his own conversation with the stranger. "He—we—will not say another word until you answer my questions!" He was wearing a very determined look.

The strange man bowed to Chaz, and then bowed to each of the young people in turn. "I am Almasty," he repeated. "I am an eternal but human being. I have, of late, been meditating on a remote mountain top in the Himalayas—one of the lower ones, you know—I like mountain goats, so I have to keep the altitude reasonable if I am to expect the goats to hang around.

"I was disturbed, awakened, by something some days ago and was compelled to find out just what that something might be.

"I think I've found it. Or part of it. It feels like just half of it, really."

He ceased his rambling and pointed at Chance. "It is you. You—and perhaps one other like you—have awakened me." He crouched down to put himself on Chance's level. "So, who are you?" he asked. His look was every bit as determined as Chaz's.

"Just wait a minute!" Chaz shouted.

"No, Dad, really, it's OK," Chance interrupted. "I want to tell him. I want to talk to him."

His father nodded his acquiescence, but he did not look happy about it. "Go ahead, then," he told his son. "I trust your instincts." And he proceeded to look very untrusting indeed.

"I am Chance Bonner," Chance told the strange man. They shook hands.

The man recoiled from Chance's touch at first, but then got a good grip on it and pulled Chance closer.

"We are kin!" he gasped. "How is this possible?"

"Kin?" Chance and Chaz asked at the same moment. The other young people just gaped, slack-jawed with shock.

As did Denny in his aerie above them.

"Bigfoot is Chance Bonner's father," he said in awe. Unfortunately, he said it out loud.

Almasty turned his head and looked straight up at Denny. "You. Yes you, Monkey-man. Come down here directly."

Just when Chaz, Chance, and his friends thought things could not get stranger, they did.

A man who looked more like a monkey than a man was suddenly in their midst, having jumped down from a tree limb high over their heads.

What was worse, he looked familiar.

"How is it that you manifest?" Almasty demanded of him.

"He is special. The boy...or young man, I should say," Denny answered without hesitation. He was in awe of this legendary being. He would answer every question he had. He would do anything he asked. He was Bigfoot. Denny looked down at his own feet and visually ran a comparison between his and Almasty's. He sighed as he realized his own feet were nothing compared to the colossal appendages of the big man.

"Explain yourself," Almasty commanded. "What do you mean special?"

"All of the aspects of his mind, good and bad, can manifest," Denny replied. "He is unique as a human being in this. None of us knows why, we just accept our status, and act, and react, accordingly."

"Your Devil King?"

"Yes?"

"Does he also manifest?"

"He does."

"Amazing."

"I guess you could say that."

"And what is your status amongst the manifesting features of Chance Bonner's mind?"

"Oh, I am just a lowly minion," Denny admitted, lowering his head humbly. "I work with a wasp. A wonderful wasp. Lucinder, her name is. And we both work for The Beast."

"The Beast, you say?"

"Yes. He's the boss. Our boss. The boss of our little taskforce."

"What is the mission of your taskforce?"

"The King has commanded that The Beast ensure that Chance Bonner does not continue to experience such enormous good fortune in his life. We are to interfere with Chance Bonner's Buddhist practice. We are to discourage him from excelling in studies or sports. We will attempt to trip him up in his every effort."

"Are you three alone in this?"

"For now. If the King determines we cannot succeed, he will replace us."

"Will that bother you?"

"If he replaces us?" Denny asked. The man bowed his acquiescence. "Well, yes, it will bother us. We won't get another good assignment, and our team will be disbanded. I will be separated from my beloved...I mean my partner, Lucinder. The Beast will be demoted to an imp. That would be a terrible fate."

"For The Beast or you?"

"For both of us. For all of us."

"Why do you fail in your mission?"

"The boy—young man—Chance Bonner," Denny stuttered. "He is incredibly lucky. But more than that, he has the protection of all of the positive forces within himself and throughout the Universe."

"How does he merit that?"

"He chants the mantra," the monkey replied. "Chance chants."

"So, what about all this chant, chant, chanting?"

"Chance, not chants," the monkey clarified. He suddenly realized why he was not getting through to the man. "Hahaha!" he said.

"Chance. Chants. Hahaha! I never noticed that before. The boy—Chance Bonner—he chants the mantra. You know, he intones the mystic syllables." Denny gave up trying to explain at this point, and just shrugged up at the man, and giggled a little more.

"Oh! Are you saying that he intones the mantra of the Lotus Sutra?" the man asked, looking like a light had gone on in his head.

"Exactly. Yes," Denny responded. "And when he does, a maelstrom of power is released. It's really quite something."

"Yes. Yes, I know." The man seemed to make a decision on the spot. "I can do the same thing," he confided.

Now a sudden silence fell on the entire group. It went unbroken for many seconds.

"Y-y-you said we were kin," a dazed Chance said, breaking the spell. "How are we kin?"

"I do not know," the man admitted. "But I am going to find out." He made a few arcane motions with his arms and hands and disappeared from view.

"Wait!" Chance cried. "Where are you going?"

The man's wail could be barely heard. But they heard it. "Angelica!" his voice cried from afar. "I am going to find Angelica!"

While the crowd was distracted by Almasty, Denny, too, made a quick and silent escape, back up into the trees where he made sure he had a secure and invisible hiding place.

"What are you doing, you fool?" a hoarse whisper demanded of him. "Why did you tell that hairy man so much about us?"

"Sir," Denny replied. "Please just remain hidden and silent. If you are discovered by the spiders, I can't be responsible for what will happen."

"OK, Denny," The Beast acquiesced. "This had better work."

"It will," the monkey said. "Just be patient."

"Not my strong suit."

"Don't I know it," Denny said under his breath.

"What?"

"Nothing. Nothing. Now be quiet! Sir. Please."

~ * ~

Angelica ran to Almasty and threw her arms around him. "My love!" she cried, showering his face with tears and kisses.

The man had simply appeared, standing in front of her desk. When she looked up from her work to find him there, her face beamed with joy. She sprang to her feet and ran to him.

"Angelica, please get a grip on yourself," the man said. He said this, but he did not attempt to pry her arms from him or distance himself from her lips.

In fact, he kissed her back. Fiercely, even.

"Woman, I have missed you," he confessed. "I tried for the last thirteen years to forget you, and thought I was just starting to succeed.

"And then something summoned me. Was it you?"

"If it was," Angelica responded, "then you would never have been able to leave me in the first place. I have been summoning you from my heart every moment of the last thirteen years."

He gently pushed her away from him and led her to a nearby couch. They sat, side by side, hand in hand.

"What have you done?" Almasty asked her. His voice and manner were gentle, but his meaning was clear: he would have his answer.

Angelica sighed. She adjusted her seating position. She threw back her head and squared her shoulders.

"We have children," she said.

"We—you and I—have children?" Almasty repeated in disbelief. "How do we have children?"

"I found out I was pregnant with twins after you left me," Angelica explained. "I knew you would be unhappy about the pregnancy, so I hid the children. They have been brought up by other parents and lead normal, happy lives."

Almasty looked disturbed. He threw his hood back and mopped his sweating brow with another hairy cloth he extracted from his robe pocket.

"Angelica," he said slowly and carefully. "There is no way children of mine are living normal lives. You must know this at some level."

"I have kept a careful eye on each of them," she responded. "They are safe."

"They should not be."

"I knew you would feel that way. That is why I hid them. I hid them from you."

"I have found one," he stated flatly.

"How? Who?" Angelica blurted.

"A lucky young man named Chance. Chance Bonner."

"How did you find him?"

"I was summoned. I followed the summons. It led directly to him."

"Where is he?" Angelica asked plaintively. "I seem to have lost him."

"I found him in the magic fen," Almasty responded without emotion. "He is blue. Blue, Angelica."

"Oh dear...blue, you say?"

"Yes, Angelica. Blue. As in magic," he responded, his emotions reemerging. "How has he become magic? Did you cause this?"

"I certainly did not!" she objected. "He doesn't need any magic. He's lucky! Extraordinarily lucky!"

"So I have heard. Well, his luck may have run out," the man said. "He can manifest, you know. The various factions of his mind, both good and bad. They are at work. They work against him and his luck."

"I know."

"You know? How do you know?"

"I have battled the bad forces twice already. I join Chance and the good forces when the battlefield manifests itself." She took a short, reflective pause then resumed. "I have a feeling we are heading toward a third battle. I sense it. It's a pressure that builds....and this time, magic will also share the battlefield."

"You mean chaos, don't you?" Almasty inquired, leaning forward to look her in the eyes.

She shuddered and lowered her head to avoid his eyes. "Yes," she whispered. "Yes, chaos will run rampant across the next battlefield."

"Well, we'd better get ready," Almasty said softly.

"We?" Angelica lifted her head and looked at Almasty, hope in her expression. "We?" she repeated.

"Yes, my dear. We," he affirmed. "And the first thing we need to do is to find the other."

"The other?"

"The other twin. Where is he?"

"Oh, it's not a he," she said. "It's a she. We have both a son and a daughter."

"Is she lucky? Is she magical?".

"Oh, no," Angelica said with a frown. "She is neither magical nor lucky. Actually, she is one of the unluckiest people on the planet."

"You may not realize this," Almasty said in a low voice. "But that kind of horribly bad luck may also be magical...if it's bad enough."

"Oh, it's bad, all right," Angelica told him. "She can't even walk without tripping. She is a hazard to herself."

"Oh dear," the man said. "That is bad. Well, where is she?"

"She is at home with her adoptive parents. They have just recently had a scare."

"Scare?"

"It seems that Destiny—that's her name, Destiny Dyer—was abducted. But don't worry, she was returned home unharmed."

"Who abducted her?"

"Well, that's a funny thing. We are not sure. But I dispatched a few friends who were instrumental in her rescue. They sniffed her out. Found her. Brought her home. She can't remember anything about what happened...the best sniffers in my friends' group said her bad luck had a distinctive odor. That's how they found her."

Almasty interrupted at this point. "That's proof right there!" he exclaimed. "That kind of bad luck is as special as the boy's good luck! Wait a minute, though. Who are these friends of yours?"

"Rodents," Angelica said.

"Rodents?"

"Yes, rodents."

"Well, what else did they report? Did they find who abducted her in the first place?"

"No, they didn't. But they sniffed out traces of the culprit or rather *culprits*, I should say, in two different places."

"Do go on," he prompted.

"They said there was a wasp in the school bus and a monkey in the bushes."

"Did you just say 'monkey'?" he challenged.

"Yes. Yes, I did. Monkey."

"Well, this is bad," he said. "I just met a monkey. He manifests from Chance Bonner's mind. He said he is a teammate to a wasp. They form a taskforce together with some kind of beast. Their mission is to rob Chance Bonner of his luck. They intend to make him unhappy."

"I know those three," Angelica admitted, unhappy herself now. "They fight on the side of the enemy when we battle. The wasp, in particular, seems extremely spiteful.

"They serve Chance's Devil King."

"I had sort of figured that out," Almasty informed her. "In all of my long life, I have never heard of someone's manifestations interacting with another person before."

"Well, they're twins," Angelica posited. "Maybe that provides some kind of bridge between Chance and Destiny."

"A good working theory, since we don't have anything else to go on," he responded.

"Gee, thanks," Angelica said, rolling her eyes and grimacing at the man.

"You're welcome," Almasty said distractedly. He didn't really understand sarcasm, you see. Or spite. He had already fully embraced the fact that he was a father. He had already forgiven Angelica for keeping that secret for all these years...almost.

~ * ~

Samantha Swisher burst through Angelica's door in a state. Her hat was on sideways, and her left shoe was untied.

She stopped short when she confirmed what she had suspected. She clasped her hands together and danced in place.

"It's you!" she cried. "This is a dream come true!"

Almasty and Angelica sat side-by-side on the sofa in Angelica's office, holding hands. He looked the small woman up and down appraisingly.

"So, you must be Angelica's rodent friend," he said.

"Oh, yes, your majesty! I am!" Samantha replied, curtseying deeply. "I am your servant, Samantha Swisher...a squirrel!"

"So good to meet you," he said. "Any friend of Angelica's is a friend of mine."

"Oh, you're funny, too," Samantha tittered. "I already know you are friend to all living creatures of this world! You are our protector. And you are a legend! I never thought I would be so lucky. I have actually met you! In person!"

"Luck seems to be our theme today," the man whispered to Angelica.

"Well, come, sit, dear squirrel, and let's chat for a few moments," he invited. "Tell me about your mission to rescue my daughter."

The squirrel burrowed herself between the two, who smiled at each other over the little woman's head. Samantha began chattering immediately and went on conversing with her legendary hero for quite some time. As for Almasty, he found all creatures of the world endlessly fascinating and worthy of respect.

Sixteen

Avatar

Lucky waited in vain for Chance to return. Brilliant Schultz had not come back, either.

When he heard the front door open and shut, Lucky ran down the stairs full of hope, but it was just Nan Bonner, returning with the smell of armadillo on her.

"Ugh. She has been with that boy, Arthur Dillow," he realized. He reminded himself that he had promised Chance that he would be more tolerant of the other boy. The only way he could do that was to not think about him at all. That, he supposed, he might be able to do.

Lucky approached Chance's mother. She was sitting at the kitchen table, her head in her hands. When she sensed Lucky's presence next to her, she dropped one hand to rest on top of his head. She scratched it gently.

"Oh, Lucky, I have such a bad feeling," she said. "I am so worried about all of them. It's my fault, all my fault." A tear ran down her face and fell with a "plop" on the table. Lucky nuzzled her hand, attempting to comfort her.

Nan stood suddenly and turned toward the stairs. "The best thing I can do for them now is to chant," she told the dog. "I must really exert myself. This is a matter of life and death."

"Life and death" rang in Lucky's head. Things were that serious, he sensed. Nan Bonner had put the right words to his feelings.

Well, a life and death problem calls for a life and death solution, he resolved.

Using the dog door imbedded in the human door, Lucky exited the Bonner house and ran all of the way to his girlfriend's house.

She was a bodhisattva. She would know what to do.

When Lucky was a hundred yards shy of his goal, he found a deserted alleyway in which to make his transformation.

A tall, bearded man in a kilt and tan raincoat left the alley moments later. Adjusting his fedora, the man approached the small cottage just a few steps down the street, rang the doorbell, and waited.

A petite exotic beauty opened the door and welcomed him warmly. They both stepped into the house and the door closed behind them, softly but firmly.

~ * ~

Nan Bonner lit incense. She opened the door of her altar to reveal the sacred scroll. She rang her large bronze bell three times and began to chant. The smoke from the incense curled around her head. From the top of her head, it then snaked its way to the ceiling.

At the little bodhisattva's house, smoke from incense also swam and danced between the two people kneeling in front of the Buddhist altar and scroll. Lucky, in his form as Angus MacLeod, and his friend, the bodhisattva Arya Tara, chanted the mantra as well.

Lucky was not the only being transformed: Arya Tara was now dusted in gold and wore jewels in her hair and on her skin. She wore a scarlet silk gown. At her side, placed carefully on the floor, was a golden staff with a huge turquoise-colored jewel in its haft, its head honed to razor sharpness.

The smoke swirled around the chanting couple and from the top of their heads it ran in a straight line for the ceiling.

~ * ~

An aerial view of the Capitol Hill district of Seattle, Washington would show it: the purple smoke rising from two residential roofs just a few miles apart from each other.

The twin spires of smoke joined a few hundred feet up in the atmosphere and melded, performing a slow, measured, and stately pavane.

~ * ~

Almasty was still with Angelica Root in her office in Baltimore, Maryland. He was meditating...well, he was trying to, at any rate. The proximity of the delightful Angelica served to distract him.

He felt around the sub-ether—an invisible envelope which contains the Earth—with his enormous mind. He briefly held, and then discarded, many events in his search.

There! He found something of the nature he sought: focused chanting. It was quite distant from his current location. That did not present a big challenge for him, but Angelica would have to travel there by conventional methods and that would take time they really didn't have.

He reflected on his progress thus far: he had found the blue humans, including his son, Chance Bonner. And now, he had found allies of his son and his friends.

The daughter, though. She was proving harder to locate...and although he suspected that Angelica knew exactly where Destiny Dyer was, he wanted her to volunteer the information. He would not ask her for it.

His thoughts were interrupted by Angelica, herself. "Almasty," she said. "Why have you shown no interest in meeting your daughter?"

His relief was so huge it burst from him in a cascade of laughter. Angelica looked at him curiously, then began to laugh along with him after a few moments.

"Wh-wh-why are we laughing?" she asked him breathlessly.

"B-b-because it's like you were r-r-reading m-m-my m-m-mind!" Almasty declared. He got control of himself with great effort. "Phew!" he said, finally sobering. "I didn't know I was that tense. Listen, Angelica, I was just thinking that you probably knew where Destiny was, and I wanted you to want to tell me...and then you asked your question like you knew what I was thinking!"

Angelica smiled slyly. "Maybe I did know what you were thinking," she said. "I have powers, too, you know."

"I have always known that," the man replied, approaching her and putting his long arms around her slender waist. "It is a very attractive quality, you know."

"I know, Almasty. I know."

~ * ~

Destiny awoke to find her cat, Mallory, staring at her. The cat seemed to be waiting for Destiny to stir, because as soon as the girl's eyes were well and truly open, the cat turned her own gaze away from the girl's, and toward the bedroom's far wall. She glared at it, a low growl rumbling in her chest.

Destiny recognized odd behavior, especially when it came to Mallory. Purring was the cat's style. But growling? This was a first, as far as Destiny knew. It sounded like her cat was warning her of danger, or something.

What? Mallory, a "guard cat?"

"Come here, you silly thing," Destiny called. "Come here, Mallory." But call and cajole as she would, the cat would not budge.

"Destiny!" her mother called up the stairs. "Breakfast is ready!"

Breakfast! Destiny realized she was starving. So, forgetting the growling cat, she quickly threw a robe over her pajamas and ran downstairs.

She almost made it, too. She got two stairs from the bottom and stepped on one of Mallory's toys—a paisley catnip-filled rat—and slithered noisily the rest of the way to the foyer floor.

"Are you all right, honey?" her father called from the kitchen.

"You know," Destiny called back. "I think I may have broken something this time. My ankle really hurts."

"Oh dear," Dick Dyer said, running to his daughter with his napkin still tucked into his shirt front. "Can you walk?"

"I don't think so," Destiny replied. "It really hurts, Daddy."

"Dorothy!" her father called to his wife. "Call the lawyer, will you please? I am taking Destiny to the Emergency Room again."

"Yes, dear, I'll do that right now. I will join you both as soon as I get ahold of Ted. You get going now. I'll be right behind you."

"See you in a few!" Dick Dyer called as he carried Destiny to the family sedan. "Tell Ted to meet us at the ER, OK?"

"I got it! Don't worry!" Dorothy replied.

Dick could hear her talking to Ted Trueheart's receptionist as he left the house carrying his unlucky —and injured—daughter.

~ * ~

There were two doctors on duty that day at the local hospital's emergency room.

One was the physician she had seen after her abduction, a strange coincidence that Dick Dyer didn't know about.

The second doctor was a very tall, very pale woman who seemed determined to treat the girl for her injury. Her lab coat was edged in sequins and there was a light dusting of glitter in her hair.

They fought over Destiny. Each of the two doctors insisted he or she should handle the case.

"I treated this girl just the other day," the male doctor, a Dr. Hyde, informed her father. "I must insist that I continue to care for her."

"All the more reason for a fresh set of eyes," the other doctor interrupted. "I am sure this young lady will be more comfortable with a woman doctor."

"Don't be ridiculous, Doctor, uhh, Faust," Dr. Hyde replied, reading from her nameplate. "I will see to my patient, thank you very much."

Just as Dr. Faust was about the rebut this assertion, Dorothy Dyer and the family lawyer rushed into the triage area.

"Oh, no you don't!" Dorothy announced as soon as she recognized Hyde. "I don't want you going anywhere near my daughter!"

"Wh-wh-whatever do you mean?" Hyde stuttered. "I am her physician."

"Not any more you're not!" Dorothy said. "You as much as called her a liar the other day. We will be finding a new doctor for our daughter effective immediately!" She turned to face the woman doctor.

"Could you please take care of my daughter?" she asked.

"Certainly. I was just attempting to do so," Dr. Faust responded, watching Dr. Hyde's retreating back as she spoke.

Dr. Hyde continued his retreat, stepping inside a door at the end of the hallway. As the door swung shut, a small amount of sulfurous cloud wafted through it, momentarily causing many in the crowded waiting room to begin coughing and wheezing.

"What seems to be the problem?" the tall pale woman asked the girl.

"I fell down our stairs at home," Destiny began explaining. "My ankle really hurts."

At this moment, a nurse with a very thick file approached the doctor and handed her the packet. She looked at Destiny's parents warily, suspiciously, even.

"That's why we have our lawyer with us," Dick Dyer said, gesturing toward the attorney. "You see, Destiny is kind of clumsy—well, I'm sorry, honey, but you are—and she has had a lot of injuries. A lot of injuries.

"We have been investigated for child abuse several times over the last thirteen years and have always been found completely innocent, but in the interest of being able to take Destiny home with us after she is treated, Ted Trueheart here has a writ from the state attorney general requiring any and all medical facilities in the state of Virginia to allow us full and free access to our daughter."

Dr. Faust had been flipping through the big file, page by page as she listened to the anxious father.

"The bicycle accident of 2012 isn't here," she said.

"She didn't require hospitalization after that fall," her father said automatically. "Hey...wait a minute. How did you know about that bicycle accident?" Dick and Dorothy Dyer and their attorney, Ted Trueheart, looked at each other, and then at Dr. Faust. The three of them stared at her in shock and puzzlement.

Destiny moaned. "It hurts," she said.

"Let's get her to Examining Room Number Four," Dr. Faust said, gesturing for two nearby nurses to assist in getting the patient on a gurney and to wheel her down a long hall toward the examining rooms, x-ray, and laboratory. The doctor followed the gurney closely. She still clutched the file.

At the door separating the waiting room from the examining rooms, the doctor turned to face the three adults.

"We will take it from here," she informed them.

"Just wait one second," the worried mother said. "I am going in with her."

"If she requests that you be present, I will have you paged," the doctor said. "Now, you are delaying me from treating her, from alleviating her pain. Please allow me to do my job. I will have the staff keep you apprised of Destiny's condition. Now have a seat in the waiting room. Please. Now."

And with a flip of her long, white ponytail, the tall doctor turned her back on the trio and strode purposely through the door and out of sight.

"This doesn't feel right," Dorothy told her husband in a hushed tone.

"No, it doesn't," Dick replied.

"I've had my recorder on the whole time," Ted Trueheart informed them. "If anything happens to Destiny, we will have evidence to sue this hospital for medical malpractice."

"Let us all pray that does not become necessary," Dorothy said, crossing the room and taking a seat. She gestured for the men to take the seats to her right and left, which they did.

"She's thirteen years old," Dorothy told herself. "She is no longer a child. She'll be fine."

~ * ~

Nan Bonner's focus while she chanted fiercely for the safe return of her husband, son, and his friends eventually landed on just one of the characters on her sacred scroll. She had chanted mightily for the Devil King of the Sixth Heaven to be vanquished...banished, even. After many moments, though, her gaze moved from his symbol to the character representing the Mother of Demon Children. The moment she made the shift, she felt the jolt of power which comes from chanting with correct focus.

She was connected. She would maintain this focus and chant for the power behind the character to come to her aid, bringing all of the other positive forces of the Universe with it.

~ * ~

Just a few miles away, Angus, too, focused his prayers on overcoming the Devil King. He found his focus on the Devil King symbol on the scroll wavering, however, several minutes into his chant. His eyes found and held the character representing the Heavenly King Hearer of Many Teachings. Focusing on this symbol, then, he continued chanting with keen focus to gain the wisdom he needed to confront the obstacles between himself and the safe return of Chance Bonner. Angus was Chance's protector, after all, and the current incarnation of the heavenly god of protection. But Angus could not protect Chance if he could not find him.

~ * ~

Back in Baltimore, Angelica felt it: the pull. "Someone is calling for me," she told Almasty, who sat beside her on her couch.

"In which form?" the wise man asked.

"Someone is calling the Mother of Demon Children," she responded.

"Seems right," he replied.

"I know," she said. "And I will respond. It will mean flying to the West Coast."

"I will meet you there."

"What about Destiny?"

"I think we should bring her with us, don't you?"

"I do. I do, but I don't know how we would be able to accomplish that, short of kidnapping her."

"Leave that to me," Almasty told her. "Just make your reservations and meet me at the Bonner house."

"Do you know how to find the Bonner house?" she asked.

"I will find it. It is the source of much of the signal which pulls at you, and it is very close to the other signal which calls to me. It pulls irresistibly."

"I feel that way, too," she said. "It compels me to go there."

"Then go we must. I am off." And Almasty simply blended in with his surroundings until he could not be seen any more at all.

"Almasty?" Angelica called. There was no answer. He really was gone.

"I wish I could do that," the woman said to herself as she keyed up her computer to make her travel arrangements.

~ * ~

Almasty reappeared in Examination Room #4 in a fashion identical, but in reverse, of the way he had left Angelica's.

"Reveal yourself!" he cried to the creature in the lab coat hovering over a teenage girl on a gurney.

Dr. Faust jumped a full two feet off of the floor in surprise and shock. As she did, she kicked up sprays of multi-colored glitter which littered the floor. She turned to face the intruder in her examination room.

"How dare you," she began to say, her words freezing in her mouth as she twirled around and took in the sight behind her. "Wh-wh-who are you?" she struggled to ask. She had begun shivering in fright, and in something else.

Suddenly, she exploded. Her masquerade as a human doctor could not be maintained in her state of agitation. She became The Beast. Destiny's Beast. On either side of the gurney, two companion explosions occurred, revealing one of the orderlies to be a zebra, the other a bee.

Destiny rested comfortably, sleeping lightly, thanks to Dr. Faust's administration of a mild sedative.

"Explain yourself!" Almasty demanded. "What are you doing here? Why have you manifested?"

"I-I-I am Destiny's," the unicorn said, her voice small and scared. "I have every right to be here."

Almasty opened his eyes in surprise. "So, you're telling me that this girl lying here is Destiny Dyer?" he asked her.

"That's right."

"What's wrong with her?"

"Broken ankle."

"Foul play?"

"No such thing. She is just desperately clumsy, and unlucky."

"Ah, so it's true."

"What? What is true?"

"She is unlucky."

"Oh, yes, very."

"Then how do you explain my being here to rescue her from you?" Almasty grinned, taunting The Beast.

"You seem familiar."

"I should."

"Do I know you?"

"All of the creatures of this world know me."

"I am not truly from this world," she explained. "I am what you would call a 'derivative'."

"Nevertheless."

"Well, from the looks of you, I would say you just might be the legendary Bigfoot." She was walking around Almasty now, making a big show of looking him up and down, her examination stopping at his feet. She stared at his gigantic cowboy boots for many long moments.

"I might be. I prefer the other names, however."

"Yeti?"

"That's all right."

"Almasty?"

"That's the one. That is what I prefer to be called."

"Well, I am the foremost of Destiny's Devil King's minions," The Beast announced. "I lead the effort to trip this girl up, but, frankly, she doesn't need much help in that department!" She laughed briefly and without humor. "Why is it that you think you can take her from me? I go everywhere with her. I am her. Well, part of her, at any rate."

"I realize you will have to come along. What I was referring to was your previous avatar. Who were you pretending to be?" He got closer to examine her name tag. "Doctor Fillien Faust. Nice.

"Well, Doctor Fillien Faust," he continued. "Have her admitted. Go talk to her parents. Tell them she has been given something for the pain and you are going to keep her for observation."

"Why should I do all that?" The Beast contested.

"I get the feeling you are underworked and overpaid," Almasty said.

"What is that supposed to mean?"

"I think you need to actually do something—accomplish something—or your Devil King will fire you and replace you with someone more effective. Someone who is not as 'high-maintenance' as you." And Almasty took his turn looking The Beast up and down, resting his eyes for several moments on her glittering horn.

"Oh, very well," The Beast capitulated. She quickly reassumed her guise as Dr. Faust and left the room. The orderlies, however, remained unchanged. They maintained their former positions and just continued to stare at Almasty in shock and awe.

Destiny's Beast returned a few minutes later in somewhat of a huff. "These people are going to be hard to lose," she told Almasty. "They want to see her. They won't leave until they do."

"Well, admit her, as I just told you to, and let them see her," he instructed. "But hurry, won't you? Time is precious!"

"All right, all right!" the harried Beast replied. "I'm on it...give me a second, would you?" She busily signed an admission form and left the room with it. Moments later, an orderly came in, fiddled with the brake on the gurney, and then wheeled Destiny out of the examination room. He could not see the "fake" orderlies in their manifest state.

Almasty had camouflaged himself, blending in with the ivory walls of the room. As Destiny was taken away, he began the process of transporting himself. He would be in her room before she even arrived there.

~ * ~

It took three days, but Arthur finally got the little girl to jump rope with him. She enlisted the aid of one of her classmates and the two girls twirled the rope while Arthur tried to jump.

"You're not very good at this, are you?" his little friend asked. "I mean you jump really well, but you keep stepping on the rope."

"Practice, practice, practice!" Arthur cried. He wasn't really enjoying himself, but he knew he would eventually master this 'game,' just as he had so many others.

"Just keep twirling!" he cried. "I won't give up!"

Seventeen

Changes

Chance felt weird. He could not put his finger on exactly why, except that he was blue and living in a magic bog.

He was sick of mushrooms, that much was certain.

He and his friends were growing apart, their conversations short and meaningless. Even his father seemed distracted.

"Stretched," is the word Chance supplied himself. He tried it on. It felt right. No, the feeling was wrong, clearly wrong, but the word "stretched" seemed to fit. It was the right word.

"You need to stop eating the mushrooms," a voice whispered in his ear. Startled, Chance looked around himself to find the source of the voice.

"Up here," he was prompted. He looked up. There! In the tree. The familiar-looking little man, all in brown.

"How do you keep your hat on hanging from a limb like that?" Chance heard himself ask.

"Oh, it's not really a hat," the little man said. "I just sort of extrude a hat-looking thing out of my skull."

"Oh. I see," said the teen dully.

"You really need to stop eating the mushrooms," the little man repeated. "They are magic. Many of them together are exponentially magic."

"Are you magic?" Chance asked.

"Oh, no, I am not random," the man replied. "I am a manifestation."

"A manifestation?" Chance asked, his curiosity aroused. "A manifestation of what?"

"Why, of you, of course!" Denny said, laughing.

"Of me?"

"You need to stop eating anything that grows here," the man said, now frowning. "It's making you stupid."

"What is?"

"The food you are eating," the man said, growing exasperated. "It is making you stupid!"

"Should I tell the others?"

"Yes, immediately!" the man cried. "Every one of you blue humans needs to stop eating and drinking things that come from here. Immediately!"

"Whoa, don't hurt yourself," Chance said, backing away from the man. "You're getting a little excited."

"I'm sorry!" the little man hastened to apologize. "I didn't mean to yell, it's just that I am worried about you, all of you. Something bad is going to happen to you if you stay here."

"You mean we can leave?" Chance's mouth didn't close after he opened it to speak.

"You can go anywhere you like!" Denny exclaimed. "You are not imprisoned here...are you?" Now it was the monkey's turn to sound confused.

"Are you eating the bananas that grow here?" Chance asked teasingly.

"There are bananas here?" Denny asked, looking all around himself like there were banana trees growing in places he had not noticed.

"No, I was just kidding!" Chance said, laughing. "It's just that you said I was getting stupid from eating mushrooms and drinking bog water, and then you, well you…then you…" His words drifted off. "I forgot what I was going to say," he admitted, shamefaced.

"Get your father and your friends together," Denny instructed firmly. "We have got to get you out of here!"

Chance ran off to gather his group as the monkey had instructed.

"Why did you do that?" The Beast called down from above. "What are you doing interacting with the humans?"

"Look, Boss," Denny said, hands on his hips. "We need Chance Bonner back in the same condition he left in. This is not working. He is becoming dull. Listless. Unimaginative. Dumb."

"What's wrong with that?" The Beast asked.

"Oh, now you're getting it, too!" Denny cried.

"Getting what?" The Beast asked. "I don't understand you all of the sudden, my good Dennison!"

"Stupid," Denny said.

"What did you say?"

"I said you—we, I mean—are growing stupid here in this magic fen. I think that it's part of Arachimedes plan to get rid of the blue humans."

"That seems pretty smart," The Beast observed, dropping from tree limb to tree limb until he stood facing Denny on the ground. "How come you're not stupid?"

"Venom," the monkey posited.

"Hunh?"

"Spider venom," Denny said with more assurance. "I think it is protecting me from whatever carries the source of this stupidity."

"Well, I have to admit you sound a lot smarter than usual," The Beast acknowledged.

"I don't think Arachimedes meant to hurt either of us," Denny informed his team chief. "But we would end up like Chance Bonner, his dad, and his friends, eventually.

"We're not really people. We are manifestations of one of those people. It is inevitable that we would mirror his life condition. If Chance Bonner goes all stupid on us, we will go stupid as well. It is only a matter of time."

The Beast appeared to think this over. "I've forgotten what we were just talking about," he admitted finally.

Denny reacted. "I am getting you out of here first!" he exclaimed, grabbing his boss by one wrist and preparing to "poof" away.

"Let me go, you buffoon!" The Beast cried. "I can do this much by myself!" He freed himself from the monkey's grasp and poofed away, leaving only a paltry little sulfurous emission behind.

"Finally!" a voice from a nearby cluster of tree roots exclaimed. "I thought he'd never leave!"

"He thinks we plot against you," Denny told the spider which crawled out of its hidey-hole. "I had to go along. You know, as part of the act you asked me to put on?"

"I know, I know," reassured Arachimedes. "But I must ask you another question now."

"Ask away!" the monkey said with enthusiasm.

"Did you say that you were going to take the blue humans away from here? That you were going to leave the magic fen?"

"I was just saying that to get The Beast to leave," Denny informed the old spider. "Do you see the blue humans gathering to leave as instructed?" Denny made a show of looking all around. "Of course, you don't. I am sure that Chance Bonner forgot my instructions mere seconds after I gave them to him!" The monkey began to laugh. "It was all for the benefit of The Beast, Arachimedes. Now we must ensure that he cannot come back here...do you know how to do that?"

"I can put up some defenses," the spider said. "They are not foolproof, but he will find it very difficult indeed to return to this place!" And with this, the spider clambered up a neighboring tree and disappeared from sight.

Denny, now alone, turned and ran in the direction Chance Bonner had taken.

"I hope it's not too late," he muttered to himself as he ran.

~ * ~

Dr. Fillien Faust ushered the Dyers and their lawyer to the room where Destiny slept.

As they entered the room, a short, wiry, dark-haired nurse was fussing around with the chart at the foot of the girl's bed.

"That will be all, nurse," the doctor said stiffly. "I will take it from here."

The nurse looked startled, and then something worse: she looked guilty. She practically ran from the room, dropping the chart along the way.

Dr. Faust bent to pick it up. The Dyers were already at Destiny's bedside, stroking her cheeks and hair.

"As I told you, I have made her comfortable," Dr. Faust told the worried parents. "She needs rest, and I will see that she gets it. Please do not worry. Your daughter will receive the best of care. If there are no complications, I am certain you will be able to take her home tomorrow."

She gave them a few more minutes, and then quietly and professionally prompted them to leave.

"She needs quiet," the doctor emphasized. "And a full night's rest."

The three adult humans left, but not without backward glances at the sleeping girl. Dr. Faust closed and locked the room's door once they had finally exited.

Almasty appeared gradually, materializing out of the baby blue wall.

"OK," he announced. "Let's go!"

~ * ~

A few moments later, a key scrabbled in the lock of the door and the small, dark nurse peeped into the room.

"That is just an empty shell of Destiny Dyer!" she exclaimed after getting a glimpse of the "girl" sleeping in the bed. "They have taken the real her. The King is going to kill me, or worse!

"Think!" she exhorted herself. "Think, Lucinder, think! What should I do?"

She entered the room and re-locked the door behind her. A look of cunning suddenly washed over her sharp little features.

"Where else would they take her?" she muttered. "To the boy, of course! Her twin. They've taken her to unite her with her twin brother, Chance Bonner! I know this is true!" She indulged herself in a little titter of glee before she grew totally sober.

"But I've lost him. I've lost Chance Bonner. I don't know where he is." She fell into thought again, slumping into a nearby chair and dropping her sharp chin onto her clenched fist.

Bolting upright, she "poofed" from the room. "Denny!" she shrieked as she disappeared. "Denny!"

Eighteen

Make a Wish

Chance had, indeed, forgotten why he was running, so he stopped. He continued in the direction of his friends, but at a dignified—okay, a slow—pace.

"Hey, Dad," he said as he entered the beautiful glade that served as the group's common area.

"Hey, son," his father responded listlessly.

"Where is everybody?" Chance asked, looking around the glade. He could not see anyone but his father.

"No clue," his father responded. Chaz Bonner didn't even look up at his son but continued to gaze at the blue mushroom in the palm of his left hand.

"What are you going to do with that mushroom?" Chance asked, just to make conversation. He really wasn't interested in anything having to do with mushrooms.

"I don't know," his father said. "I think I'm going to eat it."

Something tickled at the back of Chance's memory. "I'm thinking you don't want to do that," he said tentatively.

Now Chaz looked up at his son. "Why not?" he asked him.

"Not sure, Dad," Chance responded. "Just a hunch, I guess."

"Well, your hunches are usually pretty good," his father allowed. He threw the mushroom into the nearest thicket of bushes. "I guess I won't be eating it after all."

"What's going on?" Chance asked, again looking around for someone—anyone—other than himself or his father.

"I guess we could go look for your friends," Chaz said, looking like that was the last thing he wanted to do.

Suddenly, they heard a voice. Several voices, actually, and they were raised in anger.

Chance and Chaz walked toward where the noise was emanating. There...they could see all of them now. Chance's friends appeared to be fighting with one another, and many of them brandished sticks or tree branches.

"Hey, hey, hey!" Chance called, running toward his friends. "What is going on here?"

Like a bucket of cold water had been thrown on them, the young people stopped what they were doing and stared at the objects in their hands as if they hadn't ever seen them before. Stefan dropped his stick and, instantly, ripped open a velcroed pocket to get to his hand sanitizer and skin moisturizer.

"I don't know what I was doing," Kelly finally admitted.

"Me neither," Millicent and Sarah both said.

"I was minding my own business," Stefan said. "I was looking for my sister when I was ambushed by these three." He gestured toward Kelly, Millicent and Sarah.

Astra Schultz stepped out from behind a tree. "Stefan, that most certainly is not true!" she said. "You started the entire thing! You came at them with that tree branch, yelling 'en garde!' and jabbing at them. You were speaking French, Stefan...French! Since when do you know French?"

Stefan, in his defense, looked astonished at what his sister had just revealed.

"I don't remember any of that," he said.

"What is the last thing you do remember?" Chance asked.

"Hmmm, well, I was just walking around bored out of my mind—or what's left of it—and wished I could be a musketeer. You know, like Athos, Porthos, or Aramis? Perhaps D'Artagnan even."

"You wished? You just thought about and it happened?" Chance pressed.

"Well, I might have said it out loud," Stefan said, blushing up to his ears.

"Try it again!" Chance told his friend. "Make another wish and make it out loud!"

"OK," replied Stefan. "Here goes: 'I, Stefan Marquis Schultz, wish that I had a large five-cheese pizza fresh from Domino's.'"

And, without fanfare or flourish, a Domino's box fell from nowhere onto the ground at Stefan's feet.

"Open it! Open it!" Kelly urged him.

Stefan stooped down and picked up the box. He threw back the lid. "Oh my gosh, it's a large five-cheese pizza!" He cried in wonder and glee. "And it's pre-sliced! Here, have a piece..." He didn't get a chance to finish his invitation. His friends fought each other to be the first to grab a slice of the piping hot pizza.

Chaz Bonner did not participate. Instead, he said out loud, "I wish I had a Pizza Hut Personal Pan Pepperoni Pizza," and with a slight whoosh a box bearing the Pizza Hut logo was in his outstretched hands.

"Oooooh," the young people around him said.

"Open it! Open it!" Kelly cried.

He opened it. Inside the box was a perfect personal pan pepperoni pizza. Its delicious aroma wafted through the glade.

"I wish for onion rings!" Millicent said next. Nothing happened. "I wish for Burger King onion rings!" she tried again. Nothing. "I wish for a large order of Burger King onion rings," she said, and a big box of hot onion rings in a Burger King container plopped into her hands accompanied by the sound of a single ding of a tiny chime.

Sarah Stengler, half eaten piece of five-cheese pizza dangling from one hand, stepped forward.

"I wish for a medium-sized Dairy Queen Oreo Blizzard!" she said loudly. With a plop, the frozen delectable was in her hand. Unfortunately, it was the hand which already held the cheesy pizza slice.

Sarah laughed. "Oh well," she said, putting the now-greasy Blizzard in her free hand and taking another bite of her pizza. "Next time I'll tell it what hand to deliver it to."

"It?" a puzzled Chance asked. "What do you mean 'it'?"

"Gosh," Sarah replied, looking puzzled herself. "I don't know. What is making this happen? Isn't it an 'it' of some kind? You know, like a wizard or a god or even a fairy?"

"It's you," Denny said, at that very moment barging, at a run, into the middle of the human group. He was slightly out of breath, so he took a moment to collect himself. The blue humans made a wide berth around the monkey-man, creating a circle with Denny in the middle.

"You have become so magical you have powers," he informed them. "If you don't stop eating and drinking blue things from this bog, you will never be able to escape! You will be trapped here, and you will get bluer by the day."

"How do you know this?" Chaz challenged him.

"I have it straight from the spider's mouth," Denny said, lifting his chin in defiance. "I speak the truth. You need to listen to me."

"Go on," Chaz urged. "We will listen, at least. Please continue."

"How many of you know Arachimedes?" Denny asked, looking around the group for a show of hands.

One blue hand shot up. It was Brilliant...rather, Astra, Schultz.

"Ribetta introduced us," she told them. "We spoke for a bit and then he gave me permission to find a place to live. Here, in the magic fen. We only spoke the one time. Well, he has sent other spiders to deliver messages. You know, like, 'stop changing the fen,' 'take those nasty flowers back to where they came from,' and 'no birds of any kind in the magic fen,' you know, that kind of thing." She slowed down and stopped speaking, looking at the monkey expectantly.

"And what did you do in response to these warnings?" Denny asked.

"Made more changes. Planted more flowers. Imported more birds," she answered. "You know, drained the swamp."

"Oh dear," the monkey-man said, looking worried.

"Why 'oh dear'?" Astra challenged. "He's just a spider. He is not the boss. Well, OK, he may be the boss of the bog, but he is not the boss of me!"

Denny looked even more worried. "Arachimedes is the King of the spiders," he said softly. "He is ancient and he is powerful, and he doesn't like you blue humans. He schemes to rob you of your magic powers, even if he has to kill you to do it."

The humans all gasped. The blue nearly drained from Astra's face.

"Kill us?" she repeated. "He would kill us? Are you sure that is not just inflammatory rhetoric designed to excite his constituents?"

Denny considered. "I admit he is a bit of a blowhard," he said thoughtfully. "And he loves a bit of theater, you know. But this time, I think he has gone too far. He has made promises he can't renege on. It could mean impeachment for him, or worse, if he can't deliver."

"Just how is it that you know this?" Chaz asked him. He wore a skeptical look. His body language communicated weariness. He slumped.

"Well, you see," Denny hesitated. He looked up at his audience with pleading eyes.

"Go on," Chaz urged, squaring his shoulders.

"Well, you see," Denny continued, "I sort of—well, kind of—plotted your demise with him. We're friends."

"Who are friends? Do you mean you and us?" Millicent asked.

"No. Arachimedes and I are friends," Denny clarified, shuffling his feet and trying to kick up some dust. This was impossible in the super-moist fen. It hadn't seen dust in millennia.

"You are aware we don't want to be here, right?" Astra asked, her temper rising.

"Then why do you stay here?" Denny asked in return.

"Where else do blue human beings dwell?" Astra demanded. "I was told this was my world now, too!"

"Oh, I see," the monkey responded. "Well, blue magic belongs here, and as long as you have blue magic, technically this is your home...but even the spiders don't stay here all of the time. They visit the human world, where they say the buffet is delicious."

The blue humans gasped again. Sarah gagged and Millicent sidled over to her and held her hand. The pizza and the Blizzard had long been discarded. No one was hungry now.

"At what point are we too blue to leave?" Chance asked.

"I don't know, really," Denny replied. "But with the powers you now have, you may have already crossed the line." He turned to address the Bonners. "Try going back to your home," he urged Chance and Chaz. "Just concentrate on where you want to be and then command yourself to move."

Chance and Chaz both closed their eyes and appeared to be trying to do something. Their mouths grimaced. Their brows lowered. Their faces turned purplish with their efforts.

Nothing.

They did not budge.

Almost simultaneously, they opened their eyes and looked around themselves, disappointment written on their faces.

"So," Chance said. "Too blue to travel, huh?"

"I am afraid so," the monkey said. "But don't despair! You can shed some magic by using it. Continue to eat nothing and drink nothing from the fen," he instructed. "And use your powers until they don't work anymore."

"You mean, just wish for stuff?" Kelly asked.

"Exactly, young lady," Denny replied with a bow.

Kelly tittered a bit and looked at the monkey with kind eyes.

"You're funny," she said.

"Excuse me?" the confused simian asked her.

"You are funny," she said, smiling broadly. "Who are you, anyway?"

The monkey looked astounded...and worried. "You are not supposed to be able to ask me that question," he told her.

"What?" Now it was Kelly's turn to be astounded.

"I am a manifestation from Chance Bonner's mind," the monkey explained. "I have the power to bemuse other human beings. It's like camouflage. You're not supposed to really notice me."

"We all see you," Millicent announced. Everyone in the circle around Denny nodded in agreement.

"Give it a moment," Denny said. "I will stop speaking. You should forget all about me in a few seconds."

A few seconds ticked by. The humans continued to stare at him. Their gazes did not waver.

"You're still funny," Kelly told him.

"Egads!" Denny exclaimed. "While you gain powers, I lose mine!" He began to wring his hands in distress.

"It's a Natural Law," Stefan announced stuffily. He grabbed both of his lab coat's lapels with his hands, a sure sign they were all in for a lecture.

The young people groaned in anticipation. Chaz Bonner returned to what little was left of his personal pan pizza. He made a wish for a small Wendy's Vanilla Frosty and a large diet coke and proceeded to make a Coke Float with them.

"It's energy," Stefan began. "It all has to even out in the end—our gain is someone's loss. It's a zero-sum game."

He was done. The young people exhaled audibly in relief. It had been Stefan's shortest lesson ever.

Denny was listening raptly. "So if you all keep shedding your magic, I might get my own powers back eventually?" he asked.

"That is the theory," Stefan replied. Then he said, "Desk, table lamp, and personal computer from my apartment, Nineteen-o-two Boyer Street, Seattle, Washington, Apartment B-two."

The items Stefan requested were suddenly there in the fen.

"I need power," Stefan said next. "Wireless is preferred."

The lamp and computer both came on.

"Could you bring my computer desk chair from the same apartment as before?" he asked.

The chair was just simply there, pushed against the table in its accustomed position.

"I might get to like it here," Stefan announced to no one in particular.

The stunned group who had witnessed Stefan's achievements leapt into separate actions of their own. Within just a few minutes there were walls, floors, beds, tables, closets full of clothes, and a recreation area equipped with video game consoles, a ping pong table and a foosball game.

Astra took one look at the hodge-podge of rooms and wished the entire collection into an integrated floor plan. She covered the collection with a house...well, it was more like a mansion.

The moment the mansion was complete, gaslight street lamps appeared and bright lights twinkled from both within the house and without.

A carriage drawn by two ebony stallions pulled up in front of the mansion.

It waited.

A few moments later, a freshly coiffed and gowned Astra stepped out of the mansion and into the carriage.

"Monkey-man," she called out from the carriage window.

"My name is Denny," the monkey-man informed her. "Or Dennison Desmond DeWitt, if you prefer."

"Well, then, Denny," Astra said patiently.

"Yes, my lady?" He bowed deeply.

"You're funny," Kelly said, bending down herself to look the monkey in his eyes. He winked at her. "You are not so bad yourself!" he told her. She dimpled in reply.

"Please take a ride around the fen with me, would you?" Astra asked him sweetly. "We need to talk."

"Nothing would please me more," Denny replied, walking to the carriage and nimbly hopping up the steps to join her.

As soon as the monkey was in the carriage, an invisible driver urged the stallions to proceed and the carriage rolled away from the sparkling mansion and into the far reaches of the fen. The horses snorted and threw their heads back proudly. Their forelegs high-stepped in perfect synchronization with each other.

Nineteen

Disenfranchisement

"How is it that you can carry the girl with you?" The Beast asked. "Didn't you tell me that Destiny's mother had to travel to meet you by conventional means?"

Almasty sighed. They had materialized in the back yard of the cottage of the bodhisattva, Arya Tara. He held the inert form of Destiny Dyer in his arms. Her Beast was still manifest and now was peppering him with questions.

"She is special," he explained with a patience he did not feel. "You of all beings should know this."

"I do. Nevertheless..." The annoying Beast left her question hanging.

"Very well," a nearly exasperated Almasty said. "I left part of her back in that hospital room. I have only brought her internal self with me. Her external self still lies asleep and under sedation at the hospital. Are you satisfied?"

"No," The Beast responded, clearly puzzled. "I am even more confused than before. But you know what? I am just going to watch and wait. Maybe I will be able to make sense of it by myself."

"Now that's a plan I can get on board with!" the hairy brown man replied. Well, his robe was hairy and brown, at least. He turned once again to the house, his companion now silent and cooperative.

"Do you hear that racket?" The Beast asked, breaking the silence with her harsh bray. "It is hurting my brain!" she cried. She began to sniffle and hold her head.

"They chant the sacred mantra," Almasty informed her. "This is the power which drew me here."

"Well, it's giving me a migraine!" The Beast insisted. "I am going to have to go. I cannot take this...this...this noise one more second!" And she poofed away, leaving an enormous cloud of glitter behind. It settled on every bush, flower, and blade of grass within a five-foot radius of where she had previously stood.

And on Almasty, of course. He managed to shield Destiny from the worst of it, but he could not protect himself. The stuff stuck to his goat hair robe like snow. Almasty inhaled a nose-full of it and began sneezing out twin rainbows from his inflamed nostrils.

The back door flew open and a large bearded man bounded down the steps, grabbed Almasty by his robe and proceeded to shake him. This only served to make more of the glitter airborne, and inevitably the big man began to sneeze, too.

A beautiful, petite, black-haired woman took one step out onto her back porch and assessed the situation. She made many swift and arcane motions of her delicate arms and hands as she danced across the porch. A strong, steady breeze arose. It cleared the air, and even dislodged and blew away much of the glitter clinging to the intruder's robe.

"I came in response to your summons!" Almasty cried, wiping his eyes with his sleeve.

"We did not summon anyone," the big man stated emphatically. "We most certainly did not call for you!"

"Did you not chant the mantra to the Heavenly King Hearer of Many Teachings?" Almasty asked the man, watching his face very carefully.

"Yes. Yes, we did. Well, I did, at any rate," the man answered. He gestured toward the woman and continued. "My friend may have had a different focus." He looked at her and she smiled and shook her head. So she, too, had been focused on the same symbol on the sacred scroll.

"Wait a minute," Angus McLeod said, a challenge in his voice. "Are you telling me that you are Heavenly King Hearer of Many Teachings?" The look on his face said it clearly: he was not prepared to believe the strange, hairy man. But something nagged at him, dragging his attention downward.

He looked down at the slightly shorter man's cowboy boots.

"Wow," he said admiringly. "Those are some big boots you have there."

"You ought to see the feet," the man said, his eyes twinkling.

"But seriously," Almasty continued, "I have someone with me. This is Destiny Dyer from Roanoke, Virginia.

"She is the twin sister to Chance Bonner.

"And I am their father."

~ * ~

Destiny's Beast appeared at her bedside, a small cloud of glitter accompanying her. She made sure the girl was still comfortable. When she turned to leave, she noticed something in the room's shadows and stopped short.

"Who are you?" she asked the small dark form hiding in a dark corner of the room.

Lucinder walked out of the darkness. She wore the same nurse's outfit she had on the last time the two had met.

"Oh, so it's you again," The Beast said. "And just what are you doing here?"

"I was going to ask you the same question," the wiry little "nurse" retorted. "There is no Dr. Faust on the staff of this hospital," she continued. "I checked. So just who are you, and what is your interest in Destiny Dyer?"

The two just stood there staring at each other, eyes glaring, nostrils flaring.

"You're a tough little monkey, aren't you?" The Beast snarled.

To her surprise, the little woman broke down in tears. She sobbed uncontrollably. "Oh Denny," she wailed. "Where are you, monkey-man?"

The Beast went to Destiny's side table and picked up a box of tissues. She carried them over to Lucinder.

"Here," she prompted. "Blow your nose."

"S-s-sanks," Lucinder said, blowing her nose and wiping her eyes. "Sorry about the outburst," she apologized.

"Oh, I get this all the time," The Beast joked. The two women laughed a little at this.

"Yes," Lucinder said. "Me, too, usually. It's just that today, I've had some major setbacks, and I've lost my monkey. I also think I'm going to lose my job."

"Why don't you tell me about it," The Beast said, steering Lucinder to a nearby chair. She, herself, pulled another chair up to face the other woman. She waited patiently for Lucinder to start talking.

"I am part of a special operations team," Lucinder began, choosing her words carefully. "We are supposed to be working on one thing—and one thing only—but the bosses keep changing priorities and assigning us extra duties. Then, today, they pulled my partner—I have no idea where they sent him! I mean, their interference—their incompetence—makes all of our efforts ineffectual! From being a once-great team, we've devolved into a bunch of bumbling buffoons!" She began to snivel again but held herself together by force of will. "And I know they're going to blame me for our failure," she concluded in a very small voice. "I just know it."

"Have you been writing this down?" The Beast asked in a voice meant to shock Lucinder into lucidity. "You need to make notes of everything they do and say. Date the notes. Put time stamps on everything. Sign them. If there are witnesses, get them to initial off on the notes. Take pictures when you can."

Lucinder was looking at her with wide eyes. "What good would that do?" she asked. "The guy at the top, the King, he's the one giving us—well, me, at any rate—extra assignments!"

"Did you say 'the King'?" The Beast asked.

"Yes, yes, 'the King'!" Lucinder responded emotionally. "There, I've said it. And now you think I'm crazy, don't you?"

"Is the other boss, by any means, called 'The Beast'?" The Beast asked in a slow voice. She winced a little like she was afraid of the answer.

Lucinder's jaw dropped. "How did you know that?" she squeaked.

"Show yourself!" The Beast cried, transforming herself from human doctor to glittering unicorn...well, sort of. She still stood upright; and she had some human features, after all. But her glittering horn and shining white mane unmistakably identified her for what she was.

Lucinder could not resist the command, and a second later, a large angry wasp hovered in the air over the chair she had just sat in.

"Who do you represent?" the unicorn-woman asked.

"Chance Bonner!" the wasp cried.

"What?" the unicorn said. "Speak up! I can't hear you!"

Lucinder poofed back into her human form. "Chance Bonner!" she shouted.

"Ouch! Wow, you almost broke my eardrums!" The Beast said. "You don't have to yell. Wait a minute," The Beast hesitated, dropping her hands from over her ears. "Did you say 'Chance Bonner'?"

"I did."

"Who is Chance Bonner?"

"Destiny Dyer's twin brother."

"No."

"Yes."

"Impossible."

"Not just possible, but true!"

"Well, I represent Destiny Dyer," the unicorn announced. "I am her Beast."

"I am Lucinder Vespida," Lucinder said. "I am just a minion. I have no special rank."

"I have a couple of you," The Beast responded in a distracted manner.

"Excuse me? You have wasps?" Lucinder asked.

"What? Oh no, not wasps, per se," The Beast responded, still clearly deep in thought. "I have a zebra and a bumble bee...."

"My Beast is a yak, a red one. My partner is a chimpanzee. Denny is his name."

"Sounds like a good team."

"Well, we used to be. Now The Beast is off on his own mission, the King has me trying to kidnap Destiny Dyer, and Denny has just disappeared!"

This got The Beast's full attention. "Did you just say that your King has commanded you to kidnap Destiny Dyer?"

"Yes. Yes, he has."

"Well, she's lying right there," The Beast said, gesturing toward where the girl lay. "Why don't you take her?"

"You know that's not the real her," Lucinder answered bitterly. "That body is an empty shell."

"Well, it just so happens I know where he's taken the real her," The Beast said, cleverly baiting the other woman.

"What? Where? Wait—'he'? Who is 'he'?" Lucinder looked like the combination of hope and confusion was going to cause her to implode.

"I accompanied him. Just came back from him...Almasty, that is. Almasty has her. He went to some little bungalow in Seattle, Washington," The Beast said. Her distraction cleared at that moment. She'd had an epiphany.

"Why don't we become partners?" she asked the wasp-woman. "I'll introduce you to my minions, and we can team up. I want to get Destiny back to normal, and you need to find her, the real her. We might be able to iron out a deal. I think it will depend on what your King wants her for to begin with."

Lucinder wrinkled her dark brow. "Haven't the foggiest," she said. She looked up at the other woman. "What special attribute do you ascribe to Destiny Dyer? What makes her remarkable?"

The Beast laughed out loud. "I'll tell you what makes her outstandingly 'remarkable'," she said. "She is the unluckiest human alive!" and she continued to laugh and laugh.

Lucinder did not look amused...quite the opposite, actually. She waited for the other woman to calm down, then announced in a solemn voice: "Well, that's it, then. Destiny is unlucky. But Chance is lucky—very, very lucky.

"I think my King wants a merger," she continued. "I think he intends to destroy Chance Bonner's good luck by orchestrating the union of him with his twin.

"His colossally unlucky twin, Destiny Dyer."

The Beast sobered. "Well, that would mean Destiny would become less unlucky, then, too, wouldn't it?"

"This is all guesswork," Lucinder said. "I can't know for sure."

"Well, it's worth a try, don't you think?" The Beast said. "You want to trip Chance up and defeat his spirit, which you cannot do while luck favors him. And we want to have a hand in the destruction of Destiny, whose bad luck so far has made us totally obsolete."

"It's tempting." Lucinder was weakening.

"Let's do it!" The Beast cried.

"OK, then—partners!" Lucinder agreed, holding out her bony little hand.

The Beast took Lucinder's hand in both of her own oddly delicate white hands. "It's a deal, partner!" she crowed. "Let's start planning!"

"You got it!" Lucinder agreed, forgetting her missing team for the moment...and many, many moments afterward.

~ * ~

"The blue humans are still here," the grumpy old spider hurled at Arachimedes. "What are you going to do about it, and when?"

Arachimedes had been made aware, thanks to his network of small spies, that his constituents were growing more and more anxious and angry about the presence of the blue humans in their fen. He was ready for the confrontation.

"Where is your committee's report?" he counter-demanded.

The spider was cowed; he dithered. "Well," he finally spat out, "we haven't come up with any ideas yet."

"Maybe you need to elect a new leader," Arachimedes slyly suggested.

"What? But I am the leader. Oh, forget I ever said anything!" and the old grump skittered back to his own hidey hole.

"Just as I wished," Arachimedes said to the grinning little spider on his shoulder. "Morpheus thinks he is old and wise, but he forgets that I am older and wiser." And the pair chuckled companionably for some time.

"I hate to break the mood," Arachimedes eventually said, "but what news of the monkey?"

"He seems more solid somehow," the tiny spider responded. "You know, before he went to work on the blue humans, you could easily forget he was even around, but now? Now he is very much present. Oh, and he's riding around in some shiny new coach with that blonde blue lady. Astra, I think she calls herself."

"A coach?"

"Yes. A coach pulled by two big black horses."

"Horses?"

"Yes, sir. Horses. Oh, and the blue humans are importing all kinds of foodstuffs and furnishings."

"Furnishings? What in the worlds do they need with furnishings?"

"They have constructed a huge house...a mansion, they call it."

"Oh, have they?" Arachimedes' ire was up. "And just how are they importing all of these things?"

"They use magic."

"Magic?"

"Yes. They wish for something and it happens."

"And just how long did you intend to withhold this information from me?" Arachimedes by now had reached a level of high dudgeon.

"The monkey wished it, sir."

"The monkey wished what?"

"The monkey wished that none of us volunteer any information about him or the blue humans to anyone, especially you, sir."

"Then why have you told me?"

"I am not sure," the little guy admitted. "But I think your magic must trump the monkey's."

"The monkey has magic?"

"He does. It seems that as his form became more concrete, he grew more like the humans. They, sir, are as blue as indigo by now."

"You don't say?" Arachimedes said distractedly.

"Oh, I do say, sir!" the little spider exclaimed. "I overheard them say they might be trapped here...you know, that they are so blue they might not be able to leave the magic fen."

"You don't say?" Arachimedes repeated, still deep in thought.

"But I do say, sir!" the little spider said in exasperation. "Are you listening to me, sir?"

"So did the monkey say anything about me?" Arachimedes demanded. Now he appeared to be paying rapt attention.

"No. No he did not mention you."

"Tell him to come see me."

"I will do so immediately, sir."

"See that you do."

"You doubt my service, sir?"

"You withheld vital information from me."

"And you just ignored two important pieces of information I just tried to give you!"

"What pieces of information? And watch your attitude...you grow impudent."

"I told you the humans may have become too blue to leave the fen. I told you they have become as blue as indigo."

"Ah!" a light seemed to go on inside the old arachnid's brain. "So, Denny does still serve me! I am certain this is his doing!"

"I don't understand, sir."

"The monkey has trapped the humans for me. I don't know how he did it, but he has caused them to pass the blue line."

"The blue line?"

"Yes. The blue line. It is the limit of blueness a being can acquire and still be able to maneuver outside of the blue—in this case, 'the blue' being the magic fen." An evil smile snaked across his features. "They have crossed the thin blue line. They are trapped. They are mine." He cut short his evil reverie and addressed his spy once more. "Go. Go now and summon that monkey. Do so in complete secrecy. It is vital the humans never find out that the monkey and I are partners, that we work together to engineer their demise. Otherwise, I could simply summon him here. But that might risk our being discovered."

"Yes, sir." The little spider saluted, caught the next favorable breeze and was gone.

"Good old Denny," Arachimedes said, a lazy smile taking over his expression. "Good monkey."

~ * ~

"I told the old spider that I would spy on you for him," Denny was just saying to Astra. "But I was only in on it for the venom."

"The venom?" Astra turned up her nose at the abhorrent thought.

"Don't knock it until you try it," Denny told her. He did not have any sense of humor when it came to venom. He was going through withdrawal as the two travelled the fen in their fancy carriage.

"Look, I like you, Astra, or whatever you call yourself," Denny continued. "But Chance is the most important thing to me. I am part of him."

"See, that's something I can't understand," Astra replied. "You keep saying that you are part of Chance, but how does that make any sense?"

"Chance is special."

Astra laughed. "Oh, I know that much!" she cried. "But so are you, right?"

"Well, yes, I guess I am," the monkey allowed. "Most humans cannot manifest their natures."

"You see, there you go again. 'Manifest their natures.' What in the world does that mean?"

"Humans are so complex that they do not understand the workings of their own minds," the monkey explained. "All of you have Devil Kings, Beasts, and millions of minions, but only Chance Bonner's natures can manifest." Denny held out one hand to halt Astra from interrupting him. "Do not ask me why," he said. "He is special. That is all. And that is why I try to protect him even as the rest of my team tries to destroy his happiness. Happiness. Simple, right? But that is the penultimate goal for a human being: to become happy."

"I don't have a problem with that," Astra replied. "Just because it's simple to say doesn't mean it's simple to do."

"Very wise," Denny observed. Astra smiled at the little man, pleased with his praise.

"So, what do you intend to do now?" she asked him.

"You all must continue to wish and wish," Denny said. "You must get your blue levels down, drastically down. Be diligent. Don't give up. Your survival depends on it."

"Our survival?" Astra looked skeptical.

"Arachimedes will be able to rule you once you are trapped in his world, this world, the magic fen. Blue magic is the product of the spiders here. They can influence outcomes if the blue magic is involved. Arachimedes wants the magic you have accumulated. He will do anything to get it."

"But we are trapped!" she stated matter-of-factly.

"Yes, but he doesn't know that," Denny reassured her. "And he won't learn that from me. If we work fast enough, you will return to a manageable level of blue and I will become a non-entity once again. I will then simply leave without being noticed. You will be able to go anywhere you want."

"But how do we get back to normal?" Astra cried. "We don't want to be magic any longer."

"Do you know how much luck was involved in your transformation to begin with?" Denny asked. She shook her head in the negative.

"It is entirely unprecedented," he said. "It has never happened before. There is only one explanation for it."

"What is that?"

"Not what, dear, but rather who: Chance. Chance Bonner."

"Oh."

"Yes, 'oh'." Denny's attention was grabbed by something hanging just outside of his carriage window. He reached his hand out and snatched the distraction from the air. He kept his fist strongly clenched.

"Spying on me?" he said to his fist.

A muffled sound could barely be discerned. It emanated from his fist.

Denny pried his thumb up and spoke into the hole in his fist that resulted. "Could you repeat that, please?" he said.

"I didn't get a chance to," the little trapped spider told him. "I admit that I was trying to."

"Well, I wish you had never been here," Denny said and when he opened his fist a moment later there was nothing in it.

"Why don't you just banish them altogether?" Astra asked him.

"Oh, they have their uses," the monkey responded mysteriously. "I routinely use them to disseminate false information."

"Oh," Astra said, her admiration for the monkey's cleverness clearly captured—and communicated—in the sound.

~ * ~

Angelica Root finally arrived at the Bonner house. She carried an overnight bag...an overnight bag with a squirrel in it, that is.

She put the bag down in front of the house's porch stairs and opened it.

Samantha Swisher stepped out of the bag and brushed the wrinkles from her clothes.

"Shhh, listen," Angelica told her, holding one index finger up to her lips. "Do you hear her?"

"I do," the squirrel replied. "She's been at it for hours, hasn't she?"

"Yes, and that's what got us here," Angelica said, closing and securing the near-empty bag. "Let's go in."

The front door was unlocked. Except for the sound of the chanting from over their heads, the house was completely silent.

They walked up the stairs and entered the room where Nan Bonner knelt chanting in front of her Buddhist scroll. Incense continued to swirl around the woman's head and up to the ceiling where it seemed to disappear.

After just a few moments, Nan Bonner rang her big brass bell and finished her chanting session. She rose, closed the doors to the Buddhist altar, and turned to leave the room.

When she saw the two women standing at the doorway to her room, she gasped.

"Angelica! Samantha!" she exclaimed. "How long have you been here?"

"We only just now arrived," Angelica reassured her. "As we approached you, you finished chanting the mantra. It was no coincidence."

"Yes, I know," Nan replied. "Once you begin practicing this Buddhism, it's hard to think anything is coincidental." She smiled at her visitors.

"Part of the reason I stopped—for now—is that I haven't eaten anything today, and I am feeling weak and unfocused. Would you like to join me for a snack?"

"Black coffee would be great!" Angelica said.

"And I would just love some of the beans," Samantha chimed in. "Do you have any whole bean coffee?"

"This is Seattle," Nan said with a straight face. "I should ask you which of the three different kinds of whole bean coffee in my pantry would you like to have." She laughed. "I have Columbian, French Roast, and Espresso."

"Ooooh," Samantha said. "Espresso, please!"

"You've got it," Nan told her. "Let's go down to the kitchen."

"May I stop in Chance's room?" Angelica asked.

"Sure," Nan said. "Samantha and I will just go downstairs. Join us when you're ready."

"Thanks," Angelica said.

Nan wordlessly nodded in reply. She motioned for Samantha to precede her down the stairs and then followed her.

Angelica carefully opened the door to Chance's room and poked her head through the door.

"Stanley?" she called out.

A rumbling sound responded to her call. With a "poof" Chance's Beast appeared. He wore a huge business suit and tie. He carried a shiny black attaché case. Tendrils of sulfurous smoke trailed behind him.

"At last. It's about time someone showed up," he grumbled, clearly out of sorts. "I've been waiting here by myself for an eternity. My minions are all AWOL." He stopped to look Angelica over. "And you were the last person I expected to see here. What exactly are you doing in the Bonner house?"

~ * ~

"I am lonely," sniffed the little blue gerbil. "Why am I so alone? Why does no one—either rodent or human—care where I am, wonder what could have happened to me?" He continued to munch the huge blue mushroom he held in front of him with both of his hands. It provided some small comfort to the miserable creature.

Twenty

Two Buddhist Gods

"What brings you here?" Nan asked Samantha. The two "women" were sitting at her kitchen table. Nan had a hot cup of coffee in front of her. Samantha nibbled on dark, crunchy beans from the small bowl in front of her.

"Angelica said something called her," Samantha said. "Maybe I should let her explain it. I think it's something personal that she could do a better job with."

"I understand," Nan said. "I'll wait for her, then. In the meantime, tell me about yourself. We didn't get much of a chance to chat last November when we first met."

Samantha laughed lightly. She was thinking about her role in the epic battle Nan was just referring to. "Well, apparently I am the general in charge of the renowned Baltimore Brigade of the Rodent Army!" she exclaimed. "We haven't seen much action in the last four months, but we have conducted drills to maintain our readiness."

Her smile vanished when she continued. "We just recently worked with the Roanoke Brigade to recover a girl who had been abducted by her school bus driver."

"Her school bus driver?" Nan echoed. "How odd! Those drivers are vetted so thoroughly—what bad luck for her to run across a bad one!"

"I guess you could say that," the squirrel-woman muttered.

"Excuse me?" Nan queried. "I didn't hear you."

"I said you picked the right words to describe the girl," Samantha clarified. "Bad luck. That's her."

"I'm afraid I am not following you," Nan said.

"It's not a long story, because she is only thirteen years old," Samantha began.

"That's the same age as Chance!" Nan observed.

"Uh, well, yes, she is precisely the same age as your son," Samantha replied. "Precisely."

"I am lost again," Nan admitted. "How is it that some girl you saved is 'precisely' the same age as Chance?"

"I will let Angelica tell you about that, too," the squirrel-woman said. She looked up to the kitchen ceiling as if she could see through it to the floor above her. "What's keeping her?" She threw a handful of coffee beans in her mouth at this juncture and chomped nervously.

"Do you have any decaf?" she asked. "I'm already a little tense."

Nan laughed. "I'm sorry. I wasn't laughing at you, Samantha," she explained. "It's like I said before: this is Seattle. We don't 'do' decaf."

Samantha nodded in understanding. She didn't really like decaf beans, either. It's just that the tension was getting a little hard for her to bear.

"Do you want me to see what's keeping her?" she offered Nan.

"No, just relax," Nan replied. "I'll go see what she's up to." The human woman arose from the table and mounted the nearby stairs.

Samantha quickly stuffed all of her remaining beans into her cheeks. "I'll just save these for later," she said to herself.

~ * ~

"I was summoned here," Angelica explained to Chance's Beast. "Nan Bonner chanted to the Mother of Demon Children. That's me. I heard her and I came in response to her prayer."

"You? The Mother of Demon Children?" The Beast exclaimed. He immediately fell silent, obviously pondering something big and complicated. Angelica, for her part, also remained silent to give him a chance to think through what she had just told him.

"I guess I can see it," he eventually admitted. "You are the mother of these two special humans. I guess that qualifies you to be the Mother of Demon Children. OK, let's accept the premise. So what? Why did the Bonner woman chant for you? What does she think you can do for her?"

Angelica responded. "First, let me ask you one question: do you know where Chance is?"

"I do, actually," The Beast replied, seeming pleased with himself.

"Well?"

"Well, what?"

"Where is he? Where did you see Chance last?" Angelica was struggling to keep her cool.

"Oh. That. Chance, his father, and his friends are all in the magic fen."

"The what?"

"The magic fen. Talk to the Bonner woman. She knows all about it—she made quite an impression on the spider in charge, too."

"What are you blathering about?" Angelica was close to losing it entirely.

"I am in my human form," The Beast, speaking now as Stanley Greenleaf, attorney-at-law. "Let's go downstairs and talk to Nan Bonner."

"Just how am I supposed to explain how I found you in Chance's bedroom?" Angelica demanded.

"Good point," The Beast allowed. "I'll just jump out this window and ring the front doorbell." Before she knew it, the big man had both thrown the window open and himself through it.

Angelica ran to the window and peered from it to the ground below. "Ten points!" she called down to the man who had just pinned a perfect landing. He was straightening out his lapels and smiling up at her from his place on the Bonners' front lawn. Two deep divots were now embedded in the otherwise flawless lawn.

Angelica closed the window and turned to find Nan Bonner standing directly behind her.

"Ten points?" Nan asked her. "What about 'ten points'?"

"Oh, I was just teasing those kids out there," Angelica lied smoothly. "You know, they were doing cartwheels on their lawn, and I was giving them a gymnastics score...you know, a 'perfect ten'?"

Nan was looking through the windowpane at the part of her neighborhood visible from it. There were no children outside in any of the yards she could see.

There was, however, a gigantic man striding up the walkway leading to her front door. All thoughts of child gymnasts flew out of Nan's head. All she could think about was that big man.

"He looks familiar," she said, causing Angelica to look through the window, too.

"Oh, that's my lawyer," she told Nan. "I asked him to meet me here. I hope that's okay with you."

"Why do you need your lawyer?" Nan asked. The two women were making their way out of Chance's room and down the staircase to the house's ground floor. The doorbell rang as they descended.

"Yes?" Nan queried, opening the front door. "Can I help you with something?"

The man handed her a business card. "I am Stanley Greenleaf," he announced. "I am here to see Angelica Root. I believe she is here?"

"Yes, she is," Nan said, gesturing to Angelica, who stood right next to her. "Please come in. We will go to the kitchen...it's at the end of this hallway."

Stanley Greenleaf preceded the two ladies down the hall. Nan grabbed Angelica by one elbow and repeated her unanswered question: "Why do you need your lawyer here?"

"He has information about Chance," Angelica told her in a whisper. "I thought you'd like to hear it."

"Of course, I would!" Nan exclaimed. She dropped the other woman's elbow and hastened down the hallway after the lawyer. Angelica followed at a pace only slightly slower.

"Well, good day, my dear rodent!" the lawyer was saying to Samantha as Nan and Angelica caught up to him. "I trust you are having a good visit?"

Samantha was sizing the big man up. "I am not sure how to address you," she admitted. "But you're pleasant enough, so I will say that I am doing just fine and am enjoying your fair city." Her cheeks bulged with beans. There were shards of chomped coffee beans between her square teeth. She continued to stare at him, trying to identify whether he was truly human or not. She surreptitiously sniffed the air around him.

"I understand you have information regarding my son...and maybe about my husband as well?" Nan interrupted.

"I do, I do," the lawyer replied. "Might I bother you for some of that delicious smelling coffee?"

"Of course," Nan said, opening a cabinet and removing a large mug. She poured the steaming liquid into the mug and plopped it down on the table. "Sit," she directed the man, gesturing to a chair nearest to the mug of coffee. Angelica had already taken a seat at the far end of the table.

The lawyer placed his large face directly over the steaming coffee and inhaled mightily. He put both of his hands around the hot ceramic mug and left them there, a blissful look on his countenance. He sighed with satisfaction.

"I hate to be rude, Mr. Greenleaf," Nan said, referring to the business card to remind herself of his proper name, "but what about Chance? What have you found out about him? Is he with my husband somewhere?"

Stanley Greenleaf looked up from his mug. His face had turned reddish from the steam rising from the coffee. "I know exactly where your son is, Mrs. Bonner," he said. "And you know, too." Nan sputtered in protest. "Think, woman," the lawyer commanded. "Your son is blue. Your husband is blue. All of your son's friends are blue. Where do you think all of those blue humans would be?"

Nan appeared to be having trouble coming up with an answer. She visibly struggled with herself and was rewarded with a half-memory. "The Fen!" she shouted. "The Magic Fen!"

"Exactly," the attorney acknowledged. "The magic fen. Where, I believe, you made a very good friend when you visited there yourself?" he asked insinuatingly. He stared directly into her eyes. He did not blink.

"A friend?" Nan asked, her brow once more furrowed in thought. "I think I did, actually. Oh, why can't I remember clearly?" she asked, looking at the "people" at her kitchen table one at a time.

They all simply stared back at her. They were holding their respective breaths. Everyone in the kitchen could hear a distant old-fashioned wall clock somewhere in the house ticking away the seconds.

Stanley Greenleaf was the first to break. "Yes, a friend," he prompted her. "One with oh, I don't know, maybe eight legs?"

"Arachimedes!" Nan shouted. "I remember! It was an enormous green spider—Arachimedes!"

Her rediscovered memories made her smile. "How could I have forgotten Arachimedes?" she asked herself out loud. "We hit it off immediately. We had such great dialogues. Simpatico," she said, now looking around at her guests with a warm smile on her face. "We were completely simpatico."

"He misses you, too," the lawyer said softly.

"You know him?" Nan demanded. She had risen to her feet in her excitement.

"At one time, I considered us friends," the lawyer said, a note of sadness in his deep voice. "But we have drifted apart."

"Sad," Nan acknowledged, once again taking her seat.

"Tragic, really," the lawyer admitted. "But that does not mitigate the fact that he has designs on the blue humans who have taken up residence in his magic fen."

"Designs?" Nan asked.

"The humans have become very magic," the big man explained. "Arachimedes wants the magic returned to him. He feels the humans have no rights to possess magic. He will destroy them to release the magic if something isn't done to stop him."

"If you and the spider have had a falling out, how do you know this?" Samantha asked.

"The monkey," Stanley Greenleaf announced flatly.

"The monkey?" Samantha asked. "What monkey? You know, the rats reported monkey scent at the girl's house in Roanoke."

She looked up at Angelica, a look of panic on her honest face. "Oh, Angelica, I'm sorry," she blurted. "It's not my place to bring the girl up."

"The girl?" the lawyer roared. He caught himself mid-roar and lowered his voice again. "The girl?" he repeated in a more moderate tone. "Do you mean the twin? Chance Bonner's twin sister, Destiny Dyer?"

Nan's jaw dropped. She was stunned speechless.

Angelica frowned at her lawyer and turned to address Nan instead. "Nan, I was going to tell you," she started. "I wanted to be the one to tell you," she continued, trying to establish eye contact with the shocked woman. She threw a frustrated grimace in the direction of her lawyer. He closed his eyes and returned to bathing his face in steam.

The coffee had gone cold. He pushed it away from him in disgust and disappointment.

Nan finally looked up and met Angelica's eyes with her own. "Why didn't I know Chance had a twin?" she asked. "Where is she? What is she like?"

"I hid the twins from their father—and each other—shortly after their birth," Angelica explained emotionally. Tears sprang to her eyes as she spoke. "I knew he would be unhappy with me...he didn't want children, you see. But more than that, I thought he would take them away and raise them apart from humanity."

"You're going to have to explain that to me," Nan said. "What do you mean by 'raise them apart from humanity'?"

"He is Almasty," Angelica disclosed.

Nan's face communicated confusion. "Who?" she asked.

"The Sioux called him 'Elder Brother,'" Angelica added. Nan shook her head.

"The native peoples of this very region you now live in called him 'Keeper of the Earth'," Angelica continued.

Nan shook her head.

Angelica sighed loudly before announcing, "Sasquatch."

Nan's eyes flew wide open. She found herself slack-jawed once again.

"Big Foot?" she asked in amazement.

"He doesn't like that one," Angelica informed her somewhat primly. "But yes, he is Big Foot.

"He resides in woods and on mountain tops. He meditates. He avoids humans as much as possible. He says they distract him from his mission."

"Humans?" Nan repeated. "So he is not human?"

"No," Angelica said. "He is not truly human, although he is a remote relative. He is immortal."

"You had children together," Nan said. "How could that happen?"

"Well, I am not completely human myself," Angelica confessed.

"Nor am I," Samantha piped up.

"Nor I," Stanley Greenleaf announced solemnly.

Nan looked around her kitchen table, taking in the non-human humans sitting around it. Under the table she pinched her arm as hard as she could to make sure she wasn't dreaming.

It hurt. A big bruise was already blossoming.

She wasn't dreaming.

After several silent but awkward moments, Nan's three guests all arose to leave.

"Gotta meet someone at the airport," Samantha Swisher said, bustling out of the room. She must have left noiselessly through the pet door, because no sound accompanied her exit from the house.

"Gotta meeting...a conference," Stanley Greenleaf huffed pompously. He departed swiftly and quietly for such a large man.

"Got a hot date!" Angelica announced. She had a dreamy expression on her face as she, too, made her abrupt departure.

Nan continued to sit at the table well after her visitors departed. Her facial expression said it all: she had a lot of pondering to do.

~ * ~

Almasty carefully placed the still-sleeping girl on the couch in Arya Tara's bungalow. The bodhisattva and the large Scot watched him just as carefully.

"How is it that you are the father of this girl and of Chance Bonner?" Angus asked. "I have been with Chance for two years now and I have never seen nor smelled you."

"That's an odd thing to say," Almasty responded, rising and turning to regard the speaker. "'Smelled' me?"

Angus transformed himself back into a dog. Briefly. Just long enough to demonstrate to Almasty why the reference to smell.

"Ahh, I see," the enlightened visitor said, a look of comprehension washing over him. "You are Chance Bonner's pet then?"

"Chance Bonner and I have an understanding," the big man said, reappearing in his kilt and coat. His hat hung on an ornate coat rack just inside the bungalow's front door.

"I can smell that this girl is related to Chance," Angus admitted. "But you...you smell like nothing I have ever come across."

The hairy man laughed. "I should hope not! I've been on a Himalayan mountain top meditating on the state of the planet for thirteen years!"

"Chance is thirteen," the Scot said.

"So is Destiny," Almasty confirmed. "I told you. They are twins."

"If you are their father, then who is their mother?" Arya Tara asked. "Is it for us to know?"

"It will be known to all in the near future," Almasty announced, "so I will tell you. The mother of Chance and Destiny is a woman calling herself Angelica Root. She is not a normal person. Heck, Angus, I'll just have you sniff her when you two meet, and you will know that for yourself!" Almasty returned to laughing.

"I do not have an advanced sniffer," the little bodhisattva told him. "Can you tell me how she is not fully human?"

"She is old but appears to be young. She knows things that are unknowable. She is prescient. She can speak to animals...that is the quality which attracted me to her in the first place. Those are all the words I have to explain, I'm afraid," he concluded. "I realize you wanted or expected more, but that is the best I can do. I haven't talked to a human being in thirteen years. I am rusty." And he laughed some more.

Arya Tara and Angus McLeod found themselves relaxing around the strange man. His good nature seemed sincere. His laughter was contagious.

The girl began to stir, and the trio gathered around her. When her eyes opened, she looked first at Arya, then at Angus, and finally at Almasty.

"Daddy?" she asked. "Is that you?"

In his haste to hold his daughter, Almasty leaned down at the same time that Destiny sat up. Crack! Their heads crashed into each other like a pair of ripe coconuts.

"Ouch!" cried Almasty, holding his head with both hands.

"Ooooch!" Destiny cried, allowing herself to fall back onto the couch.

"I guess it's true," Almasty said, raising his head and looking into his daughter's eyes.

"What's that, Daddy?" she asked. Both of them had big matching bumps on their foreheads.

"Your luck," her father said. "It's spectacular, isn't it?"

"I like that word," Destiny said. "'Spectacular.' Yes, Daddy, I guess you could say that my luck is spectacular...if by 'spectacular' you mean amazingly bad." And the pair of them laughed and laughed.

Soon, Angus and Arya were laughing right along with them.

~ * ~

"I go by a lot of names," Almasty later explained to his daughter and their new friends. "But the one that is closest to correct is 'Keeper of the Earth.' My proper honorary title is 'Heavenly King Hearer of the World's Teachings'."

Arya and Angus both turned to look at their sacred Buddhist scroll, most particularly at the symbol which had been the focus of their recent chanting.

"That's right," Almasty confirmed. "You two summoned me. Both of you.

"And now that I am here, we need to figure out what our next steps are going to be. We must rescue Chance Bonner, his father, and his friends.

"Time is of the essence. Angelica said she sensed looming danger, and she is rarely wrong.

"We must save them. We must save them all."

Twenty-one

The Monkey

Dennison Desmond DeWitt was one of many monkeys occupying niches in Chance Bonner's psyche.

He understood that it was no accident he had been chosen from all of the other monkeys to work with The Beast and Lucinder in bringing ruin down upon the lucky Chance Bonner.

But he also understood it is the nature of negative forces, of which he was one, to trip each other up in their efforts to cause distress. He took solace in this knowledge, for he had been purposely trying to undermine The Beast and Lucinder since joining their team, even though he felt bad about it.

It was not random. Luck was not at play. It was deliberate. Denny understood he was a negative force. But negative forces are not meant to plot or scheme. They merely act, and therefore, sometimes act against each other.

It is a Universal Law.

The positive forces run into each other, too, but two positives colliding just make for more positivity.

Not so with negativity. The collision of two negatives makes a positive.

At the root of Denny's actions was just one thing: he admired the fighting spirit of Chance Bonner. He did not want to harm the boy... and now, facing a situation he had never imagined he would be in, Denny was actively trying to help Chance Bonner.

"He has to get back to normal and return to the human world or we're all out of a job," he told himself. He was prepared to tell The Beast and Lucinder the same thing and was confident they would have to agree with him. He told himself this over and over. And over.

His help was in advising and cheerleading. He had no practice in either of these, but found within himself some kind of natural ability.

"Keep wishing for things, the bigger the better!" he cried loudly to all of the humans. He was already surrounded by cars, boats, recreational vehicles of all types, clothing, jewelry, and yard ornaments of every shape and size wished into existence by the humans.

"You are fading!" he encouraged them. "I can see it! The more magic you spend, the less blue you become."

It was true. The blue humans were no longer indigo, but rather merely royal blue.

"What are you doing?" a voice without a body asked.

Denny jumped and turned all around, looking for the source of the sound.

"You've forgotten the sound of my voice?" the voice asked.

"Arachimedes?" Denny asked tentatively.

"Of course," the old spider replied, stepping out of the tree bole he had secreted himself within. "Did my great-great-great-great grandson not tell you to come see me?" he asked the monkey.

"Your great-great-great-great grandson?" Denny replied. "No, I am certain I have not spoken with any of your messengers."

"Hmmm," the spider mused. "Strange, that. When he returned from the task I had given him, the spiderling had forgotten where I sent him, then forgot why. He's too young to have such a bad brain, so I suspect magic was in play. Was it you, monkey-man?" he asked. "Did you use magic to disarm my agent, my precious great-great-great-great grandson?"

"Me?" Denny said incredulously. "Magic? How could someone like me have magic, Arachimedes?" He tried to keep his voice even, but he could hear the fear in it.

"Have your eyes always been blue?" the spider asked, training his many eyes on Denny's two.

Denny laughed nervously. "Now I know you're pulling my leg," he replied. "My eyes are not blue..." He left his denial in mid-air as he wondered if his eyes had really changed color.

"Of course, I'm joking!" Arachimedes said with a laugh of his own. "Say, monkey-man, how about a nibble for old times' sake?" The spider rose on his back six legs and motioned Denny to approach him with his two forelegs.

"I've just about gotten over my addiction," the monkey said sadly. "I am sorely tempted, Arachimedes, but I am trying to quit the venom."

"Just a little nibble?" the spider urged. "I won't take much."

"Take as much as you like," Denny replied. "Just don't leave anything behind...no venom!"

The spider leapt up onto Denny's shoulder and clamped his jaws on the monkey's neck. "Can't do one without the other," he cackled evilly.

Denny's eyes glazed over and his face went slack.

"OK, now let's have the truth!" the spider cried. "Did you use magic on my great-great-great-great grandson?"

"I did," Denny said sloppily. Now he wore a silly grin. "I really did, Arachimedes, you should have seen me."

"I knew it!" the spider crowed. "Now you're magic, too! What of the humans...are they trapped here in the fen? Have they crossed the blue line?"

"They have," Denny said, becoming sad. "They really have. But I am trying to help them."

"Help them how?"

"They expend great quantities of their magic in an effort to reduce their blue balance. I encourage them. I keep them working."

"Denny," Arachimedes became deadly serious. "I need to recover the blue magic. I need to expel these pesky humans from my fen. I will do this by any means. Do you understand me, Denny?"

"I understand," the monkey replied. "By any means. Got it, Boss." And he slumped to the ground unconscious.

Arachimedes approached the monkey and lifted one eyelid with a single hairy foreleg. "He's out cold," he said to himself. He backed away from the slumbering monkey and faced the woods.

"Advance!" he cried loudly, "and take your positions!" An enormous horde of spiders of all colors and dimensions immediately poured forth from the underbrush. Like floodwaters, they flowed across the clearing and down into the blue human region which had been reclaimed from the swamp. They crawled up into bushes and trees which surrounded the human encampment and there they waited, an army of over a million angry spiders.

"We're taking our land back," they muttered to each other. "When Arachimedes issues the order, we attack!"

~ * ~

"Lonely, so lonely," sniveled the blue gerbil. "So, so lonely. Hello! What's this?" And the little rodent snugged himself into Denny's jacket pocket where he curled into a tight, furry ball, and promptly fell fast asleep.

~ * ~

Denny came out of his coma hours later with a crashing headache. "Oh, no," he groaned, pushing himself up into a sitting position. "What happened?"

As his memory returned, the monkey moaned and clutched his head. "So where did he go?" he asked himself, looking around for the old spider. The turning motion caused his pain to peak. He did not repeat the motion a second time.

After several painful minutes, Denny hauled himself to his feet and began the long walk back to where the blue humans resided.

"I need to encourage them," he told himself. "We need to get out of here as fast as we can."

Unheard by him, his words were being repeated from bush to bush and tree to tree. "Get out of here as fast as we can," they reported to one another.

"They will not leave here with one shred of our blue magic," a voice vowed. This message, too, was picked up and repeated and repeated over one million times.

"Not one shred," the voices eventually settled on. It became a rallying cry that was employed throughout the night.

~ * ~

Denny climbed over mountains of gold bars and precious gems in order to gain access to the blue human camp. He stepped over the humans, too, who apparently had fallen asleep in place, on the ground.

"Oh, my goodness, but you're all so pale!" he cried. "You've nearly done it! You're almost back to normal!"

"What?" a bone-tired Chance Bonner said, raising his head from where it rested on his crossed forearms. "Oh, it's you, Denny," he said dispiritedly. "I didn't see you there for a moment."

"That means I'm almost back to normal, too!" the monkey cried, excited and elated by the news.

"What?" Chance asked blearily.

"Never mind, never mind!" the monkey replied. His answer went ignored. The humans were having a hard time seeing him.

He ran up to Chance and put his hands on the young man's shoulders. "Chance Bonner," he said loudly. "Let's gather the humans and try to leave this fen!"

"What?" Chance asked. He seemed to be having trouble keeping his eyes open. "What did you say? Do you mean we can leave this place?" A sign of hope lit up his face. "Stefan!" he cried. "Kelly, Millicent, Sarah, Brilliant—Dad! Come here! Come quickly!"

Sounds of people stirring and slowly approaching could be heard. Finally, when all of the humans had gathered around him, Chance spoke. He gestured toward Denny. "This monkey..." He paused and turned back to face Denny "What did you say your name was again?"

Denny just smiled and shook his head. "Anyway, this guy here says we can leave the fen—we are almost back to normal!"

"Concentrate!" Denny cried. "Concentrate on the Bonner house... the kitchen. Close your eyes and will yourselves to relocate."

The pale blue humans certainly appeared to be concentrating. Their faces were all screwed up with the intensity with which they thought. They clenched their fists. Their bodies shook with the strength of their effort.

But nothing happened.

After several minutes of effort, they quit trying, one at a time. They stood in place and just stared blankly at each other.

A stool with three bright blue legs popped into the center of their loosely knit group. A moment later, a lumpy old lady dressed all in blue appeared with a "pop," sitting unsteadily on top of the stool.

"Ribetta!" Denny cried. "Thank goodness you're here!"

"I told you people that you were permanently magic!" the frog-woman cried. "What are you playing at? You can't drain your magic away and survive here—you are now made of magic! Without it, this place will eat you up!"

Ribetta was the only being in the clearing who heard that her words were picked up and repeated in the surrounding bracken, bush, and arbor. "Eat you up," she heard, over and over again. She looked up. She looked around herself. Even though she could not see the sources of the many voices, she was certain she knew what they were and what they were doing there.

"You are in danger," she whispered to the humans. "You are in grave and immediate danger." She grabbed Astra by the hand. "Everyone grab a hand...you, too, Denny. I haven't forgotten you, even if you're trying to be invisible.

"OK, hang on to each other. I'm getting us out of here!" And with great effort and its resultant great power, Ribetta transported all of them out of the fen...

...and into a giant arena.

The next great battle had begun.

Twenty-two

The Arena

If you are familiar with Chance Bonner and his previous battles, you will already know the layout of the arena.

For the sake of those of you who are here in your first adventure with Chance, a description follows:

The arena is concrete. It has been burnished until it glows like silver.

It is rectangular, with four great white marble pillars in each corner and two on each side. The pillars bear engravings and labels identifying them as Heavenly King Hearer of the World's Teachings, Heavenly King Upholder of the People, Heavenly King Wide-Eyed and Heavenly King Increase and Growth. The two pillars positioned on the sides of the arena bear the names Wisdom King Craving Filled and Wisdom King Unmovable. Each of the six pillars displays the graven images of human men and women who are famous for their support of art, science, philosophy, charity, human rights, and exploration.

Behind and around the pillars which define the field of combat there are rows and rows of spectator seating, and returning to our story's point in time, these seats were full of spectators already. These spectators were bejeweled and robed. Their long black hair was beautifully oiled and elaborately coiffed.

They were countless numbers of Bodhisattvas of the Earth.

Ribetta was the only one in the Bonner party who had never seen the arena, and she was absolutely flabbergasted.

"What? Where are we?" she cried. "What are we doing here? I aimed us directly at the Bonner house!"

"Could it be luck?" Denny asked from his place at the back of the group.

Ribetta was frantically jumping up and down in her excitement and alarm. Her filmy gown floated in the air in a counter tempo to her leaps. When the fabric of her skirt actually blew up over her face, she stopped jumping and smoothed her garment down where it needed to be. Her legs still twitched, but she managed to keep herself on the ground, for the moment.

"It has to be magic. You can call it luck if you like, but is it good luck or bad luck?"

"Chance is here, so it must be good luck," Chaz Bonner said. The other young people standing around him nodded their agreement with his assessment.

"Good luck?" Ribetta repeated. "Good luck? I don't detect anything good here, and who are all of those shining people? What are they waiting for?"

Ribetta had turned to surveil the audience. When she turned back to face the Bonner group again, she gasped at their transformation.

They were all clad in leather and metal—silver, gold, and bronze. They were armed with large spears, each of them sporting huge colorful jewels in their hafts.

There were ten Brilliants. The first of them glowed a light blue, identifying herself as Astra. Each of the Brilliants differed in skin and hair color. Each of their long spears bore a different precious gem.

"Who are you supposed to be?" Ribetta asked Astra.

Astra threw back her head and laughed. "I am truly revealed here, creature of magic!" she declared. "I am the Ten Demon Daughters!"

Angelica Root, likewise garbed and armed for battle, stepped out from behind the tenth Brilliant and spoke.

"And I am the Mother of Demon Children!" she announced.

Astra and Stefan Shultz looked at each other, shock written large on their faces.

"Mom's not going to be happy about this," Stefan whispered to his sister.

"You are right about that!" Josephine Schultz the Elder said, striding up to Angelica and staring into her eyes. Mrs. Schultz was olive green, and her eyes were bright red. She was in full battle gear.

The two tall women stood facing each other, nose-to-nose.

Without speaking a word, Angelica took a step to her left and indicated the newcomer should join her there. Mrs. Schultz stepped readily into the breach and the two women squared their shoulders and faced the rest of the group. They did not say anything, but their body language communicated readiness. Resolve. Determination.

Chance looked puzzled. "I'm confused," he confessed. "I don't know what I'm doing here this time. There is no enemy here. Who are we fighting?"

Ribetta cocked her head, hearing something that was still outside of human hearing range. She groaned. She shuddered. If it were possible, she looked greener than usual.

Then Angelica heard it. Her pale face paled further and two bright red spots appeared in her chiseled cheekbones.

"Do you hear that?" she asked her human companions. "Listen… listen closely!"

It took many moments, but soon the humans were nodding. They could hear something. The sound was coming into human hearing range.

"Not one shred! Not one shred! Not one shred!" they heard from countless voices, in an endless repetition. As the words got louder, another sound could be heard: the tramping of approximately eight million feet.

"Oh no," Ribetta moaned. "It's spiders—spiders! A million or more!"

"Spiders?" Chance echoed. "Why so many? Where have they come from? Better yet, why do they come here in the first place?"

"The fen," Denny said, fear making his voice quake. "They inhabit the magic fen. They come for their magic—their blue magic!"

"How is it they approach this arena?" Stefan asked. Like his mother, his skin was olive green and his eyes were a piercing crimson. Unlike her, however, he still sported his natural blond hair. It was slicked straight back and held in place by a layer of gel that had dried to helmet strength. He was not wearing his glasses. He didn't need them here.

Ribetta stood forward to command everyone's attention. She held one hand up, indicating that she required silence.

"Spiders go where they want. They are magical creatures...usually that means that their comings and goings are random, their behaviors chaotic.

"The spiders you hear approaching now—they are not behaving chaotically. They have united and they are focused. This is unprecedented. Do you understand me?"

To a person, everyone listening to her shook his or her head in the negative. That included a few hundred of the closest bodhisattvas sitting in the stands.

Ribetta sighed in frustration and gave it another try. "This is the result of some legendary bad luck: the spiders want their magic back. They don't like human beings and they don't want you to possess any of their precious blue magic—"

Stefan interrupted. "You keep saying 'blue magic' specifically. Are there kinds of magic other than blue magic?"

"Of course," Ribetta replied. "Now let me continue, young man. Please restrain yourself."

Stefan looked peeved. Peeved and even more curious than before. He would bide his time, but he would have his answer in the end.

"The spiders are coming here because this is where you blue humans are," Ribetta continued. "It's that simple.

"I have told you repeatedly that you are permanently magic. If the spiders want to get every shred of their blue magic back, they will have to kill you."

"Wow, talk about bad luck!" a little voice interjected. "And I thought I had it bad!"

Almasty, still robed from head to heel in goat hair, strode forward holding a skinny little blond teenager by the hand. She came with him willingly, even though she took three steps for every one of his. He looked down at her fondly. "I told you to stand on my boots, Destiny," he chided her lovingly. "You didn't have to walk here on your own."

Destiny looked up into the hairy man's kind face. "With my luck, I would have scuffed them or worse," she replied. "Probably would have caused you to trip," she added as an afterthought.

The pair was nearing the Bonner group when it happened. As Destiny approached her twin, an arc of blue light sparked into being. At one end of the arc stood Destiny Dyer; at the other—Chance Bonner. The arc crackled with static, causing their hair to stand on end.

The twins stood staring at each other, the arc's blue light dyeing their skin identical cyan shades.

Like a dam bursting, the spider horde breached the arena and scattered. The entire floor, ceiling, and each of the sacred pillars were covered with spiders small and large; spiders black, brown, green, and red.

But not blue. There was not a single blue spider among the million.

"Can I return to my question now?" Stefan asked Ribetta.

"I said to restrain yourself," Ribetta spat out through clenched teeth. "Can you not see the trouble you're in right now?"

"The arc protects us," Stefan said flatly. "The spiders don't dare attack now. They will be fried by the super-blue."

Ribetta broke form. She looked confused. "The super blue?" she asked Stefan. "What are you babbling about?"

"The super blue is the power created by the joining of Chance Bonner and Destiny Dyer," Stefan told her tersely. "It is not magic—

even if it is blue. It is pure power. It occupies the void between Chance and his twin. Now that they are close, it concentrates...it becomes super. Super blue." He turned from Ribetta dismissively and faced toward Almasty. "You, sir, the big hairy man," Stefan called above the heads of his shorter comrades, ignoring the frog-lady entirely which irked her no end. Almasty looked at the tall young man in surprise and touched his breast with a long index finger. "Who, me?"

"Yes," Stefan answered "You. Bring that girl closer to Chance Bonner."

The hairy man looked at Angelica Root, who shrugged her shoulders. "OK," he said. "Are you all right with that, sweetie?" he asked his daughter.

"Yes, Daddy. But who is that boy on the other end of this arc?" Destiny asked.

"That is your brother," Almasty informed her gently. "Your twin brother. His name is Chance. Chance Bonner."

"Who are you?" Chance called over the void which separated them. He had to shout to be heard over the arc's static. "Do I know you?"

"Apparently, I am your twin sister," Destiny called back, taking steps toward him. The arc sparked and crackled louder with each step.

"I have a twin sister?" Chance asked, looking at his father for confirmation. His father shrugged. He didn't know anything. So, Chance looked to Angelica. He knew she was his birth mother.

She nodded in the affirmative. "She is your twin," she said softly to Chance.

"I am Destiny Dyer," the girl called out once more. "Are you Chants Bonner?"

"I am," Chance replied. "Did you say your name was "Dire?"

"Yes," the girl answered. She was getting close. The arc bent at an almost impossible angle. As the toes of her shoes touched the toes of Chance's shoes, the arc became a stable thick vertical line for the briefest second, then popped into non-existence.

The brother and sister hugged, albeit a little awkwardly. As they did, Chance's blue-tinged skin returned to normal flesh tones.

"You did it!" Kelly cried excitedly. "You're back, Chance! You're not blue anymore!"

"Me next! Me next!" cried Sarah, Millicent a half-step behind her.

"Here, touch my arm, both of you!"

Destiny reached out and grabbed Sarah's arm. She watched as the blue tint of the girl's skin was replaced by her normal peachy complexion. "I have the negative luck," Destiny said. "I can eliminate the good luck, the magic, in your case. Chance is too lucky. His touch will only worsen your problem."

She turned to face Chance. "No offense intended," she told him.

He was stunned. "None taken," he said.

Millicent stepped forward wordlessly, and the act was repeated. Her blue tint retreated just as Sarah's had.

Kelly, Stefan, Chaz and finally Astra stepped forward one by one. Destiny, by her mere touch, changed them back to fully human.

"Good-bye to Astra!" Brilliant Schultz announced gleefully. She returned to join the other nine Demon Daughters, resuming her place at the front of the formation.

"We now have no shred of blue magic!" Chance announced to the spider audience. "Are you satisfied?"

"We are not!" called a loud voice. The humans could not make out which of the spiders spoke—there were simply too many of them. "There is blue magic with you, and we will have it! Spiders...on the ready!"

~ * ~

Denny poofed away, not out of cowardice, but because he needed to alert The Beast and Lucinder to what was going on in the arena. This time, they would need to fight on the side of the humans. If they did not, Chance Bonner would die.

When he materialized, he was surprised to find not just The Beast, but also Chance's Devil King in the cavern.

"Sir!" he cried. "And Sire!" he added, bowing deeply to their regent. "We must assemble our forces! Chance Bonner is facing a crisis. He will surely be killed if we do not intervene!"

"Calm yourself, young Dennison," the King drawled, drawing an emery board across one long thumb nail. "Whatever are you blathering about? Are you telling me that you have located that troublesome lucky boy?" The tall, crowned man leaned down close to Denny. Denny could feel the King's hot breath on his face. His waxed and pointed goatee tickled the monkey-man's upper lip.

"I have found him!" Denny cried. "Come with me, I will show you."

"Lead away!" the Devil King commanded. "Stanley," he said as he turned to address The Beast, "assemble the troops and follow us. Hasten." The Beast did not move but rather seemed to be lost in thought. "That means hurry!" the King screamed in his face. The Beast disappeared immediately in a giant cloud of sulfur.

"Gads, I wish he'd change his poof signature!" the King remarked to Denny while trying to clear the air by waving both of his arms about. "Let's go, young Dennison!"

And with that, Denny and the Devil King of the Sixth Heaven disappeared with a quite unremarkable "poof." The Cavern was empty.

For a moment or two.

The Beast's sulfur trail had hardly settled when, with another poof, this time accompanied by approximately two hundred fluffy balls of cotton candy, Destiny's Beast and Lucinder appeared in the cavern.

"Seriously," Lucinder told Destiny's Beast as they waded through the pink and blue sugary heaps. "This is a big improvement over the glitter, don't you think?" She scooped up a big blue puffball as she walked and munched on it greedily. "Mmmmmm," she said. "Yummy!"

"Well, I don't know about that," Destiny's Beast replied, "but it's a lot easier on the lungs."

They strode clear of the sugary clouds and looked around the cavern and Chance's room to make sure they were truly alone.

"So, what's next?" an excited Lucinder asked The Beast. "How do we retrieve the boy from that magic quagmire?"

"You have a way with words, Lucinder," The Beast responded admiringly. "'Quagmire.' That's a really good word."

Lucinder blushed, although it was hard to see through her ebon cheeks. "I learn a new word every day," she confessed. "I used to do it to impress Denny, actually."

A surprised Beast interrupted her. "Denny? Who is Denny?"

Lucinder hung her head. She carried an unexpected burden of sorrow over what she had to report. "I mentioned him to you. He was my partner," she told The Beast. "Just a monkey, really, but a very, very, very good monkey."

"Any human has thousands of monkeys in their heads," The Beast said without emotion. "How could just one of them be so special?"

Lucinder responded thoughtfully. "Truly, I think it's because he thought I was special," she said. "There are more wasps than there are monkeys in your average human head. But Denny thought I was special. He never said it out loud, but I knew. And I cherished him for it. And now he's gone."

"Well, maybe we'll find him when we find his human, you know, Chance Bonner," The Beast offered with just a hint of empathy.

"That would be just great!" Lucinder responded, perking up instantly. "So how do we get started?"

The Beast had been looking around the room during the preceding conversation. She was fixated now on just one thing.

"We start with that glowing silver door over there," she said, pointing at it. "Has that always been there?" she asked Lucinder, turning her gaze on the little wasp-woman.

Lucinder gasped. "How could I have not seen that door?" she marveled. "No. No, it has not been there before. It is new!"

"Well, let's see where it goes," The Beast announced. She led the way. The two "women" went through the door arm in arm.

As the door closed behind them, it disappeared. A single ball of lavender cotton candy slipped through its crack just before it was entirely gone.

~ * ~

"She went this way!" The taller and leaner of the sniffer rats called back confidently to the general. After his announcement, he immediately got back on the trail.

"This is almost too easy!" he said to his partner rat. "Her bad luck is so stinky, she is impossible to miss."

And then it happened. They missed her. Her unique scent vanished. It was there one moment and gone the next.

The entire Baltimore Brigade of the Rodent Army was stopped in its tracks.

"Take a short break, everyone!" General Swisher announced. "Get some water. Eat while you can. Rest. We will camp here until we pick up the trail again."

The Army was back in Seattle. They had once again stowed away amongst baggage and foodstuffs on a direct flight from Baltimore International to Seattle-Tacoma. They were stalled in a human memorial garden not far from the airport.

She turned to the rats. "So, what happened?" she asked.

"Don't know, General," the shorter of the two sniffer rats responded with a smart salute. "It seems her luck may have changed."

"That would be very bad luck for us," the general confided in her scouts. "And if it's bad luck for us, then it's bad luck for Angelica, Almasty, and their human charges."

"So, they are human, the children?" again, from the shorter rat.

"As odd as it may seem, they apparently are completely human," the general said. "They are special, or so I am told, but they are one hundred percent human."

"Odd," said the shorter rat.

"Very odd indeed," said the taller rat.

"I hate 'odd'," the general said. "Keep sniffing, my good rodents. Let me know the moment you pick up any trace of that girl!"

"Roger, ma'am, roger wilco," both rats responded simultaneously. Their salutes were delivered with speed and snap.

The general returned the salutes and went in search of her old and wise Sergeant Major.

~ * ~

"SMAJ, you're a genius," the general said a little while later. She had located her trusted senior NCO and had briefed him on the tracking problem.

"I shook his hand several times before I left Angelica's," she continued. "I am sure to have his scent still on me. And you're right—it is unique in all of the world!

"I'll take it to the tracker rats right this instant. We will be back on the trail in no time!"

~ * ~

"The scent leads here," the rats informed their commander some time later. It had been many miles from the airport to their current location.

The advance party stood in the back yard behind a tiny bungalow. "He is no longer here," the short rat said.

"We need to get inside of this house," the general said. "Any ideas?"

"We can get in anywhere," the thin rat said with confidence. "It's getting the rest of you in that's a problem."

"Is there anyone inside?" the general asked.

Both rats sniffed some more. "No, ma'am," they both responded.

General Swisher turned toward the bushes and trees that surrounded the property. She knew her entire brigade was hidden nearby.

"Bring the Beavers forward!" she commanded.

Twelve bristling beavers marched out from behind a large larch. Within one foot of the general, they stopped, came to attention, and saluted her.

"Yes, ma'am. Beaver Company reporting as ordered!"

"I need you to open that door," she told them, pointing at the bungalow's rear entrance.

"Yes ma'am," the beavers responded in unison. They proceeded up the porch stairs, and then constructed a ramp to the door's knob using their own bodies.

The ranking beaver, a young captain, used the beaver-body ramp to reach the knob. He grasped it and wriggled it with both of his hands.

"Locked, ma'am!" he announced.

"Oh dear," she responded. "I guess we'll have to use brute force."

"Give me a moment, ma'am," the captain interrupted. He whispered to one of his subordinate beavers who then ran to the bushes, returning with a large grey and white porcupine.

"Soldier, this is going to hurt me more than it will hurt you!" the captain proclaimed. He bent and pulled one of the porcupine's bristles out.

"Ouch!" cried the porcupine. "Hey, sir, I'd do anything for the mission, but you could have warned me!" he complained, carefully rubbing the spot where his quill had once been.

"That will do, Private!" the captain replied severely. "Dismissed!"

The porcupine saluted and retreated back to the bushes.

The captain had inserted the quill into the lock and was manipulating it with his clever hands. They all heard the "click" when he succeeded in throwing the lock's tumblers.

Tossing the now useless quill behind him, the captain grasped the door's knob once again. This time, it completed its turn, and the door yawned open.

The beavers lined the stairs to the now open door and saluted as their general walked between their neat columns up the porch and into the bungalow.

"Well done, men!" she said. She heard a little gasp and halted her progress. "Please forgive me," she said after a moment's observation. "Well done, men and women!"

At this, the Beaver Company cheered. "Please take cover, Beaver Company," General Swisher said. "I am going in alone."

"Oh no, you're not—with all due respect, ma'am!" said the old grey squirrel who was her sergeant major. He ran up as fast as his arthritic legs would allow and stood in front of her. He saluted.

"I am going in with you, General!" he announced.

It brought a smile to her lips. She relented. "Very well then, Sergeant Major. Come along. Let's proceed."

"Yes, ma'am," he responded. "I'll go in first—you are too important to risk. I will go in first and secure the site. I will let you know when it is clear. Then you may enter."

She hiked an eyebrow at the old NCO. "Oh, then I may enter?" she said. "No, SMAJ, here's how it will go down. We will enter together. You may precede me if you insist, but we go in together, do you get that?"

"Yes, ma'am," the old squirrel replied. "I get you, ma'am." His admiration for her glimmered in his beady little eyes.

He turned and entered the bungalow, General Samantha Swisher on his heels.

The bungalow was empty of life. The owner's possessions were few and orderly. The place was spotless.

Only one thing was out of place. It wasn't messy or anything...it just didn't belong.

It was a large, shimmery, silver door.

"Alert the Army," the general commanded the old squirrel. "We go through that door as close together as we can. The Baltimore Brigade will charge!"

"Yes, General, I will give the command!" and the old sergeant major ran back out of the bungalow to relay the general's order to her battalion commanders.

Mere moments later, the general could see that her army was assembled at the foot of the porch stairs.

"Ahead, march...double-time!" she shouted. Her call was picked up by the battalion commanders and then the company commanders and then the platoon leaders.

The Rodent Army marched with speed and precision through the shiny silver doors; they were led by their esteemed commander, General Samantha Swisher, who crossed the doorway first.

As the last rodent crossed that threshold, the door shimmered briefly and then disappeared. A single acorn bounced across the lintel just as the door noiselessly vanished. One second behind it, a small espresso bean squeezed through, spinning wildly for several moments on the polished wood floor, the only moving thing in the now deserted little bungalow.

~ * ~

Back in the arena, chaos reigned.

"Halt!" cried the spider voice, still from a source the others in the arena could not identify.

A hush fell across the entire hall. The spiders halted as one, frozen in place.

"The blue magic is gone!" the voice cried. "Stand down. I repeat, stand down. Hold your positions while I consult with Arachimedes!"

Not a sound could be heard now. The spider horde had fallen completely silent and motionless. Still, an enormous tension remained and was experienced by everyone, spider and non-spider, across the arena and into the spectator stands.

With a "poof" and a small mountain of blue and pink cotton candy, Lucinder and a very tall, very pale, horse-faced woman with a glittery horn projecting from the middle of her forehead appeared.

They were as astonished at what they saw as the people in the arena were to witness their sudden and startling arrival.

"Retreat!" the spider voice cried. The spiders skittered back across the gleaming floor and climbed back up the columns, and otherwise resumed their former positions.

The tension did not wane. Rather, it waxed as a thrumming sound began and grew louder and louder.

With a "pop!" Samantha Swisher and her Rodent Army swarmed the arena, taking up the very spaces just made available by the retreating spider horde. It was the sound of the marching militant rodents which had shaken the foundations of the arena just prior to the army's arrival.

"Status?" General Swisher asked Angelica.

"Unsure," Angelica responded. "We have yet to clearly identify our cause."

"'Our cause'?" General Swisher repeated.

"Yes, 'our cause'," Angelica responded. "Even Chance Bonner cannot figure out why we are here and what we are battling."

"Not one shred! Not one shred! Not one shred!" the spider horde began chanting. Samantha strained to make out the words, and when she heard them—really heard them—she readdressed her tall friend.

"Why do they shout so?" she asked her. "Are they the enemy in this battle?"

"They only seek to regain what is theirs by right," Angelica said. "And Chance, his father, and his friends would gladly relinquish it to them, but they no longer possess it!"

"And what is this 'it'?" the general persisted.

"Magic. Blue magic, to be specific," Angelica replied.

At that moment, with a thunderous "poof" and an enormous cloud of sulfur, Denny, The Beast, and the Devil King made a splashy appearance in the center of the arena, accompanied by a host of minions, all brandishing weapons of every make and kind. The spiders retreated around them, but not fast enough to spare them the sulfurous poison. Many thousands of them fell over on their backs, feet twitching in the air.

The Devil King beat mightily at the air around him, coughing and wiping tears from his eyes as he did.

Something aroused the spiders not overcome by the sulfur. "It's back!" the unidentified spider voice announced. "There is blue magic here once again! Spiders, fall back and assume attack positions. Await the order! Each of you take a fallen comrade with you!"

The human and not-human contingent members looked at each other and then turned to stare at the newcomers.

"Which of you possesses the blue magic?" Almasty demanded of them. "We were free of it until you appeared here. Which of you is it?"

The answer to his question did not come. Instead, there was another appearance which interrupted the interrogation: Nan Bonner. Nan Bonner appeared without noise, cloud, candy, glitter, or any other fanfare of any kind.

But she was blue. She was very blue.

And on her shoulder rode an enormous green spider.

Twenty-three

Nan and The Spider

After Angelica and Samantha had left her house, Nan Bonner sat and worried for some time.

Then, with a look that spoke wordlessly of inspiration, she rose and went to her refrigerator. She opened the vegetable crisper.

There. Inside a baggie in the crisper: a single glowing blue orb.

Without squandering a second thought, Nan Bonner swallowed the orb and willed herself to travel. It was the fen she wanted. The magic fen.

She had clenched her eyes shut to envision her destination, and when she opened them, she was there: the fen.

"Arachimedes, my friend!" she cried. "It's me, Nan Bonner! Are you here?"

"Nan!" a voice called. "I am here. Give me one moment, and I will come to you!" and mere seconds later, he appeared, jumping from one tree limb to the next until he dropped to the fen floor not two feet from where Nan stood.

"Oh, it is so good to see you, Nan Bonner!" Arachimedes cried. "I have missed you so!"

"And I you!" the woman replied, holding her hands open so that the enormous spider could climb up into them. "How have you been?" she continued. "Where is everyone? Are my son and husband here, by any chance?"

"You have just missed them," the big spider told her. "But yes, they were here for quite some time. They had other blue humans with them."

"Where have they gone? Do you know?" Nan asked.

"I have sent every one of my spiders after them," he responded. "I am waiting for word from my scouts as to their current location."

"Do you intend to go to them?" Nan asked.

"I must," the spider told her sadly. "I am afraid I may have to harm them in order to retrieve what they have taken from me."

"Oh no!" Nan exclaimed. "What have they taken?"

"Magic," he replied. "Blue magic."

"But they didn't know that it belonged to you!" Nan explained. "They found it in my refrigerator. They only took it so that they could find Josephine."

"Who?"

"Oh, yes. I forgot she has many names. She is the sister of the tall blond young man in the lab coat, Stefan. Stefan Schultz."

"Oh," the spider said. "You mean the girl named 'Astra'."

Nan laughed. "Well, that's a new one. 'Astra,' huh? I guess I'll have to add it to the list."

"You are such a pleasure to talk to," Arachimedes said to the woman. "But where have you been? Why did you not at least say goodbye?"

"It turns out that I was only temporarily magic," Nan informed her friend. "So when my husband, my son, and my son's friends began to chant the sacred mantra for me, I was pulled back to the human—I mean 'non-magic'—world. I could not resist the pull, Arachimedes. I did not have full magic powers then...but I do now. Until you decide to banish me, I am magic now. Permanently magic!"

"Sounds like an invitation to an adventure!" her friend responded. "You make me feel young again!" he declared. "What shall we do? Shall we join my legions and search for your husband and your son?"

"You are so kind to me, my good Arachimedes!" Nan cried. "Yes, let's do that!"

"May I ride upon your shoulder?" the spider asked.

"Of course, old friend!" Nan replied readily. "Hop aboard!"

Once Arachimedes had perched securely on her right shoulder, he instructed her to close her eyes and use her magic to find her son. "You will be able to sense your son, in particular, because you are of the same blood."

Nan started. The spider felt her tremble. "What is it, Nan Bonner?" he asked. "What is wrong?"

"Chance and I do not share any blood," she admitted tearfully to the spider. "Chaz and I adopted him. He comes from another bloodline entirely."

"Well, that is a poser," the spider responded thoughtfully. "Let's try this, then: I have many thousands of offspring in the spider horde. Let me try to sense where they might be...zounds!" Arachimedes suddenly exclaimed. "Danger! They are being harmed! Oh, how dastardly!"

"What?" Nan asked anxiously. "What is it?"

"Gas," the spider replied. "Many of my offspring have been viciously attacked by someone—or something—spewing out poison gas."

"Well, can we go to them?" Nan urged. "Let's go! We might be able to save them."

"You are right, and oh, so good," the spider responded admiringly. "That is just what we should do. I will direct our travel. Just lean forward ever so slightly and close your eyes."

And the pair silently disappeared, travelling the magic ether to a destination unknown.

They travelled fearlessly, knowing that danger awaited them. They went unhesitatingly to rescue Arachimedes' kith and kin.

Twenty-four

Tensions Mount

A single moment before Nan Bonner and Arachimedes made their appearance in the arena, Denny decided to act. Just as Almasty was demanding to know which of the three of them—The Beast, the King, or the monkey—was carrying the blue magic, Denny made the snap decision. "I am going to find Arachimedes!" Denny told The Beast and the Devil King. "I'll be back as soon as I can." And off he "poofed."

"The blue magic is gone again!" the disembodied spider voice announced. "Stand down, spider horde! Stand down!"

The Beast and the Devil King looked askance at one another.

"Is it the monkey?" the King asked The Beast from the corner of his mouth. He was trying mightily not to move his lips or be overheard.

"What?" The Beast asked loudly. "Sire, I cannot hear you. What was that you said about the monkey?"

All heads in their vicinity turned to watch them—and to listen.

"Hey!" cried a huge man in a kilt and raincoat. "Where did the monkey go? When did he leave?" Angus McLeod had been standing right next to Denny mere moments before.

"Monkey?" the Devil King asked, shrugging and assuming a confused look. "What monkey?"

"Monkey?" cried Lucinder from across the arena. She ran toward where The Beast and her regent stood. "Was Denny here?" she cried. "Denny! Denny!" She frantically looked around for her erstwhile partner, and friend, in vain.

He was not there.

"Monkey?" cried the green spider on Nan Bonner's shoulder. "Was it Denny? Was Denny here?" He jumped from Nan's shoulder and skittered closer to where The Beast and the King stood.

"You again!" he said, looking The Beast up and down with his lip curled in distaste.

"You again!" said The Beast, looking angry—and hurt.

The spider looked from The Beast to the Devil King and back again. "I know you both. You are the bigwigs in charge of Denny's team," he announced archly. "What has happened? Has he evaded you once again?"

"You know," The Beast responded, shooting his regent a look which kept him silent. "He said he was going to go looking for you! And you know what? Your spider horde, or whatever it is you call them, just announced that one of us was carrying blue magic! When the monkey 'poofed' away, your spoke-spider announced that the magic was no longer in the arena. What exactly do you think that means?" The Beast insinuated snidely. "Could it be that your precious monkey possesses blue magic? Could it be that he smuggles blue magic in and out of the magic realm? Hmmmm?" And with this, The Beast lowered his head and stared directly into the spider's multiple, many-faceted eyes. "Well?" he prompted him smugly.

"Denny be damned!" the magic creature cried, demonstrating his fickle, chaotic nature. "All of you be damned!" He ran back to Nan and crouched down in preparation for jumping back onto her shoulder.

Something stopped him. Something random.

"Damn you, too, Nan Bonner!" he cried. He turned and ran into the spider horde, soon becoming just one of a million spiders...each one of which was magic. Chaotic. Random. At least in their basic natures they were.

Nan looked stunned. And devastated.

And scared. She realized she was blue, that she carried the blue magic, and that she had lost her protector...and friend.

A short, slight, blonde teenaged girl emerged from the pack of two-legged contestants in the arena. She held her hands out to Nan, who felt compelled for some indefinable reason to take them in her own. As their hands touched, Nan could feel the blue leeching from her. As the last of the magic left her body, she fell to her knees.

"Are you all right?" the girl asked her. Chaz Bonner rapidly approached and helped his wife up onto her feet. Chance wasn't far behind him. He put his arms around his mother. "Mom! Mom!" he cried. "Are you okay?"

"Chance. Chaz," she replied. "I am so glad to see you! I have been so worried." And with that, she fainted dead away in Chaz's arms.

Chaz Bonner hefted his wife's body up into his arms and looked desperately for a place where he could lay her down.

"Dad, take her home," Chance urged him. "We need to make sure she is well. And safe." He pulled on his father's sleeve. "Please, Dad. I'll be all right here. This arena is mine, after all. These creatures, good and bad, they're mine, too."

Chaz finally nodded his acquiescence. He carried his wife across the length of the arena and out through a door seemingly made from pure light. Chaz had been in this arena before, too. He recognized the door he had used to enter it two different times before. Those were other battles. Battles that had made sense at the time.

Battles that did not feature the elements of chaos. Randomness. Magic.

~ * ~

Denny appeared a few moments later in the same place from which he had disappeared. "He's not there," he said as he materialized.

The Beast and the Devil King were both staring angrily at him. Steam was exiting The Beast's flaring nostrils.

"What? What is it?" the monkey asked his superiors. He turned and looked around only to see various unfriendly looks directed his way.

"What is it?" he demanded of the crowd. He didn't get his answer. Instead, he was hit from behind. Something was on his shoulder. Something that was biting his neck.

"Ahhhhh," the monkey sighed, his eyes rolling up in their sockets. "Arachimedes," he said. "I've been looking all over for you." As he fell into a swoon, several hundred large spiders caught him on their backs. Once they had secured the monkey, they ran, sweeping him into the midst of the spider horde.

It happened so fast that the non-spider bystanders were unable to act to intervene.

"What just happened here?" a dazed Almasty asked anyone within earshot.

"We just got our cause," Chance announced. "This is why we are here.

"We must fight the forces of chaos and rescue their captive.

"Let's save the monkey."

"For the Monkey!" Angus McLeod seconded. His cry was picked up by everyone on the arena floor over the next few seconds. In the stands, the cry was beginning to be taken up.

Chance strode forward and turned to face the spider horde. "For the Monkey!" he cried. A great roar from the spectator stands greeted his announcement.

Behind him, his team was solidifying. New combatants were materializing to supplement those already there. Prominent among them was Destiny's Devil King, dressed as a samurai. He made his way to her Beast's side, brandishing a razor-sharp katana. Chance's own Beast was garbed all in leather and steel, a gigantic mace in one meaty claw. His Devil King wore red polished leather and held a large glistening battle axe. The essences of his parents were there, wearing armor and carrying spears much like his own. The Rodent Army, Baltimore Brigade, stood steady and ready.

And Arthur. Arthur Dillow. Arthur wore the cloth, leather and chain mail kit of a hobbit. In his hand, he yielded his weapon of choice.

A jump rope.

~ * ~

By anyone's count, Chance's forces were outnumbered a thousand to one by the spider horde. It would have seemed impossible odds to any person facing them, anyone but Chance Bonner, that is.

"Destiny," he said, approaching his sister. "Stand with me, okay?" he asked her. "Your bad luck will protect you, I think." He looked at her with a hint of doubt which communicated itself to her through his eyes.

"I will be okay," Destiny replied. "My protectors are here." She gestured behind herself to reveal her parents, Dick and Dorothy Dyer, both armored and armed to the teeth. Behind them was the tall and heavily muscled Ted Truehart, the family lawyer, carrying a shiny black leather satchel full of nasty looking darts. He wore a Kevlar vest and a much-used army helmet carrying the logo of the 101st Airborne Division.

Behind Ted Truehart was a being which could only be described as a battle zebra. On his back, in a richly ornate red lacquered saddle, rode a plump yellow and black lady sporting a shiny black motorcycle helmet. She held a crossbow.

And it was cocked and ready.

Twenty-five

Attack!

Unlike previous battles, this one was not a clash of evenly matched foes; this battle was a lopsided contest between a million eight-legged, unpredictable, magic creatures and a loose coalition of rodent, human, immortal and manifested beasts who had never worked together before—well, not completely.

The non-spider contingent had one binding force, and that was Chance Bonner. It was Chance who was the focus of his own manifested creatures. It was Chance who was the focus of his parents, both by birth and by choice, his trusty guardian, Angus McLeod, and of his newly discovered sibling, Destiny Dyer. On her part, Destiny commanded the protective forces of her own parents, both by birth and by choice, her trusty avatar, Ted Trueheart, and her own manifested creatures.

Then there was the Rodent Army. Its allegiance was to Samantha Swisher, and it trusted her judgment to commit it only to causes worth fighting for. Samantha had come to support Chance's cause in his most recent battle with the negative forces which sprang from his own head; she and her army additionally opposed those negative forces which abound throughout the Universe, attacking the course and quality of sentient life. And in both scenarios, she and her army fought beside avatars representing the positive forces of the Universe which had been excited into protecting Chance Bonner by his chanting of the sacred mantra.

This time, however, there was another important factor in her decision to fight: Almasty was here. He was the legendary protector of the Earth and its non-human creatures. She would die protecting him and his family. She was honored to do so.

"Charge!" called the unmistakable voice of Arachimedes from deep within the spider horde.

The order given, nearly a million spiders of all sizes and colors—except blue—mobilized. The larger spiders carried smaller ones on their backs. They carried no weapons; they *were* weapons. They threw webs and bit and clawed their way into their opponents' main body. They dropped from the ceiling like rappelling special forces soldiers; they spun sails and flew through the air like paratroopers. They disappeared and reappeared in different places at will.

Or was it at will? As soon as their formation broke, it seemed the spiders all returned to their natural states. They resumed their randomness. Their chaos. Their individual identities. It was no longer a unified front which faced the non-spider combatants, but rather a huge mob of angry and disorganized anarchists. Some of the spiders actually turned on their own, devouring them greedily.

"They are one in body, but many in mind," Chance observed aloud.

"What?" his sister asked. "What did you just say?"

"It is a tenet of Buddhism," Chance replied. "The Daishonin says that if we are many in body and one in mind, we can achieve anything. But watch those spiders...they've lost their unity. They are now one in body, being the spider horde, but they are many in mind. They have lost the one thing which would have guaranteed them victory: each other."

Destiny struggled to get her mind around the wisdom which Chance had shared with her.

"I think I understand, but Chance, your army...it is very diverse. Does that mean that your own forces are 'many in body and one in mind'?"

Chance laughed. It was an expression of joy. He was not making light of Destiny's own wisdom. "I sure hope so!" he said, readying his spear to take on the swiftly approaching enemy. "Stand behind me, Destiny. I will protect you!"

Destiny took her turn to laugh. Chance turned to find out what caused her laughter only to see her, her parents, Ted Truehart and the battle zebra duo form a unit of their own. Destiny wore her glasses—her actual glasses—and spun a double-headed spear much like Chance's own weapon.

"I can see again!" the girl exclaimed, spinning her spear, and deflecting hundreds of charging spiders. "Isn't that great?"

"Yes...it is," Chance managed to respond before taking on multiple attackers of his own.

The battle was engaged in earnest.

Jeweled spears spinning, the Ten Demon Daughters deflected charging spiders, most of which disappeared at the moment of impact, only to reappear elsewhere in the arena. Many of them were catapulted into the stands, where the robed and bejeweled spectators performed swift dances with intricate arm gestures to generate winds to propel the nearly weightless spiders up and out of the arena.

The spectators had begun to chant the sacred mantra. The sound grew and grew until it became the driving tempo for the drama on the field below.

On Chance's shoulder, left and right, the two miniature Chances appeared once again, taking turns at recording events, and then popping away to file their reports with the archives on Eagle Peak. They wore saffron robes and their heads were shaved, but they were clearly tiny copies of Chance, himself.

They were called Same Name and Same Birth. All humans have Buddhist gods like them on each of their shoulders, but Chance's analysts were visible to him at times of crisis. Chance would have a full report of his life, every action, and every word, once his essence departed his current lifeform and traveled to Eagle Peak, to rest and renew for relaunch into his next life.

The two Mothers of Demon Children fought shoulder to shoulder. Their demon children surrounded them, both fighting the enemy and protecting their precious mothers: Stefan and Brilliant and her nine clones fought for Josephine Schultz; Chance and Destiny fought for Angelica and each of their adoptive mothers.

Supporting Stefan and Brilliant were their father and their friends: Kelly, Millicent, and Sarah. All of Chance's friends fought as one, fiercely and fearlessly.

Supporting Chance and Destiny, Chaz and Nan, the Sasquatch Almasty parried spider blows and returned as good as they got.

And then there was Arthur. Arthur Dillow had approached the two Devil Kings and convinced them to twirl his jump rope. "D.K.s Unite!" he cried. "Pardon me, young armadillo," Destiny's fussy king said. "But are you a 'D.K.'? A Devil King?" His face said it all. He knew this puny little creature with his pathetic rope could not be a devil king.

"Of course not!" Arthur cried. "I am D.K., the Donkey Kong! Now twirl that rope with everything you have!"

As the kings twirled the rope, it caught fire in several places. This excited them to twirl the flaming rope faster and with more panache. Spiders running into the spinning rope caught fire and poofed out of existence in great numbers. Eventually, surviving spiders would not even approach the flaming weapon. The regents twirled the rope slower and slower and finally came to a complete stop.

Arthur walked up to the kings and thanked them for their support. "I'll have my rope back," he told them, his hand out, palm up. They put the still-pristine rope in his hand. They bowed to the young creature as they did so. "Nicely done," Chance's King said. "Yes, very nice indeed," admitted Destiny's King with a pained expression.

The two kings looked at each other suspiciously. Thanking someone for doing something was not in their nature. It is the nature of the Devil King of the Sixth Heaven to take credit for the accomplishments of others, and to never accept blame for anything that is unsuccessful. They dropped their eyes after a few moments, turned, and walked dejectedly away from one another. Chance's Devil King was shaking his head and talking to himself. Destiny's Devil King was promising revenge upon the lousy armadillo-boy. He just needed to find someone to do the actual work that would entail.

Chance's Beast approached Arthur, a strange look on his face. It could have been admiration, but that sentiment didn't seem in character for The Beast. "Arthur Dillow," he said, "How is it that you are on the side of Chance Bonner in this fight? How have you developed such skill with this rope?"

Arthur patted The Beast on his kneecap, which was as high as the young creature could reach. "You did it," he said. "You told me to be like Chance. I practiced. I also practiced my video games and jumping this rope." The boy paused to look up into The Beast's wondering eyes. "I found out that if you practice enough, what you're working at becomes a habit, something actually real inside of you. You change. I've changed!" At this, the young armadillo laughed gleefully, turned on his heel and ran back into the fray.

It was a bemused Beast who himself turned back to the battle. He put his gigantic mace to good use and managed to frighten some of the enemy away by wielding a beaming smile he couldn't seem to wipe from his face.

"For the monkey!" Chance shouted. His words were picked up by all of the beings on his side of the battle until, without any command being issued, and as one, they transitioned to intoning the mantra which the spectators had started. With all of their voices thus engaged, the sound of the mantra shook the very foundation of the arena and its stands.

All of the non-spider combatants were actively engaged in repelling, stabbing, or slicing at the attacking spiders. The organized forces of human, beast, and rodent were becoming overwhelmed by the forces of chaos. It was not just that they were so outnumbered, it was that chaos in battle prevents strategies from working. The non-spider combatants coordinated a rush, and the formations they rushed suddenly weren't in place anymore. They fell back to regroup only to meet with savage resistance from spiders which just suddenly appeared behind them from out of nowhere.

Chance paused to collect his thoughts. "Denny!" he cried. "We must get to Denny!"

He led his team toward the very center of the spider formation, hacking, hewing, stabbing, swiping—doing anything and everything to clear the way for an advance. Samantha Swisher approached and positioned herself to his immediate right. She spat out espresso beans from her mouth with great force and precision. Not one bean failed to take out at least a single spider.

They seemed to make very little progress. Moreover, they were all becoming fatigued, even the immortal Almasty and the almost-immortal Angelica.

A loud noise announced it: something big was about to turn the course of the battle.

A huge dark blue gerbil had exploded into being. The giant indigo rodent's advent blasted away hundreds of thousands of spiders. His advance toward Chance's forces squashed many of thousands more.

It appeared that nothing could stop him. He shook his head and slapped his ears sporadically, as if to clear them of the sound of the chanting which still dominated the arena. It looked like he was swatting gnats. Chance's forces stopped to watch the gerbil's actions, trying to ascertain if he were friend or foe. That's when they saw it. Him. They saw Denny. The monkey dangled from the gerbil's left ear. It seemed that one of Denny's jacket pockets was stuck around the ear...and he wasn't alone. On his neck, fangs sunk in deep, was the big, old, green leader of the spider horde—Arachimedes was clinging to Denny's neck, seemingly stuck, at least for the moment.

The giant gerbil looked around the arena and froze. "You!" he said, pointing toward Samantha Swisher and her rodent army. "You! You abandoned me! You left me for dead on that school bus! I must exact revenge! I must and I will!"

Samantha sidled up to the old squirrel. "What is he talking about?"

"Beats me," her sergeant major told her. "I'll confer with our commanders, if that suits."

"It does," his commander concurred. "Hurry."

She turned back to address the gerbil. "Are you—or were you—part of my forces, young gerbil?"

At this, the gerbil looked angrier, if that were possible. "No. No, I was not part of your forces," he spat out. "Your recruiters said I was too young to join your stupid army."

"So what brings you here?" Samantha pressed.

"I told you. I was abandoned. I was kidnapped. I've spent an eternity in some bog somewhere, all by myself. I was the only rodent in the whole place!" and now the blue giant was sniveling in earnest.

"How did you survive such an ordeal?" the general asked, her genuine sympathy evident in her tone of voice.

"Mushrooms, mainly," the gerbil replied. "Blue mushrooms. Many, many, many blue mushrooms." He lapsed deep into a reminiscence of some kind, his attention mysteriously diverted from the current conversation.

That was when Arachimedes made his move. Releasing his fangs from Denny's unresponsive body, he made a leap for the gerbil's neck.

Arthur Dillow had been watching the proceedings with great attention. Now he sprang into action. Using his rope as a whip, he struck the big spider with its far end. The handle which formerly ended the rope had morphed into a large claw which grabbed the spider, capturing him in its grasp.

With a flick of his wrist, Arthur whisked the captive spider away from the gerbil's neck and landed him neatly in front of Chance Bonner.

"That was awesome, Arthur," Chance told him. "That's another move from the Mario Party game, isn't it?"

"You know it!" Arthur cried, grinning from ear to ear. "I have been practicing, you know."

"Well, it shows!" Kelly said, moving over to Arthur to give him a congratulatory slap on the back.

Arthur's grin grew until it almost split his face.

Chance turned his attention back to the spider commander. "So here is the source of the blue magic you seek!" he said, gesturing toward the giant blue gerbil. "It was not us, not us formerly blue humans at all! What have you to say for yourself now?"

The big green spider puffed himself up and straightened his jointed legs to stand taller. He was still captured in the rope's claw. There was no escape.

So he decided to bluster.

"This rodent," he said glaring with a curled lip at the big gerbil, "is obviously a human spy...a pet, no doubt, of one of you. He acts as your agent. As such, you are as much to blame for his possession of blue magic as if you had stolen the magic yourself."

"Objection!" Ted Truehart cried, stepping forward out of the pack and standing in front of Arachimedes. "This is clearly a specious accusation propounded in an ill-considered effort to defend an extremely tenuous premise!"

The spider stared up at the lawyer, his jaw agape. "Huh?" he asked.

"You're jumping to a conclusion without any evidence!" the lawyer clarified. "How can you assume that this noble animal," and here he paused to bow to the stunned gerbil, "is someone's pet? That he is just a tool to be used by any human?"

Samantha Swisher ran up. She was oblivious to the legal discussion just occurring, for she had obtained crucial intelligence which she needed to share with the gerbil.

"Are you from Baltimore?" she asked the huge blue creature.

"I am," the gerbil said proudly. "I am the valued friend of one Jessica Smith of one-ten River Walk Drive." He held his head up and placed his hands on his hips.

"Did you stow away in the Baltimore Brigade's food stores when it deployed to rescue Destiny Dyer?"

The gerbil slumped a bit but remained defiant. "Perhaps I did," he admitted. "Perhaps I had to because you would not let me join the army!"

"Just how old are you?" Samantha asked next.

"I'll be eight next week," the gerbil replied, lifting his chin once again.

"Eight years?"

"No," the gerbil replied. A blush rose in his chubby cheeks. "Eight months."

There was a gasp from the rodent army.

"There is a minimum age of one year for a rodent to join the army," Samantha informed him. "Were you informed of that?"

"Yes."

"And you could not, or would not, accept this condition?"

"I could not."

"Can you tell me why not? Were you mistreated at your home on one-ten River Walk Drive? Did your Jessica Smith starve you or demand that you perform tricks without reward?"

"N-n-no."

"Then what? What caused you to run away from the comfortable safety of your nice home to stow away with a field army on the march?"

"I heard the army was looking for a girl. A teenaged girl...a missing teenaged girl..." And with this, the gerbil began to cry loudly and messily.

"Are you saying that your human friend, Jessica Smith, is missing?" Samantha demanded. She needed this gerbil to come forward with the full truth, sooner rather than later. She knew it was nothing short of a miracle that the battle's cessation had lasted as long as it had.

"Y-y-yes," the gerbil confessed. "She is missing. I haven't seen her in over two weeks. I can tell her parents are extremely worried—everyone is just beside themselves."

Samantha turned to the old squirrel. "SMAJ," she said, "get those sniffer squirrels back to Baltimore. Have them pick up the scent of the teenage girl who resides at one-ten River Walk Drive. Then put them on her trail." The old squirrel executed a smart salute and hurried off to relay the general's orders.

She faced the gerbil once again. "I will keep you apprised of their mission," she informed him. "Now how is it that you accuse our army of abandoning you? You said we purposely left you on the school bus.

By that, I take it to mean the school bus we found Destiny Dyer on? The one we rescued her from?"

The gerbil regained some of his ire. He picked his head up and said, "Yes. I was asleep in the girl's sweater pocket one moment, and in a dark, dirty corner of the bus a moment later. The army must have found me and removed me from the girl's pocket. Instead of taking me with them, they left me...alone. Hungry. Cold. Thirsty..."

"I can attest to his whereabouts," Lucinder said, stepping forward. Destiny's Beast was still at her side, listening intently to her words. "I found him on that bus under one of the bench seats. Can't attest to the cold, thirst, or hunger, but he was abandoned on that bus."

"Hey, aren't you my bus driver?" Destiny asked, also stepping forward to stand in front of Lucinder. "And you," she added, looking now for the first time in the eyes of her own Beast, "you look familiar, too. Do I know you?"

Before either of the creatures could respond, the crowd standing around Destiny gasped and began calling out to one another.

"Do you see that?"

"What is happening? Who or what are those things?"

"Are they spiders?"

"They look like little people—there, on her shoulders. One pops in and the other pops out at the same time."

Destiny's twin gods, Same Name and Same Birth, had manifested. They were tiny little Destinys, robed in scarlet silk. They had hair, but it was black, glossy, and elaborately coiffed.

Destiny's Beast took advantage of the distraction to fade into the background. She sought out her minions. In moments, she was standing beside the Battle Zebra and his buzzing, armed, and helmeted rider. The proud minions nodded at The Beast in acknowledgement and respect. She nodded back in a rare display of respect for what her two minions had accomplished that day.

Lucinder and Destiny were still eye to eye.

"I asked you a question," Destiny prodded the wasp woman. "Weren't you the bus driver the day I was abducted?"

"Of course not!" Lucinder lied.

The gerbil stooped to look at the tense little lady. "I think you are," he said, peering closely. "I think you're that pretty little bus driver who found me. I am almost certain you are the one."

He put one huge blue finger out and pointed it at Lucinder. As he did, he lightly brushed his paw across Destiny's shoulder.

At contact, the gerbil's size and hue began to shift. As he shrank, a bright blue streamer erupted from him. It flowed like a river of color carried in the air of the arena.

"Catch it! Catch it!" screamed Arachimedes. "Don't let it get lost in this world between worlds! It will be lost to the fen."

Arachimedes stopped abruptly when he saw Ribetta. She was holding her three-legged stool in front of her. She had swathed it in layers of her diaphanous gown. She was netting the blue stream like it was a run of bait. The gown grew bluer and bluer until the stream finally came to its end.

Ribetta addressed the old spider. "I'm off to the fen, my friend," she said. "I will see that all of your blue webs are restored, just as they once were!"

With a "pop" and leaving a residual odor of mildew, the frog-lady was gone.

The gerbil, no longer blue, was also returning to his original size. He looked at his brown little arms and paws and sighed happily.

Runners approached Samantha Swisher. They saluted her and the elder of the two delivered his intelligence.

"General, ma'am," he said. "Reporting as ordered. We located and interrogated the original search party members. They confirmed there was evidence of a stowaway in the supply wagon; the scent confirmed gerbil. Ma'am, no one remembers seeing a young gerbil on the school bus. The girl was searched before the team carried her back home. There was nothing in her sweater pockets but some little black specks and a ball of lint."

"The mesmer," Lucinder muttered.

"What?" Samantha Swisher asked, spinning on one heel to look at the wasp-woman.

"Nothing. I said nothing," Lucinder lied once again.

"You said 'mesmer'," Sarah Stengler interjected "I heard you clearly. You definitely said mesmer."

"We have been mesmerized," Stefan added. "By someone who looked a lot like you. We don't remember what happened while we were in that trance...we only remember waking up. By that time, you and the little brown man were gone. We've talked about it many times...me, Kelly, Millicent, and Sarah. Our memories are all the same. Little black things flew from your fingers into our eyes, and we don't remember anything between then and when we woke up. Is that what you did to Destiny? Did you make your flying black specks put her in a trance?"

"I am not answering any more of your questions!" Lucinder screamed, looking all around her for an ally of some kind—any kind.

Regina prodded Brody forward. "You haven't answered even one question yet!" she cried. "Are you even capable of telling the truth?"

Lucinder recoiled from the buzzing intruder. Then she took in the whole package: the armor, the crossbow, the motorcycle helmet and the caparisoned zebra.

"Who are you?" she shrieked. "What are you? And how dare you talk to me like that?"

"Hear ye, hear ye, humans, non-humans, and countrymen," the bee-woman began, one hand held high, index finger pointing straight up at the ceiling. She paused to listen to her steed, who was speaking. "What? Too much? Okay, I'll tone it down a bit."

She put her hand down, raised her head, and directed her next comments just to Lucinder. She was well aware that her voice carried throughout the arena and into the stands.

The mantra was still being chanted in the stands, but in a much tamer manner. It now provided a backdrop to events rather than being a driving force.

"I know your mesmer," she began. "I know it because I have one just like it. You can shoot stingers from your fingertips, can't you?" She looked doubtfully at the silent Lucinder.

"Oh, you can't? Well, I can! Would you like me to demonstrate?" She glared at Lucinder, her mood and volume thunderous.

"Okay, okay," Lucinder broke. "I mesmered the girl to keep her still while I ran an errand. So what? The mesmer does not have a permanent effect, she's perfectly fine."

"And what about creatures who run into the stingers you leave lying around? Could they be affected by the mesmer?"

"Well," Lucinder replied thoughtfully. "I suppose there might be some residual power. They might cause a dulling of the senses, for example."

"Or hallucinations?" Regina prompted.

"I suppose that's possible."

"Could a sleeping gerbil be mistaken for a ball of lint under such circumstances?"

"I should object," Ted Trueheart whispered to Destiny. "This bee is leading the witness something terrible."

"No, please don't, Mr. Truehart," Destiny said. "I need to get involved. Thanks for making me realize that."

"No need for thanks."

"Oh, I think we both know that's not true," Destiny replied, giving her family's lawyer a direct look and a sincere smile.

"I think I can add something to this story," Destiny announced, raising her voice to be heard. She stepped forward to stand next to Regina and Brody. "I have a vague recollection of fumbling in that sweater pocket. I must have been coming out of the mesmer, because I remember finding a little mouse or something. I held it in my hand. It was sleeping so peacefully. Then I dozed back off again myself. I must have dropped that poor gerbil to the floor. And for that, I am very, very sorry. It's my luck, you see," she concluded, her head hung in embarrassment. "It is bad. It is very, very bad."

She turned and bowed to the gerbil. "I am very sorry," she said. "You must have rolled under the seats. It's my fault."

The gerbil was struggling with his emotions. "I think I have jumped to some conclusions," he finally admitted. "And for that I am very, very sorry." He bowed to Samantha Swisher. "Please accept my apologies," he said to her. "It seems I accused your army of abandoning me when it appears they never knew I was in that bus to begin with."

"You are forgiven," the general said. "More than that, I will see that you are going to be rewarded for your contributions today. You have single-handedly defeated the spider horde.

"You will be awarded with our army's highest medal, The Rodent Medal of Freedom. This medal is rarely awarded to a combatant rodent, let alone a civilian. I hope you will accept it with our thanks."

The gerbil was blushing. He hung his head. "Shucks, ma'am," he said, "I didn't do anything that any normal rodent wouldn't have done if he were taken to an enchanted realm and fed magic mushrooms."

"So, you do remember being fed!" Arachimedes shouted, pointing at the gerbil with one forearm. "You ingrate! I fed you those mushrooms! I kept you blue and healthy! And what do I get for my trouble? You turn on me and my spider horde! You disappeared hundreds of thousands of my troops!"

"If I understand the nature of chaos...of magic," the gerbil said, standing his ground and looking the old spider in the eyes, "then you should have expected the unexpected. Under your care, I became a random element. Even you do not command the chaos!"

The old spider sputtered wordlessly for some moments. Then, in one of his own random events, he appeared to come around to accept what the little rodent had just said.

"Just so," he said, nodding his head up and down. "Just so, young gerbil. You have cracked the code. Too bad you're not magic anymore!" and with this, the old spider collapsed his segmented legs so that he was no longer imprisoned by the jump rope's claw. Once free he was able to "poof" away.

"He may have fed me, but he was terrible company," the gerbil said to anyone who was listening.

Nan Bonner stepped forward. "I thought he was excellent company," she said. "I think we all should pause to consider just what has happened here. Whether we wanted to or not, we acquired something that belonged to Arachimedes and his people. It was not wrong for them to want it back. But we were unable to give it back. We didn't know then what we know now...that the blue magic was luck. We did not have the agent to undo our luck...not until we found

Destiny. Destiny Dyer. We could have ended our problems with the spiders of the magic fen if we had known that the blue magic and its effect on us humans were due to luck." She turned to face her son. "Chance. You are the luckiest of all of us. I firmly believe it was your luck which caused this entire series of events to occur."

Chance looked shocked, then abashed. "I didn't mean for any of this to happen," he said in a low voice. "And I don't think you're being completely honest, Mom."

"What?" a perplexed Nan Bonner asked her son.

"It was you who was targeted by the negative forces in my head," he pointed out. "The seamstress was using the blue thread to alter your clothing. You were inspired to cut those clothes apart. You discovered the blue threads. You collected them and put them in our vegetable crisper." The boy was talking calmly and matter-of-factly. He was not accusing his mother of any wrongdoing. Rather, he was trying to take them all back to the start of things...the cause of what they had all just recently experienced.

"Why?" he asked. "Why you, Mom?"

Nan Bonner could not respond. She was, frankly, dumbfounded. Every word Chance had just uttered was true. Why didn't she see that before?

Chaz Bonner came forward. He approached his wife and put his arm around her shoulder. "You make Chance vulnerable, honey," he told her. "His negative forces have lost to Chance twice in as many years. Don't you think that introducing magic into our family dynamic was a ploy to separate us? Chance's luck probably saved him from being their prime target this time. They are clever. They are sneaky."

Both Kings, both Beasts and all of the represented minions gasped. They were offended.

At first.

"Well," Brody said first. "We are good at it. You know, being sneaky, that is."

Soon, they were all beaming with pride. "Yes, we are very sneaky!" Chance's Beast said, speaking for all of them.

Chaz continued. "They picked you because you have no guile. You suspect no one of the least bit of treachery. You are also a little vain."

"Vain? What do you mean I am vain?" Nan demanded.

"Your weight," Chaz said kindly. "You have always been too weight-conscious."

"Oh, I see...that's vanity?" Nan asked her husband in disbelief. "How about healthy? Wouldn't that be both kinder and more correct, Chaz?" She had begun to snivel.

"I found the brochures, Nan," Chaz told her. His voice communicated his words and his feelings. He loved her. He wanted her to know it. "All of those brochures about craze diets, diet pills, liposuction clinics..." He allowed his sentence to die unfinished when he saw the look on Nan's face.

"I thought you brought those home," she said, looking shocked and confused. "I thought you were leaving me hints that I was getting too fat."

"What?" Chaz explained. "Why would I do something that stupid? What am I, suicidal?" He laughed.

It was the right thing to do. It completely broke the ice. Nan started laughing. Then Chance started laughing. Soon, everyone in the arena was laughing, including the thousands of spectators.

"Well, if they're not mine, and you didn't bring them home, where did they come from?" Nan asked as soon as she was able to speak again.

"Chance?" his father asked him.

"Oh, no!" Chance said. "Never. I would never bring something like that home. I mean, where would I even find stuff like that?"

"At the gym," Arthur Dillow said, weaving through and around the taller members of the crowd to make himself seen, and heard. "I got those at the gym," he repeated. "I go to Theo's gym when it rains so I can practice jumping rope. I left them at your house, Mrs. Bonner. I stuffed them into your mailbox." He hung his head, ashamed. "I'm sorry."

"Why would you do such a thing?" a horrified Nan Bonner asked.

"You lied to me," Arthur said, raising his head to look her in the eyes. "You told me that your husband and Chance had to go to Baltimore for a funeral."

"And?" Nan prompted the boy for more.

"And all of them were missing!" Arthur cried, pointing to Chance, Stefan, Kelly, Millicent, and Sarah. "What...did they all go to Mr. Bonner's uncle's funeral?"

Now he had a look of defiance and hurt. It still stung that an adult he actually looked up to would betray him like that.

"Wait a minute, Arthur," Chaz Bonner said, interrupting the boy. "Those brochures were left at our house well before Nan lied to you. Sorry, honey. I mean well before our disappearance. Oh, you don't know about that, either. Well, let's just say your timing is off by several days. How do you account for that, son?"

Arthur didn't answer. He couldn't. He did not know the answer.

"Time travel?" he guessed lamely. He shrugged. "I don't know," he finally admitted.

It was strange. Everyone believed him. Even Chance's Beast, who was his employer. He believed the armadillo, too.

That's because he knew. He knew who left those brochures...and when. There was no disturbance in the timeline.

At this juncture, Denny rose groggily to his feet. "Whasshappenin'?" he said before he fell back to the ground in a swoon.

Lucinder ran to him and put his head in her lap. "Denny!" she cried. "Denny! Are you all right?"

"I am now," the little brown man said, a goofy smile plastered across his face.

The Beast felt the need to get his minions away from the Bonners before someone let out information that would compromise him. He gestured to his regent that he was going to round up his people and go. It was a pantomime that was completely lost on the Devil King, who just shrugged and made his own departure rather than ask The Beast to repeat his vaudevillian act.

When Destiny's Devil King saw the other royal depart, he followed suit.

Chance's Beast relented and walked over to where Denny and Lucinder were. "Let's go," he said, waving his arms around and making hand gestures. The trio disappeared in a cloud of sulfur so thick it caused the remaining combatants to run toward clearer air.

When the sulfur dissipated, there were only two people left in the arena. Even the Bodhisattvas were going, dancing as they went.

Chance and Destiny turned to face each other.

"It was so nice to meet you," Destiny said. "I don't feel unlucky when I am with you."

"I felt it, too," Chance said. "I felt more grounded when you were with me. I was using my brain more. I was less reliant on my instincts. It was weird."

"Yeah," Destiny said, smiling at her twin. "We don't look anything alike," she pointed out.

"No, we don't," Chance agreed. "But I think you look a lot like our dad."

"And you favor our mother, I think," Destiny added.

"That's weird, too."

"Yeah. It is."

"Well, I guess it's time to go. Will you return to Roanoke?"

"Yes. Soon. Daddy will be taking me back." At this, Almasty approached them through the dwindling sulfur, coughing and wiping his eyes.

"Ready, Destiny?" he asked as he neared the girl.

"Yes, Daddy. I'm ready," she replied, smiling up at her tall, hairy father. "This time, I'll stand on your shoes if that's all right with you," she added. "I am a little bit tired."

"Chance, my boy, I didn't get much of an opportunity to talk to you," the hairy man said. "I left you a present back at your house, though. I'll teach you how to use it the next time I'm in town."

"Okay, sir," Chance replied. "Thank you, sir."

"Let's not be so formal," Almasty objected. "If you can't call me Dad or Father, call me Almasty—it's the name I prefer. I would consider it an honor, son."

"Okay, Almasty, then," Chance agreed. He held out his hand. Almasty extended one of his own and the two shook.

With tears in his eyes, Almasty dropped Chance's hand and picked Destiny up. He positioned her feet on top of his gigantic boots, and they strode very quickly out of sight.

Twenty-six

Homecoming

"Well, Ribetta, you've got things back to normal," Arachimedes said. "It's almost like none of that nonsense ever happened.

"Oh, we still have plenty to do," the frog-lady said. "I have to turn all of those things the blue humans wished into being back into the blue, after all. That will take a while." She hummed cheerily and fussed about, untidying flower beds and squashing little dams and aqueducts Astra had constructed to drain the swamp. She was soon squelching around the restored bog just as before.

"It's good to be home," Arachimedes said. "Why don't we pop out later and bite something?"

"Sounds good," Ribetta replied, still bustling happily around the fen un-arranging things. "Sounds good."

~ * ~

"Nan, it's the oddest thing," Chaz Bonner said, coming back into the house from his trip to their mailbox.

235

"There is a bundle of brochures here, all about diets and all kinds of drastic weight loss techniques and tips. I think these are the brochures Arthur was talking about."

A puzzled Nan took the mail from her husband and started to sort through it.

"Well, if Arthur didn't leave those others, where in the world did they come from?"

"Beats me, honey," Chaz replied. "Beats me."

~ * ~

Stefan returned home with his sister. "Mom, we're home!" he called out as they entered the apartment they shared with their parents.

Nothing.

"Mom?" he repeated, just as loudly as before.

Nothing.

"Hey, Stefan," Brilliant said. "Here. Mom has left a note."

"What does it say?"

Brilliant Schultz continued to pore over the note, a look of consternation on her face.

"Brilliant. JB," Stefan repeated. "What does it say?"

Brilliant looked up at her brother, shock in her eyes. "She's gone, Stefan. She and Dad are both gone."

"What do you mean, 'gone'?" the young man asked.

Brilliant suddenly laughed. "I am such a good actress!" she crowed, swatting at Stefan with the note paper.

"They've just moved, that's all," she updated him. "The apartment is ours until the lease runs out, she says."

"Where did they move to?" Stefan asked, tearing the note out of his sister's hand and poring over it himself.

"The Spite House?" he read aloud. He looked up wonderingly at his sister. "The Spite House came up for sale after all of these years?"

"It would appear so!" his sister replied. "Mom has been jonesing after that house since we were little kids, Stefan...isn't this just wonderful?"

"I'll say it is!" her brother said. "I have dibs on the master suite!"

"Oh, sure, as if," his sister said dismissively. "You know that's a non-starter! You are still a minor, little brother—that means you have to move with Mom and Dad into that tiny little house." She laughed again, with just a hint of malice. She was enjoying her brother's discomfort.

After letting him suffer for several moments, Brilliant relented. "You'll be fourteen next month, Stefan. You can choose where you want to live. You can stay here with me if you want."

She went over and put her hand on his shoulder. "It is completely up to you, Stefan. But I would like it if you stayed here. With me."

~ * ~

Kelly O'Hara went to hang her coat up on the hook in the hall she always used. That's when she noticed.

There was another coat on the hook already.

No big deal, she told herself. Maybe Dad's finally got a girlfriend.

She hoped it was true. Her mother had been gone for nearly two years. It was time for her father to sober up and start over again.

She heard the sound of a beer can being opened in the kitchen. This distinctive noise was all too familiar to her by now.

"Dad!" she called, walking toward the kitchen. "I'm home!"

She stopped at the kitchen door, rooted to the floor by surprise.

And dismay.

There were two beer cans on the kitchen table. One sat in front of her father, who smiled sloppily at her.

The other sat in front of her mother.

"Just where have you been, young lady?" her mother asked.

"I might ask you the same question," Kelly answered with attitude. "What are you doing here?"

"Come on, honey," her father said, still smiling goofily. "Lighten up! We're celebrating! Your mother has come home!"

"We were doing just fine without her," Kelly told her father. Her mother began to smirk.

"Well, I'm back and I'm staying," she said, grabbing her husband's hand and giving it a squeeze.

"If you stay, I will leave," Kelly announced. She turned and left the doorway. She took the stairs to the second floor two at a time and ran into her bedroom, slamming and locking the door behind her.

She threw herself on the bed and hid her face in her pillow.

Her shoulders heaved for many long moments until Kelly fell into an exhausted sleep.

She slept through the rest of the afternoon and the entire night. When she awoke, it took a few minutes for her memory to remind her of what had transpired.

"I will leave," Kelly said. "I have to leave."

~ * ~

The Beast, Lucinder, and Denny were back in the cavern. Denny was still very groggy but was slowly coming to.

"Nice work on those brochures," The Beast told Lucinder. "They nearly did the trick. If it hadn't been for the cursed luck of that dratted boy, we would have succeeded in ruining his mother...without her, he would never practice that blasted philosophy."

"Forget the philosophy," Lucinder spat out. "It's all that lousy chanting that is killing me."

"Kill me," Denny said drunkenly. "You kill me, Lucinder." And with that, he slumped back to the cavern floor and began to snore.

~ * ~

A little armadillo cavorted in the dry underbrush, sniffing out beetles and grubs. "Yum, yum, yum," he repeated to himself as he munched and crunched.

"Now to go lie out in the sun for a while," he said, again to himself. "This is the life!"

As he basked in the mid-morning sunlight, he dozed.

That is why he did not detect the presence of the two feral pigs who hid themselves in the bushes surrounding his sunning spot.

"Is this the being you spoke of?" one pig said to the other.

"Yes," the second pig responded. "This is the being."

~ * ~

Lucky had but one more task he needed to accomplish prior to returning to the human world: he needed more of that Love Potion.

He caught the old squirrel just as the Baltimore Brigade was leaving the arena on its way to SEATAC International.

The squirrel recognized the man inside the dog suit. "Here," he announced, holding out a vial of shimmering oil, "I thought you might be wanting some more of this...it's my own recipe, after all."

Lucky took the vial in his mouth and bowed deeply to the old squirrel.

"Oh, you're more than welcome, young man!" said the sergeant major. "It warms the heart of an old squirrel to be an accomplice to a love affair!" The old squirrel looked at his departing troops. "Well, I've got to dash, my good man, or I'll miss my flight. See you soon, son!"

The squirrel ran off, limping just a little and griping about his lumbago. Lucky pivoted and trotted off to rejoin the Bodhisattva Arya Tara who waited for him at the arena door. As the pair stepped through the misty doorway, the dog morphed back into the big Scotsman.

"I thought I'd see you soon!" the little Bodishattva cried, clapping her hands together in joy.

As they disappeared from sight, the man removed a small shining glass vial from his mouth and slipped it into his trench coat pocket. He turned to salute the retreating army. "See you soon," he said softly.

~ * ~

Chance was composing an email to send to his sister.

Behind him, hanging in his closet, was Almasty's gift—a hooded goat hair cloak. His father had not made an appearance yet to teach Chance how to use it.

Chance wasn't worried...he was elated. He had a sister! It was still a marvel to him. He finished up his short note and hit "send."

"What now?" he asked himself. He was not considering the far future but was wondering what he should do next—in the now.

His personal computer chimed. He had mail! He was delighted to see that it was a reply from Destiny. She was home from the hospital. It seemed that when she woke up from the sedation, she had a cast on one leg. She told Chance that she was very clumsy, something he had not witnessed himself in the arena. She also told him that her glasses were missing again and that she was very nearsighted. He could hear her frustration in her typed words.

He composed a short, encouraging note back and powered down his computer.

He got up and went to his bedroom window. On a whim, he threw the window and peered out, looking toward the O'Hara's house next door.

Kelly was not in her room, but he saw evidence of disarray. There were clothes scattered around, some of them hanging from the drawers of her dresser.

That was not like Kelly. A tomboy she might be, but sloppy she was not.

Then he saw her. She carried a huge backpack, stuffed to the gills. She had thrown a spare pair of shoes, tied together by their laces, over her shoulder.

There was a taxi at the curb. He watched as Kelly jumped into it and it roared away.

"Oh dear," Chance said out loud to himself. "What now?"

THE END—NOT

Meet Jude LaHaye

Jude LaHaye enjoyed a career spanning twenty-five years before ever turning his hand to writing. He worked hard, always putting in extra hours and effort, as an Army and then a DoD Logistician, blaming his "day job" for his inability to become a writer.

And then he got his chance: he jumped on an opportunity for an early retirement from civil service.

It was hard. That first book took him almost two years, at the end of which he questioned his life-long ambition to become an author.

But it also broke something loose. After struggling over that first book, he now writes fluidly, finishing as many as three books in any given year.

LaHaye lives a solitary life, preferring his own company to that of others, living and creating predominately in his head, and then putting many of those ideas down on paper to become the backbones of his novels.

He has a wife, Liz, who is as extroverted as he is introverted. She is his inspiration for some of his more outgoing and optimistic characters.

His four children are all as different from one another as they can be, providing yet more inspiration for good, bad—or simply *weird*.

LaHaye and his family live on an island in Washington State on the Puget Sound, where they enjoy fauna, flora, and majestic views of forests, mountains, and ocean.

Other Works From The Pen Of

Jude LaHaye

The Empty - How will far-future humanity survive the death of its sun?

Chance - Can a youth of twelve, even a very clever one, overcome the negative Universal forces which unite to defeat him?

Fat Chance - How can a youth—even a very clever one—confront and defeat the sinister forces of the Universe?

Letter to Our Readers

Enjoy this book?

You can make a difference.

As an independent publisher, Wings ePress, Inc. does not have the financial clout of the large New York publishers. We can't afford large magazine spreads or subway posters to tell people about our quality books.

But we do have something much more effective and powerful than ads. We have a large base of loyal readers.

Honest reviews help bring the attention of new readers to our books.

If you enjoyed this book, we would appreciate it if you would spend a few minutes posting a review on the site where you purchased this book or on the Wings ePress, Inc. webpages at: https://wingsepress.com/

Thank You

Visit Our Website

For The Full Inventory
Of Quality Books:

Wings ePress.Inc
https://wingsepress.com/

Quality trade paperbacks and downloads
in multiple formats,
in genres ranging from light romantic comedy
to general fiction and horror.
Wings has something for every reader's taste.
Visit the website, then bookmark it.
We add new titles each month!

Wings ePress Inc.
3000 N. Rock Road
Newton, KS 67114

www.ingramcontent.com/pod-product-compliance
Lightning Source LLC
Chambersburg PA
CBHW070635100726
47907CB00007B/1996